BIG SKY

TIMELESS
WESTERN
COLLECTION

BIG SKY

KIMBERLY KREY   ANNETTE LYON
CINDY ROLAND ANDERSON

Copyright © 2019 Mirror Press
Print edition
All rights reserved

No part of this book may be reproduced in any form whatsoever without prior written permission of the publisher, except in the case of brief passages embodied in critical reviews and articles. These novels are works of fiction. The characters, names, incidents, places, and dialog are products of the authors' imaginations and are not to be construed as real.

Interior Design by Cora Johnson
Edited by Kristy Stewart and Lisa Shepherd
Cover design by Rachael Anderson
Cover Photo Credit: Nichole Crowley Photography

Big Sky is a Timeless Romance Anthology® book
Timeless Romance Anthology® is a registered trademark of Mirror Press, LLC

ISBN: 978-1-947152-87-8

Timeless Western Collections

Calico Ball
Big Sky
Mercer's Belles

Enjoy our Timeless Regency Collections

Autumn Masquerade
A Midwinter Ball
Spring in Hyde Park
Summer House Party
A Country Christmas
A Season in London
A Holiday in Bath
A Night in Grosvenor Square
Road to Gretna Green
Wedding Wagers
An Evening at Almack's
A Week in Brighton
To Love a Governess
Widows of Somerset

And our Timeless Victorian Collections

Summer Holiday
A Grand Tour
The Orient Express
The Queen's Ball
A Note of Change

TABLE OF CONTENTS

The Cowboy's Catch _____ 1
by Kimberly Krey

Selling Her Ranch, Stealing His Heart _____ 107
by Annette Lyon

The Cowboy's Second Go _____ 197
by Cindy Roland Anderson

THE COWBOY'S CATCH

KIMBERLY KREY

ONE

Jason Keller kept his eyes and ears trained on the stage, sparks of nervous energy flaring within him. The Bransons' annual charity auction was in full swing and, any minute now, Marlee Jenkins would take the stage. Like last year, the intriguing brunette would introduce the family she'd be raising funds for on behalf of her father's trout farm.

But this year, Jason planned to shake things up. His adrenaline spiked each time the microphone moved from one announcer to the next. The old restored barn was decked out with spring daisies, fresh greens, and all the usual antiques, but the auction itself was far from formal. No program to speak of, no real order in the bidding process. Bidders simply hollered over one another while Dee Branson kept track of the winners in her trusty notepad.

If all went according to plan, sweet Mrs. Branson would be jotting Jason's name into that notepad, right beside an item, or should he say *event*, that wasn't even up for bid—*yet*.

A grin pulled at his lips.

He tipped his head to see Marlee through the crowd. Just a glimpse of her gorgeous profile sent those nerves into action once more.

"Dude," Taylor said with an elbow nudge. "I don't think you understand just how out-of-the-question this scheme of yours is. Ever seen a *Do Not Touch* sign?"

Jason shot Taylor a disapproving scowl. "Of course."

Taylor chuckled under his breath. "Well Marlee Jenkins is a walking *Do Not Touch* sign if I ever saw one. There's no way she's going to agree to this."

"This" being the date night Jason planned to propose. Taylor might have more experience with the auction, seeing that his parents ran the show, but Jason had learned that going after what he wanted often paid off. Even if he had to get creative in the process.

"I don't know why you think it's such a stretch," Jason said. "She auctioned off dates with her younger sisters last year. I'm sure she plans to do the same this year too." Of course, she had specific qualifications for the bidder: must be a city resident, must pass a background check, and must have each gal (though both were legal adults) home by 11:00 p.m. and not a minute later.

"Yeah, but notice how she only auctioned *herself* off for a month's worth of filleting as many trout as the winner could catch—not a date."

"Yeah, well tonight that's going to change." It might sound cocky or even crass, but Jason had only the best intentions: treat Marlee to a fine evening with a perfect country gentleman like himself, and give her a night away from demands far too great for someone her age.

Jason knew firsthand what it was like to have the world on his shoulders; by the grace of God, he'd escaped it. Perhaps he could help Marlee Jenkins now, a woman who'd caught his attention since he'd seen her in action at Charlie's Trout Farm. He never imagined that a group of delicate-looking women, some barely out of their teens, would be running a trout farm where they gut and fillet the latest catch for every fisher in town.

"Gonna win a date with one of those Jenkins girls," came a voice from behind.

"Good luck outbidding me," came another. "I put in overtime on the field for this."

Jason glanced over his shoulder to see a couple of Bob Branson's ranch hands, Brody and Lincoln. They were good kids, as far as he could tell. "Who do you boys have your eyes on?" Jason asked.

"Lilly," they said in unison.

Jason lifted a brow. "Is that the youngest one?"

Brody nodded. "Britt's cute too, but she's twenty-two, and girls usually don't want guys that are younger than them."

"Good point." Jason had been pleased to find out Marlee was twenty-four, like him. In fact, he had four months on her, which made him a bit older.

Bob Branson, the kind man who gave Jason his first shot at ranch life, took the mic from the Weatherly twins. The elderly women auctioned off pies of the month to be delivered throughout the year. Strawberry rhubarb for April, blueberry for May...

Jason had been tempted to bid on the pies himself, but he didn't want to make a spectacle before he bid on what he really wanted. Besides, Dee Branson had been a second mother to him since he'd come to work on their ranch over four years ago, and Dee would take it as a downright insult if he paid for another woman's desserts.

With squinted eyes, Bob stared into the section where Marlee sat with her sisters. Jason's pulse revved like a hot engine ready to rip.

"How about we get the owner and operator of Charlie's Trout Farm up here for our next auction?" the burly man thundered.

The audience cheered. Brody and Lincoln shot to their feet and whistled high-pitched catcalls as Marlee took the stage, Lilly and Britt in tow.

Her younger sisters had heart-shaped faces with round noses and cheeks, while Marlee's oval-shaped face held high cheekbones and a narrow nose bridge.

The angular features continued along her jawline, her hands, and even the well-defined slope of her delicate shoulders. No doubt all three women were beautiful, but of all the women who'd caught Jason's eye over the years, none had done it quite as effectively (not to mention inadvertently) as Marlee Jenkins.

Of course, he couldn't dismiss the other reasons for that—ones that had nothing to do with her outward appearance. The woman's generosity was evident in events like these, but at the trout farm she demonstrated genuine care for nearly every customer who came and went. *Nearly*, because her kindness had yet to extend to Jason.

It was often he overheard Marlee encouraging someone during a rough time, or laughing heartily at a joke, even if it was more of a cringer. She had a way of putting the townsfolk at ease in her company, and he admired that.

Marlee curled her fingers around the mic. "Thanks, Bob. How we doing tonight, everyone?" The woman's small-scale drawl drew Jason in every time he heard it.

She paused for the crowd to cheer once more, a gorgeous smile pulling at the corners of her mouth. Unlike her other fairly narrow features, Marlee's lips were full and her smile was wide.

"The family we're raising funds for this year couldn't be here, but most of you know the Inglesons. Danny lost his job due to a back injury, leaving his wife Cathy, who's been caring for their three small children, with a heavy load to bear in medical expenses and such. Let's see how much we can raise to help them out. What do you say?"

Jason nodded and clapped, feeling like he was in store for

a medical emergency of his own; his heart was thundering like a stampede of wild horses.

"You're going to chicken out," Taylor said with another nudge to his arm.

"Keep telling yourself that if it makes you feel better. But get ready to be surprised because this is going to be my lucky day. I can feel it."

"Face it, dude. The woman doesn't want *any* man. And as hard as it might be to understand for a guy who's had women throwing themselves at his feet since he was sixteen, Marlee Jenkins seems to especially not want *you*."

Jason chuckled. He couldn't help it; the statement was true enough on both counts. Due to his high-profile family and the Los Angeles life he lived before moving to Montana, Jason was no stranger to women wanting him if not for status alone, even here in the small town of Phillipsburg.

And then there was Marlee. Jason had often approached the counter at the trout farm with his latest catch only to find that the oldest sister had made herself scarce (yet again). At first it just seemed like a coincidence. But as the pattern continued—Britt or Lilly filleting the half dozen trout he'd caught while Jason did his best to pretend he wasn't wondering where Marlee had run off to—he'd realized the truth of it for himself: she was *especially* not interested in *him*. Which didn't make a whole lot of sense; she didn't even know him. Something he hoped to remedy very soon.

"Three hundred and ten," came a loud bid from behind. Lincoln.

Jason shot a glance over his shoulder to see the anxious cowboys were already bidding. Whoa, he'd been too zoned out to notice the bidding for a date with Lilly had already begun.

The townsfolk cheered.

"That's a new record for one of our date nights," Marlee said with a grin.

Lilly shifted her weight from one high heel to the next, a smile pasted on her blushing face.

"Do I hear three twenty?" Marlee asked.

"Three-twenty right here," Brody said.

"We're breaking records here, today," Marlee cheered. "The Ingleson family will be very happy to hear it. We've got three twenty for a date night with the beautiful Lilly, do I hear—"

"Three fifty!" Lincoln said in a booming voice. "Plus I'll do a day's worth of farm work for the family. Whatever they'd like."

Brody gave his friend a shoulder nudge. "I thought you couldn't go above three twenty."

Lincoln gave him a sly grin. "I pulled some strings."

Marlee looked stunned. Lilly had a wide smile on her face, her gaze fixed on Lincoln. "That's... incredible," Marlee breathed. "Anyone want to try to outbid that offer? Going once, going twice..."

When no one spoke up, Marlee pointed at Bob, who slammed down the mallet. "Sold to Mr. Lincoln Hart for three hundred fifty dollars and a day's worth of labor."

Britt was up next. Jason could hardly stay focused through the bidding process. All he knew is that Brody bid on the evening with the middle sister as well, giving up only when someone outbid him. Another three hundred fifty dollar bid, minus the day's labor.

"Now," Marlee said, "as I've done the last three years here at this fundraising event, I'll be offering one full month's worth of trout filleting—as much as you can catch—and we've got a beautiful selection out there this year, guys. Brown trout, golden trout, cutthroats, you name it. We've even got a few of those hard-to-catch bull trout left for those who really want to test out their skills."

Jason waited as the bids came and clapped along with everyone else as the winning amount came in at two hundred sixty dollars.

"Well," Marlee said, bringing the mic back up to her lips. "The gals at Charlie's Trout Farm thank you for your continued support, not only in fundraisers for locals like the Inglesons, but also for the generous donations we've seen appear in the collection jar for Charlie's Find a Cure Foundation as well. Your donations have amounted to a whopping four thousand dollars this year. Our father's definitely smiling from the clouds. We're so thankful to be part of this incredible community."

Jason's insides became a shaken can of soda, adrenaline bubbling beneath the surface and ready to blow. If he didn't speak up now, he might never get his chance. His eyes widened as Bob moved toward the center of the stage. Marlee extended the microphone to him.

Hurry, Jason. Do it!

"Bob," he blurted, standing to his feet. "I'd like to bid on a date night with the lovely Marlee Jenkins."

Bob's eyes grew larger than dollar coins. "You would?" The man's usually booming voice came out like a mouse squeak.

Marlee hadn't relinquished the mic just yet; she took advantage of that fact and pulled it right back to her lips. "That's not up for bid." She fixed a challenging glare at Jason, leaned on one hip, and folded her arms. Something seemed to speak to him in the gesture. An acknowledgement of who Jason was—the guy she always dodged at the trout farm.

"Five hundred dollars to Charlie's charity," he blurted.

Marlee's pretty lips parted as her jaw dropped open.

Whistles broke out over the crowd.

"That *is* a pretty penny," Bob's thunderous voice was back in full supply.

Marlee mumbled something under her breath and handed off the mic. "She thanks you, fine sir, but says she'll have to decline."

Give up, Jason. Just let it go. But he couldn't. "A thousand," he blurted. "One thousand dollars to the Ingleson Family, and another thousand to Charlie's charity."

Whispers turned into outright gasps and hushed terms of amazement.

"*I'd* pay that much to go out with *him*," one gal blurted, causing the crowd to chuckle.

"That's two thousand dollars," another piped. "She's not going to be able to turn that down."

That was precisely the idea.

Bob cleared his throat, wiped a grin off his face, and turned to Marlee, who looked like she was summoning the ability to shoot fire darts from her eyes.

"If it's any help to you, doll," Bob Branson said, "I can vouch for the man myself. Jason Keller's a trustworthy, hard-working gentleman."

"Aww, just go out with the poor guy," an older lady pled.

"Jason Keller's *not* poor, I can tell you that," another mumbled.

More comments rose up over the crowd, urging her to give him a chance.

Jason's pulse had taken up residence in the high-speed zone. He tugged his shirt from his chest to get some air and willed himself to look at ease.

At last Marlee's shoulders dropped in defeat. She snatched the mic from Bob, her forehead scrunched up in irritation. "The same rules apply, then. Back by eleven and all that . . ."

Jason brought his arm up to make a square. "Scout's honor." Thank heavens Gramps took him to scouts in his youth so he could lean on the phrase, because it seemed to impress her. At least for a second as her face softened the slightest bit.

Her lip twitched, an action Jason fixed his gaze on as she went to speak. *Yes. Just say yes, you beautiful, stubborn woman.* The truth was, if she'd have simply engaged him with some polite conversation at the trout farm, all of this could've been avoided. She'd practically forced him into taking the drastic measure.

"Fine," she finally snapped.

"Sold!" Bob ran to where he'd left his mallet. He slammed it down hard as the crowd cheered.

A flood of triumph rushed into Jason's chest like hot air in a balloon. He pumped a fist and grinned. *Yes!*

Taylor blew out a whistle and turned to him. "Looks like you got yourself one ticked-off date." He nodded to Marlee a second before she bolted into the crowd.

Jason grinned, still shocked that he'd actually gotten a yes out of her. "I think you're right. Hopefully she won't be ticked off for long."

TWO

MARLEE SPUN FULL circle before her mirror, a fresh wave of dread washing over her. She could not believe she'd gotten sucked into a date with a cocky city boy, one with Hollywood ties, no less. What could be worse?

"Thinks he can just swoop in with all his money and good looks and get anything he wants," she grumbled while scrutinizing her reflection.

Was her outfit a good choice for an anniversary party? And was that really what Jason Keller wanted to do with the date he'd paid so much money for? She'd pictured him pulling up in a limo, escorting her to a tarmac where they'd board a private jet, all to dine in some "quaint little café overlooking the water."

Not that she wanted that; Marlee Jenkins lived for the simple life. But an anniversary party that started at two in the afternoon? Which was just twelve minutes away, she realized. If Jason kept her until her self-appointed 11:00 p.m. curfew, their date could last nine whole hours! A bit of quick math said that was over five hundred minutes.

Of course, only *some* of that time would be spent at the party he mentioned. According to Jason, the dress code called for boots and jeans. It just seemed too . . . *country* for a guy who'd been raised as part of the world-famous Keller family.

Everyone knew who Michael Keller was—the plastic

surgeon starring in his own reality TV show called *Beauty and the Keller Beast*. According to tabloids and town talk alike, the man was furious when his only son quit his med-school pursuit to become a ranch hand out in the country. Especially since the famous surgeon planned to have Jason join him on the show once he graduated.

Marlee had figured Jason would grow tired of ranch life within the first year or so, but that hadn't happened.

She forced her mind back to her outfit. The turquoise top seemed too cheery for the occasion. Quickly, she unbuttoned the blouse, shrugged out of it, and tossed it onto the heap of rejects at the foot of her bed.

She hurried back to her closet and gripped a cluster of hangers. Just as she prepared to slide them to one side, giggles sounded from beyond her window. She froze in place, muscles tightening, and cringed.

Great. Britt and Lilly were home.

Marlee had purposefully given her sisters extra chores at the trout farm in hopes that they wouldn't get back until she was gone. Either they'd finished the spare jobs early or passed them onto Stone, the new guy Marlee hired to work on weekends. Of *course* that's what they'd done. Like the poor kid could actually say no to the likes of Britt and Lilly.

She tugged a sweater off its padded hanger and sighed as an image of her date floated to mind. Talk about hard to say no to. Jason Keller with all his good looks and Hollywood clout had probably never learned the meaning of the word. Which was why Marlee had wanted so badly to teach him in front of the entire town of Phillipsburg. But she couldn't do it while denying the very family she was raising money for an extra thousand dollars, not to mention Dad's charity.

Jason Keller was probably the one sneaking all that extra cash into the jar at the trout farm each week. Normally, that would be to someone's credit. So why with Jason did she have to dismiss it so entirely? A vision of her mother rushed in, reminding her of exactly why—he had a direct tie to Hollywood and all its misplaced values.

She pictured the way Jason had stood there at the auction, a cocky grin on his gorgeous face as he awaited her reply. It caused a dose of heat to break out over her skin every time. And if she were honest, it also sparked a delicious stir in her chest—the vain thrill of being the object of his desire. But that's all it was—vain—because Jason didn't even know her.

Marlee shoved her arms into the sleeves of the neglected sweater and carefully, so as not to disturb her hair, pulled it over her head.

A knock came to her door. A second later the thing burst open.

"Let's see what you're wearing, sis," Britt said.

"Oh, no," Lilly blurted as they dashed into the room. "You can't wear that old thing."

Marlee rolled her eyes and smoothed the hem around her waist. "I can if I want to." Though one look in the mirror and she agreed. As timeless as she'd once thought the sweater to be, the stretched wool and loose neck suddenly looked outdated and frumpy.

Brittany ran straight for Marlee's closet, hollering over her shoulder as she moved. "Let's find something to bring out the blue in your eyes."

"You guys know I don't care about stuff like that," Marlee said.

"You should," Lilly mumbled under her breath.

Britt barreled out of the closet as quickly as she'd moved to it and breezed past Marlee and Lilly empty-handed. She disappeared down the hall. "I've got the perfect thing," she explained.

"Holy smokes," Lilly squealed, "he's going to be here in, like, ten minutes!"

The excitement in Lilly's tone forced a streak of nervous energy right down the back of Marlee's neck. She pulled in a deep breath and held it. *Relax, Marlee. You don't even like this guy.*

"You're going to give him a chance, aren't you?" Lilly asked once Britt left.

"I don't even know what that means," Marlee said, hoping to end the conversation before Brittany came back. The last thing she needed was the two ganging up on her.

"Oh, yes you do," Lilly said with all the gusto she used while performing in the town's musical. "It might have been fun to play the bullheaded trout for a while, but if you keep doing it, you're going to be alone for the rest of your life."

"It's bull trout, not bull*headed* trout," Marlee corrected.

"Well *bullheaded* sounds better, since that's what you are."

"You don't need to lecture her," Britt said as she burst back into the room. "Dad gave her that nickname as a joke. And now she's just going to swim around trying to dodge every gorgeous guy who asks her out, including the biggest catch in town, Jason Keller."

Lilly flopped back onto the bed. "Which means he'll be available for *us* to date!"

"Right." Britt nodded to Marlee's sweater. "Take that off."

"Geez, Ms. Bossy," Marlee grumbled as she carefully pried the thing off her head. She flung it toward the growing pile on her bed and missed.

Maybe Marlee *had* been charmed by Dad's nickname. A name inspired by a few rare bull trout that somehow snuck into their reservoir years back. Season after season those bull trout lived on, seeming to avoid every hook that might snare them. They were clever, savvy, and evasive. Best of all, they never got jerked around.

"Put this camisole on first," Britt thrust a silky tank top into her hand.

As soon as she had that on, Britt handed her the blouse. "This rusty orange color will make your eyes pop."

Marlee shrugged into the sheer top and began to button it. "Geez, do you own every color of top known to man?"

"Better," Britt quipped while lifting her brows. "I own every color of top known to *woman*." She took a step back and gasped. "Wow, that *does* look incredible on you."

"It really does," Lilly added, her tone laced with reverence.

Marlee eyed her sisters; they were truly beautiful. And they were much better at keeping up with makeup and fashion trends, getting their hair done with highlights and trendy cuts while Marlee lived in ponytails and baseball caps. But as she turned to look in the full-length mirror, her hair falling around her shoulders, Marlee saw a very different woman.

"This really *does* make my eye color pop." It made her skin look better too, gave her more of an olive complexion. She shot a surprised look at Britt. "You really *should* go to cosmetology school. You're so good at all this."

Britt shrugged. "Some people say we should wear spring-like colors when it's spring; but what we should really focus on is what compliments *us,* not the season." She reached out and undid the top two buttons and pulled a gold chain off her arm. "This area right here—around your collarbone, neck, and upper chest—is called your clavicle. The Jenkins girls have pretty clavicles that are meant to be seen."

"Especially since we hardly have any boobs," Lilly grumbled.

"Speak for yourself," Britt snapped. "A B-cup is perfectly respectable." She came up behind Marlee and clasped the thin gold chain at the back of her neck. Marlee took hold of the tiny, heart-shaped pendant before letting it fall just above the camisole. It really did look pretty.

"Looks like you already put some blush on," Britt said as she came around to look at her. "Did you?"

Marlee shot a hesitant glance at Lilly before answering. "A little."

"Oh my gosh! I *knew* you secretly liked him! I mean, it's Jason Keller. *No* woman's immune to his charms, not even the old Weatherly twins."

Three distinct knocks sounded from the front door, exuding all the hype of trumpets announcing royalty.

The chatter ceased.

All movement did too.

Even Marlee was holding her breath, but only heaven knew why. Her insides went wild. Heart hammering, pulse racing, muscles clenching. Heat poured into her face like she'd just leaned over a dozen mugs of morning coffee.

"Holy smokes," Lilly hissed, breaking into the stillness.

"He's here!" Britt's declaration came out somewhere between a whisper and a shout.

In a flurry of dashing limbs and flying hair, the duo made for the hall and raced toward the door, leaving Marlee in the room with her own reflection. She half expected it to be blurry with how frantically her heart was beating.

A noise carried down the hall, and Marlee tipped her head to tune into it. Laughter. Jason's, actually.

It had been a while since the sound of a man's hearty laugh echoed down those halls.

A wave of warmth rippled over Marlee's arms. And just like that, the deep, raspy chuckle snuck right past her defenses and nestled into a quiet spot in her heart. It felt nice there. Like a combination of heat and hope.

"Marlee!" Lilly hollered. "Your date's here." Her boy-crazy little sister giggled loudly. "Not going to lie—he looks *really* good."

What a flirt. Marlee rolled her eyes. Why hadn't Jason just bid on one of her sisters? Both Lilly and Britt were interested in dating, a pastime Marlee usually avoided at all costs.

Still, she squared her shoulders, took one final look in the mirror, and blew out a shaky breath. Suddenly, a realization sank in. The necklace—the one Britt had given her—was *Mom's*.

Marlee's hand shot to her throat. Quickly, she tugged one side of the thin chain until the clasp was in front, then pinched the small lever to unlatch it. If the stupid piece of jewelry weren't special to Britt, Marlee would chuck it in the toilet and flush it; the last thing she wanted to carry was a reminder of the mother who'd abandoned them for her own selfish pursuits. Instead, she rested it next to her jewelry box and turned out the light.

Yet as Marlee stepped into the hallway, she wondered if it wouldn't have been a bad idea to wear it after all; the token might help her remember how strong the pulls of fame and fortune really were. Just because someone left the lifestyle behind didn't mean they wouldn't go back. Even if they had to leave the ones they were supposed to love most.

She wouldn't need a gold chain to remind her of that. Marlee had treated enough late-night fevers, attended enough of Britt's soccer games and Lilly's choir concerts to sear the warning right into her brain. The latest images were razor-sharp and new-scab fresh, even if they were from two years ago: caring for Dad—all but forgotten by the woman he'd sworn his devotion to—while he suffered through one taxing treatment after the next. No, she'd learned the lesson quite well: people who'd had a taste of fame were destined to seek it once more, and that included Jason Keller.

"Coming," she called. A few short steps led her through the hall and into the foyer where her date for the night stood.

Tall, gorgeous, and more muscled than she'd realized, the Keller Cowboy (a nickname bestowed by tabloids) set his eyes on her.

"Hi," he crooned. "You look beautiful."

The comment was met with enough *awwws* by her sisters to fill Marlee's face with another dose of heat. Or perhaps it was the discovery of a small dimple in Jason's cheek that made her blush.

Whoa! She was fooling herself if she couldn't admit this guy had—hands down—the most attractive smile, jaw, face, and now *dimple* she'd ever seen in person.

She gulped, forcing herself to lift her lowered chin back into place. "Hi," she squeaked. "Thank you. You too. Look nice, I mean."

Lilly giggled some more.

Marlee shot her a warning glare before eyeing Jason once more. Hesitantly then, as if she were walking the green mile, she forced herself to step closer to Jason and the door that would lead them into their five-hundred-forty-minute-long date.

One step closer. Two.

Dang, he smelled good. Like a living cologne ad for cowboys. All spice and musk and rugged good looks.

She took another cautious step.

If she didn't know better, Marlee might actually think Jason had been cowboying his whole life. The famous Keller hadn't been born there, but that hadn't stopped him from taking on the rugged quality that made cowboys so appealing: a well-defined, muscular frame that was more lean than bulk and the ability to wear a cowboy hat and jeans like he'd been born for them. Even that five o'clock shadow he wore was more country than city, where men often favored a clean shave.

Marlee stopped a few feet shy of him, reminding herself that he was, in fact, a wolf in cowboy's clothing.

A look of curiosity had replaced the smile on Jason's face. But as his gaze dropped to the space between them—a good foot and a half of gray ceramic tile and white grout—a slight tug pulled at one side of his mouth.

She watched him with curiosity of her own as Jason moved his gaze up her frame, slowly, until it rested on her face. The room went warm. He kept his eyes fixed on her, thoughtful still, before unleashing the power of that full grin once again. A broad smile with white, sparkling teeth.

Were those goose bumps forming along her arms?

Suddenly, in one smooth stride, he closed the gap between them and nodded to her sisters in turn. "I'll have her back by eleven."

"Oh, you can keep her all night long as far as we're concerned," Britt said.

Marlee was about to reply with a snide comment when Jason flattened a hand along her lower back. "My lady," he crooned.

Whoa. She was positive there'd been some sort of comeback on the tip of her tongue, but for the life of her, Marlee couldn't recall it. Couldn't recall whom she'd even speak it to if it *did* come to mind. Because all she could focus on in that moment was the warm and steady sensation of Jason's palm through the thin fabric of her blouse.

Geez, she really was deprived if a simple hand on her

back could stir such a response. A small voice repeated the sentiment as the truth of it sank in. She better keep her wits about her today. If she wasn't careful, Marlee could wind up crushing on the Keller Cowboy like every other female in town.

In the front yard, the bright sun cast moving shadows over the grass as they walked toward Jason's truck.

"Did you hear that?" He opened the passenger door. "Your sisters said we could stay out later if you'd like."

Marlee forced her eyes off the driveway and looked up to catch a wry smile on his face. Her heart skipped at least three full beats.

"Eleven o'clock is perfect," she assured.

"Suit yourself." Jason's smile only grew. He waited for her to buckle up, then gently closed the door. And as he circled around the back of the truck, Marlee could swear she heard that low, raspy chuckle once more.

Dang, she really *was* in trouble.

THREE

JASON COULDN'T WIPE the grin off his face. Sure, it wasn't polite to revel in his victory, but he'd been dying to go out with Marlee Jenkins for a long time now. And here she was, making the passenger side of his Tundra truck look better than it had since he bought it.

Her blue eyes were hypnotizing today, their reflective nature capturing the green from the fields as they passed. He couldn't believe the woman he'd been secretly aching for a solid year was actually here with him.

Taylor's comment from the auction floated to his mind. *Looks like you got yourself one ticked-off date.* By the looks of Marlee's narrowed gaze, the serious set of her brow, and the unwilling way she'd neared him at her front door, Jason would say that held true. But there was only one sure way to find out.

"So have you forgiven me yet?" he asked.

"What was that?" Marlee held a casual looking glance out the window, but she turned to him as she waited for his reply. Gorgeous olive skin, warm cheeks, and that deep mystery in her eyes—all of it lit a fire low in his belly.

"The uh, auction. Have you forgiven me yet for springing that on you?" He draped one hand over the steering wheel as he stopped at the sign. Was it just him, or were those pretty cheeks growing pinker?

"Forgiven you?" she asked in a high-pitched, I-didn't-see-that-coming tone. She bit her lip, chuckled slightly, and then gave into one of the most beautiful smiles he'd seen.

Jason didn't even know what she'd say yet, but already he was grinning back like a fool.

"I don't really have time for dating, that's all."

"So what would you be doing today?" he asked. "Instead of this, I mean. You don't work on Saturdays." Oh, shoot. He shouldn't have shown that he knew that.

Marlee did a double take, and Jason forced his eyes back on the intersection, pulling onto the road once he saw it was clear.

"Right," she said softly. "I don't work Saturdays, but I've got all that spring cleaning stuff to take care of with the house and the yard. My dad—even up to the last few months of his life—was taking care of things I didn't even know needed to be done. Cleaning out the . . . what are those things around the roof? Gutters?"

Jason was all too familiar with this himself, having just bought a home of his own last year. He nodded. "Right, rain gutters."

"Plus I do a vegetable garden, and I haven't even planted peas or lettuce this year. In fact, I've got last year's tomato corpses all shriveled up in their cages waiting for me to bury them. It's sad."

Jason chuckled. "That *is* sad." Also sad was the realization that he was the reason she wasn't making progress on the chores today.

"So far I've been focusing on deep cleaning and going through a few neglected boxes in the garage. Stuff my dad left behind."

Jason couldn't imagine going through the boxes of a loved one after they were gone. "It's a lot of work running a house of your own," he said, focusing on that instead. "Plus you've got your sisters to look after. That can't be easy." He glanced over in time to catch Marlee's shoulders soften.

"Yeah, stinkers," she said. "They should be helping me with all the house stuff. And I *do* have them help out on a few things, but they're young. I want them to go out and have fun."

Man, she sounded like his sister, Payton. How she used to be anyway: take care of everyone else. Shelve your own happiness at all costs. "What about you?" Jason was probably stepping over a line, but he couldn't help it.

Marlee stiffened. "What *about* me?"

He shrugged, blew out a paced breath as his own irritation rose. Why people couldn't recognize that *they* mattered too, he'd never understand. His own actions might have been deemed selfish where his escape from the Keller lifestyle was concerned, but Jason viewed it as not only survival, but also the pursuit of happiness.

"You're still young," he said. "You should get out and have a good time too, right? At least sometimes."

She shrugged. "I have a different personality. I'm the type who's fine being alone."

That comment was no better than the other. His irritation kicked up a notch. A million retorts shot to his mind, but he forced himself to stay quiet.

For two whole seconds.

And then the frustration won out.

"I don't mind being alone either, *sometimes*," he said, angry heat burning in his chest. "But anyone who says they never get lonely is either lying or kidding themselves."

"I never said I don't get lonely," she snapped.

The engine got louder. Probably because he'd revved it in lieu of speaking up again. But what was *this*? She'd just admitted to feeling lonely.

"My sisters keep me company," Marlee added. "And then

there's the trout farm. I'm friends with like, everyone in town." Her tone had changed, more wistful now. "They fill me in on the latest while I fillet their catch of the day . . . it's nice. I guess that's why I never minded stepping in when Britt and Lilly had a hard time with the dirty work, cutting out guts and all that—it gave me a chance to hear if Gary Bon's son made it into that fancy university he applied to. Or if the Gerald's baby girl was doing better after a terrible cold."

He liked that side of her, but couldn't help but think of how she'd never shown that sort of interest in him; it was obvious that Marlee made herself scarce every time Jason approached the small shack, bucket in hand.

"If it weren't for the trout farm," Marlee continued, "I wouldn't know who needed help when auction time came around. So yeah, I guess you could say the folks in town, the people who frequent the trout farm, they're like family."

All except for me, he wanted to say, but he bit his tongue as she continued.

"They loved my dad, always asked about him when he cut back on his hours to do treatments. Plus they know about my mom."

About her mom. He knew about her mom too—she was a famous soap opera star. But the way Marlee said it made Jason wonder if there was more to it than that. "How long ago did your father pass, if you don't mind me asking?"

"Two years ago now."

Jason nodded. "I'm sorry about your loss. I didn't have the privilege to meet him. Taylor and Luke had been trying to get me to go to the trout farm with them since I moved here four years ago, but I kept telling them I didn't like fish."

She twisted in the seat and shot him a look. "You *don't?*"

"*Didn't.* At least, that's what I thought since my parents never made me try it. I just had that idea in my head. But then

I came in after a long day of work and I got an invite from Dee to come to dinner. Fresh trout with mashed red potatoes and a lemon-herb hollandaise sauce. Had I not been so starving, I might not have tried it." He shook his head, glanced in the rearview, then sped up to pass a slow-moving tractor. "I couldn't believe how good it was. And here I'd been missing out on it my whole life. That's when I started going up there and catching my own."

He glanced over in time to see a triumphant looking grin on her face. "I love fresh fish. And I love it when people learn to enjoy it as an adult. There's something satisfying about it."

He smiled. "Keeps you in business too."

"Yes," she said through a small laugh. "It sure does."

He thought back on how they'd started this conversation. Of the way Marlee had bristled when he'd challenged her about getting lonely. Things had diffused nicely, but only because he hadn't confronted her about the way she gave him the cold shoulder when he came around.

"Do you miss your parents?" she asked. "Or does having Payton here make up for it?"

It was the first time she'd acknowledged knowing anything about him. "Having Payton here is everything. Especially now that they have Gunner. That little guy is something else. Started walking just last week. I love being an uncle."

He put his mind back on her original question. "But as for my parents, we have a better relationship now than we ever did when I lived in California. I think because they finally stopped trying to control my life and accepted that I never wanted the future they wanted for me."

Memories of that difficult time poured in. The struggle to break free from the heavy burden of fame and the endless list of expectations that came along with it.

It took him a moment to notice in the quietness that Marlee was studying him. He shot her a glance. Her face was thoughtful. The deep blue of her eyes seeming to hold beautiful secrets he'd probably never come to know. The thought sparked a longing deep in his chest. He wanted very badly to know this woman. He wanted to know how he'd managed to end up on her crap list without even doing a thing.

"You don't like me," he said softly. "How come?" He'd set his eyes back on the road now, but he sensed her discomfort upon his saying it.

"I don't . . . *not* like you," she said.

The hesitation in her denial was glaring. "Wow." He chuckled. "That was convincing." Jason leaned into the seat, angling himself toward her. "Do you want to know one of the things I like about you?"

Her eyes widened.

"I like that—unlike most women—you're not enamored with me because of who I am."

That thoughtful expression was back on her face again. "So that's an issue for you? Women wanting to go out with the famous Jason Keller?"

He nodded. "Yep. And I always know—the second they start talking about California and why would I want to be in a boring old town working hard labor on a ranch instead of being pampered in LA—that's when I know I'm on a date with a woman I'd never want to marry. I don't want to be with someone who's in love with who I used to be, or what my old life represents. I don't want to be with a woman who doesn't want to be *here*."

A quick glance at Marlee said she hadn't moved a muscle.

"That's why I've taken an interest in you," he continued. "You're definitely not enamored with the Jason Keller of LA, which I think is a very good thing. But can I ask you a tiny little favor?"

His heart tripled in rhythm as he waited for her reply.

She licked those pouty lips of hers and shrugged. "Sure." It came out in a whisper.

"Give me—the Jason Keller of Phillipsburg—a chance. You may find that I'm not so bad."

The slightest hint of a smile pulled at one corner of her full lips.

"We've got the entire day together," he added. "Might as well open up, get to know me, and have some fun. What do you say?"

FOUR

Wow. Marlee hadn't thought in a million years that Jason might do this. *This* being the way he'd called her on her crap, as Dad used to say. And now he was asking her to give him a chance. It was such a straightforward thing to ask that it took her by surprise.

Jason's brown eyes held a hint of amusement, like they had when they were by the front door. But she detected something else too: vulnerability. For the second time that day, he'd managed to puncture another piece of her heart.

She gulped and forced herself to nod. "Okay."

Jason gave her a satisfied nod as that dimple sank right back into his cheek. Swirls and twirls of heat fluttered over her skin. Sheesh! That grin should be illegal.

She set her gaze back out the window. Marlee hadn't ever considered the fact that all of his Keller status might actually play against him. Of course it would to someone who wanted to escape it. To someone who had a genuine desire to find a woman who'd love him outside the very cocoon he was trying to shed.

She couldn't help but feel as if an entirely different man sat beside her now. When she'd climbed into his truck just ten minutes ago, he'd been, in her mind, LA's Jason Keller. But to know that he didn't like using his status as an advantage—and to know that what he liked most about her was that she wasn't influenced by it—that made a difference.

What he might not know, and perhaps this didn't make her any better, is that she *was* influenced by that status. It just had the opposite effect on her. Instead of drawing her in, it repelled her to the point that she'd been rude. *You don't like me.* She cringed, hating that it'd been so obvious.

She felt bad for giving him the cold shoulder this whole time, but at least she was giving him a chance now. But a chance at friendship or at romance?

The question scattered her thoughts like ashes in a windstorm. What a dumb thing to ask herself. Of course he'd have to settle for friendship like anyone else; romance was not in the cards for Marlee.

Still, at the mere idea of becoming romantically involved with Jason, a rush of heat pooled into her face and heart and hands. She felt like some young, dumb teenager. A mess of hormones and emotions she hadn't experienced in quite some time.

Heck, it'd been over three years since she'd gone on an official, pick-me-up-at-seven type of date. Sure, a few men in town had insisted they take her for a bite to eat after a long shift, but she'd never agreed to anything beyond that.

Tommy Wilkinson—that's who she'd gone out with last. It was such a vivid time in her mind. The time when her world started to crumble. Tommy had asked her out on a Wednesday, Dad's diagnosis came on Thursday, and the date was set for Friday. Marlee had attempted to cancel; she'd just wanted to stay home with her family and . . . and circle the wagons. Come up with a foolproof way for Dad to beat the rare form of cancer.

But Dad wouldn't hear of it. *Don't you dare go canceling that date, hon,* he'd said. *You need to keep living your life, no matter what happens with mine.* His face had turned stern then. *Promise me.*

Marlee had gone on the date as promised, but she'd known even then that it'd be the last date she'd go on until Dad recovered. And when his health declined instead, it became even more clear: it was her job to be present in the home and do the things Mom should have been there to do. Take care of Dad. Watch after her teenage sisters. Make sure they didn't use the tragedy as an excuse to go wild.

Britt went through a short rebellious stint anyway, and Lilly—heck, that girl was born boy crazy—but they'd made it through. Were still making it through. Which was why she shouldn't let herself get involved in a relationship.

So there. She'd come full circle. Yes, she'd give Jason a shot at friendship, but nothing more.

Marlee repeated those very words as they pulled onto the Branson family's ranch. "When I first heard that you came to work for the Bransons, I thought it was for research or something, you know? So you could play the role of some ruggedly handsome cowboy with a chip on his shoulder."

Jason shot her a look. "You think I'm *ruggedly handsome?*"

She didn't bother replying; he *knew* he was. "What made you leave everything behind and move out here?"

Jason shut off the engine and tossed the keys into his cupped palm. "Since I was young, I knew the role I was supposed to play. I was one of the Kellers. My mom's one of the biggest names in fashion, right? And here comes Payton, and she's just on fire. She hits the runway running, if you know what I mean. She created her own fashion line and made a name for herself before I was even out of my teens."

He shifted in the seat and fixed his gaze on her, hints of gold shimmering in the depths of his brown eyes. *Phillipsburg Jason,* she reminded herself. "That's impressive," she said, but really she was thinking about how much she liked this side of him already.

"You said it," Jason said. "And here my dad is, some famous plastic surgeon starring in his own show, so what does that mean? Oh, that *I* have to go to med school, follow in his footsteps, and become the newest star in *Beauty and the Keller Beast*. Well, he would have changed it to *beasts* once I came on."

He shifted his gaze to look over a distant field. "I'd wanted the simple life ever since I could remember. I used to watch westerns with my granddad, and I'd dream about climbing on a horse and galloping over the land. I *wanted* it, but I also knew I'd never *have* it.

"Until this one day when I was messing around on the web, looking for something to do during summer break. I'd graduated high school early, with an associate's, actually, and was working on my pre-med classes.

"Anyway, as I'm checking out different vacation spots—I don't even know how—but I see this ad posted about ranch hands for hire, and I just knew."

He turned back to her, a fresh intensity in his eyes. "My whole body knew. Has that ever happened to you?"

Marlee shook her head absently, intrigued by the passion she saw in him. He hadn't been some rebellious punk like the media made him out to be.

"My entire life felt like . . . like a prison almost. I mean, I was free in one sense, of course. But it was understood that I would do what my father did. So to break them in, I told my parents I'd just try ranching for the summer, you know, get it out of my system. But that was only so that I could ease them into it gently. I knew I was never going back to that life."

"Wow." It came out in a whisper. "That was brave of you."

He grinned. "Thank you, for saying so. Not everyone sees it that way. My parents . . . they've divorced since, but they're both remarried, and they seem pretty happy now too. Happier than they were, I think."

A vision of his also-famous sister came to mind. The woman had shocked the media world by marrying Luke Branson, who was Jason's boss at the time.

"I can't believe Payton left too," she said. "What, did she just meet Luke when she came down for a visit once?"

Jason pointed at her and lifted his brows. "That's a good question. Stay there." He shoved open his door and climbed out, shutting it before hurrying over to her side. He cracked open her door and offered his hand. That illegal smile spread over his face.

Marlee rested her hand in his, welcoming the tingles that skipped through her skin at his touch. The weather was perfect out today. Sunlight, warmth, and not even a hint of the cold breezes that often made springtime so chilly.

"When I left," Jason continued, "it caused a big upset in the family. When I refused to come back, it got worse. Poor Payton was trying to salvage our reputation and save our family from falling apart all at once—most of which she blamed me for at the time.

"So she showed up late one night, demanding that I come home with her. I refused, of course." He chuckled and shook his head. "So when that didn't work, she actually told Luke he needed to fire me, which *he* refused to do. She was getting a lot of no's that night.

"Needless to say, she and Luke did *not* hit it off at first. But Luke, the caring boss that he was, encouraged Payton to stick around and see what it is I do before she made judgments about it. Long story short, the two fell in love."

Fell in love. Just like her parents. Of course, Mom gave up the life she always wanted only to resent it seven years and three kids later. Would Payton do the same?

Stop it, Marlee. Get Mom out of your head and quit assuming the worst about everyone. Obviously she'd been wrong about Jason this whole time.

The backyard was alive with all sorts of excitement. Games, food, and a whole lot of chatter. *"This,"* Jason said under his breath, "is my family of choice."

Marlee took in the crowd of people, realizing what a large family the Bransons had. It made celebrations at the Jenkins home seem pitiful in comparison.

Jason wasted no time introducing her to the few guests she wasn't yet acquainted with, and soon they settled into a shaded spot on the patio beside his sister.

"How about you get Marlee and me some of Dee's famous slush," Payton suggested, shifting her weight from one side to the next as her baby clung to her hip. Boy, was he cute. Full, pouty cheeks, big, brown eyes, and a swirl of auburn hair that was closer in color to Jason's than his mom's.

Jason looked at Marlee. "Would you like some slush?"

"Sure. Thank you."

Payton hoisted baby Gunner from her hip. "Oh, and take this little guy with you, will you?"

Jason clapped his hands before holding them out, his face transforming into a dopey grin. "You wanna come with Uncle Jay Jay? Huh?" His voice had changed too. Silly and scratchy, like a cartoon character's.

That secret corner in Marlee's heart—the one Jason kept managing to sneak into—did flips at the sight of him in uncle mode.

Gunner squealed and kicked his feet. "Jay, Jay, Jay . . ."

"That's right," Jason said proudly. He shot Marlee a wink. "Be right back."

Marlee replayed that wink in her mind at least four times before Payton came into focus.

Of all the people she knew at the gathering, Marlee was least familiar with Payton. The pretty redhead leaned in and covered the side of her mouth conspiratorially. "I'm so happy Jason asked you out on a date," she said through a wry smile. "Who cares if he paid for it? At least he has good taste."

"Oh, thank you." Marlee squinted against a ray of sun that pierced through the branches overhead. Guilt pierced through in a similar fashion. "I appreciate that. And I appreciate *him,* donating so much money to the Inglesons, and toward Charlie's cause too." It might have seemed like a hollow statement, but it wasn't; Marlee was truly grateful for the generous donations he'd made.

"You know," Payton said, "I've been here for close to four years now, but I swear I still have to pinch myself that this is actually my life." The warm depth in her brown eyes reminded her of Jason. "I'm so glad that we're raising our family here. My kids will never know the kind of lifestyle and pressures Jason and I had growing up."

Marlee couldn't deny the authenticity she sensed in those words. Was that what Jason was hoping for too? To raise a family out here in the country?

She grinned. "Yeah, that's wonderful." But something was happening. The words *raising our family* got snagged on a rusty, jagged blade Marlee hadn't even known was there. Did she ever plan to raise a family of her own? Or did she just plan to sit back and watch Britt and Lilly live a life she'd opted out of?

Her gaze drifted over the crowded backyard. Two picnic tables held bowls, pots, and casserole dishes filled with everything from potato salad to baked beans. The round table close by tempted guests with fresh cinnamon rolls, raspberry cobbler, and Jell-O hidden beneath thick layers of whipped cream.

The food and the games and the fun seemed to stretch on

for miles. And laughter. When was the last time she'd heard so much of it in one place? Or seen so many smiles . . .

Or felt so much peace . . .

Bob and Dee were teamed up with Taylor and his brother, Ross, racing hovercrafts from one end of the yard to the next. The school-aged grandchildren were busy swinging lassos over their heads and hurling them toward the stationary bull named Mabel. A game they called Rope a Bull by the Horns.

And there was Jason standing beside the dessert table. He'd run into Luke there, and the two were spooning a drippy bite of bright pink slushy into Gunner's mouth from a plastic cup. Gunner puckered his little lips before bursting into a smile. "More!" the little guy cheered as it dripped down his chin.

The men chuckled, and Luke readied the spoon for another taste.

"So cute," Marlee said under her breath. No wonder Jason called these guys his family of choice.

"It's amazing, isn't it?"

Marlee blushed, feeling as if Payton had read her mind. Still, she couldn't stop the swell of warmth and hope that rose in her chest. "Yes." She gulped back the knot in her throat. "It's wonderful."

A large banner had been strung between two trees to mark the celebration. Colorful balloons clung to the corners while paint-blotched handprints lined the edges. The words *Happy 40th Anniversary* took up the center. Some families really did stick together, didn't they?

"Ice-cold slushies for your refreshment," Jason said as he returned. He handed one to Marlee and Payton in turn. "Luke took Gunner in for a diaper change. He wanted me to ask if the diaper bag is inside."

Payton sucked air through her clenched teeth and set

down her cup. "Shoot, no. I left it in the car. I better grab it." She gave Marlee a nod. "We'll talk more later. Oh, and before I forget to have you do this . . . " She snatched Jason's cowboy hat off his head and hid it behind her back.

Jason raked his fingers through his auburn waves. "What are you doing?"

"This," Payton said, lifting her hand to toss his hair from one side to the next. "This hair is one of Jason's best features. You *have* to run your hands through it at least once."

Jason rolled his eyes. "Can I have my hat back?"

"Only if you *promise* to let her play with your hair first."

He gave Payton an exhausted look that only a fellow sibling could relate to. Payton grinned at Marlee. "Promise me you'll try it just once, and I'll give him his hat."

Jason turned a set of pleading eyes on Marlee.

Her heart reacted to the sight before she could even speak. Head lowered, a young-looking pout on his handsome face. "You've got to save me here. I have hat head."

She tilted her head to see if that was true. His hair wasn't long by any means, but it wasn't short either, the tips falling along his dark brows. Sure enough, a small dent played across the strands toward the ends.

"You can't really tell, since your hair's kind of wavy anyway." She glanced back at his sister. "But yes, I promise to feel his hair, Payton."

"You'll thank me for it." Payton smiled and shoved the hat into Jason's hand before darting toward the patio steps. "I'll be back."

"Thanks for warning us," Jason mumbled. He turned to Marlee, rested the hat over one fist, and moved his gaze slowly back to her face. Her heart pounded out an extra beat as warmth rushed into her cheeks. She took a sip of the tangy slush, hoping to counter the flash of heat.

"You don't have to play with my hair if you don't want to," he mumbled, looking even more boyish now as he looked at her through his lashes. "Payton's weird about stuff like that. She's so proud to be a redhead that she thinks everyone should be enamored with it."

Marlee grinned, enjoying his discomfort in a way. "A promise is a promise." It felt as if her heart had multiplied in her chest, as if there were a dozen tiny extra hearts hammering in there as well. She rested her slush cup beside Payton's and, with a tentative hand, reached up and hovered it over his head; there was no backing out now.

He likes you, Marlee, she reminded herself. *He donated two thousand dollars to go out with you!*

She let the thrill of that thought urge her on, and at last Marlee pushed her fingers through the gorgeous waves. She slid the tips of her fingers along the parts in his auburn hair while the strands caught streaks of sunlight. Only then did the copper color shine through. It really was a nice head of hair for a man.

"I think it has more to do with . . . the *feel* of your hair than the color," she said, moving her hands through it once more. The thick strands were cool and smooth as they slid through her fingers.

She glanced down to see a trail of goose bumps rise over Jason's arms. "Does that feel good?" she asked before she could stop herself.

Jason chuckled under his breath and made a purring sound. "Yes," he admitted. "When *you* do it, it does."

Heaven help her, but she liked having that kind of effect on him. The idea caused an entirely new thrill to shoot through her.

Jason lifted his chin until his eyes met hers. The delicious sensation grew and swelled as he held her gaze. It took Marlee a moment to identify what was causing it: *chemistry*. That's what this was. That magnetic spark of potential. It'd been forever since she'd felt anything like it.

She found herself giving him a flirtatious smile as she raked through his hair one last time, starting just above his forehead, her fingertips pressing firmly now. It reminded her of high school in a way, the forgotten feelings of attraction stirring within her. She'd missed it.

"I told you he had a great head of hair," Payton came from behind.

Marlee yanked her hand back.

Jason cleared his throat and shoved the hat back on his head.

Payton looked back and forth between them pointedly. "I think I hear Luke calling for help again." She gave them a tight-lipped smile and popped her brows. "I'll catch up with you two later."

His sister walked away, leaving the two of them standing there, the disrupted dust of desire still swirling about, looking for a place to land.

"That was subtle." Jason shook his head and took hold of her hand. "C'mon, let's see if we can ring the rope around good ol' Mable."

Bob and Dee had moved on from the drones and were lined up for the roping game as well. "How you doing, doll?" Bob boomed as they neared. "Is Jason treating you right?"

"So far, so good," Marlee admitted.

"And now he's challenging you to a match?"

Marlee glanced at Jason in question. "I don't know. Are you?"

He puffed his broad chest. "Of course."

Bob leaned toward Marlee. "Psst, you *do* know he ropes animals for a living, right? He's dang good at it too. A natural."

"Should have seen him last year at the rodeo," Dee added proudly. "He placed in three different categories."

Marlee could picture it now—Jason, riding on horseback while swinging that rope over his head. Or balancing atop a wild bull while it kicked and thrashed. The vision stirred memories of the first time she'd ever been to a rodeo. She sure knew how to crush on cowboys back then. Seemed Jason was reviving that tendency with a vengeance.

"How about we team up?" Bob suggested. "I'll have Marlee on my team, since I'm not too bad at it myself, and you take Dee on your team, Jason."

Dee scooted a set of turquoise bracelets up her wrist and cracked out a laugh. "Poor Jason," she said. "I'm all thumbs when it comes to the rope." She held up a finger. "*But* you get me in the kitchen, and there's no comparing. Not even with the Weatherly twins."

"You can say that again," Jason agreed, wrapping a loving arm around the woman. It reminded Marlee of the way he'd called her his second mother. He was sweet to her. And there was no doubt the couple had really grown to love Jason in return.

Maybe he really was a safe bet; heck, even the Branson family could vouch for him.

"Now," Bob said to her under his breath. "Let's work up a plan to beat those guys."

Marlee grinned. "You got it." Would they really be able to beat them, though? Inwardly, a bigger question came to mind: how would she beat the feelings she was starting to have for Montana's one and only Keller Cowboy?

FIVE

JASON SQUEEZED MARLEE'S hand as they walked back to the truck. In another hour or so, the sun would set completely; for now, it hovered low along the horizon, spreading its evening glow over the land. The green, swaying fields soaked in the warm colors of sunlight, making the symmetric rows appear dreamlike.

Phillipsburg offered some of the most breathtaking views he'd seen, but none could compete with the way Marlee Jenkins looked in the evening sun. He had to remind himself several times that she was, in fact, there with him. He was one lucky dog.

He glanced over, felt that heat dancing low in his belly, and gave her hand another squeeze as she smiled at him.

"What's going through that mind of yours?" she asked, that subtle twang sweetening the words.

He shrugged. "Just thinking that you were the perfect date for today."

She grinned, the action accenting her high cheekbones.

"Really," he assured. "It's refreshing to be with a woman who knows how to enjoy herself in a setting like that. You even kicked my butt in roping. I'm going to take that up with Bob later," he added with a laugh.

"He *was* a good teacher," she said. "But if I share a secret do you promise not to tell him?"

"Of course," Jason said.

She leaned in closer, propped herself onto her toes, and brought her lips dangerously close to his earlobe. Heat roared low in his belly as her lips grazed his skin. "I liked it better when *you* showed me."

At once he recalled the way he'd cupped her hip with one hand, wrapped his other around her slender wrist, and helped her get the rhythm of swinging the rope over her head. He'd liked showing her too, but even more, he liked knowing that Marlee felt something in those moments as well.

After helping Marlee climb into the truck, Jason leaned against the open door. "What sounds better to you? Going out to dinner—you choose the restaurant—or grabbing some takeout and going back to my place where I promise to be a perfect gentleman?" He put his hands up at either side of himself to prove it.

Marlee tipped her head and tapped her full lips with a finger. "Hmm... both sound good."

Dang, he liked hearing that too.

"Why don't we do takeout at your place? That sounds nice."

"My place it is," he said with a grin. Yet as he rounded the truck, an errant thought snuck into his mind: A warning was more like it. This was all happening too easily. Perhaps Marlee was just being polite, the way she was to all the folks in town.

Dread crept in. Enough to snuff out at least half of the hope he'd had only moments ago. What if he never found someone who'd love him for who he really was? And what if the chemistry between them was only one-sided?

Jason hated how very possible that idea was. Well, politeness only went so far; if that's where her feelings ended, he was bound to find out before the night was through.

Marlee lifted her roasting stick to check the biscuit dough she'd wrapped around the whittled spear. She could see, against the bright, crackling flames, that the biscuit had not only puffed up, but turned golden brown as well.

"Oh, it looks perfect," Jason said. "That boy's ready for a butter bath."

Marlee giggled. "A butter bath it is." After testing the temperature with the tips of her fingers, she carefully pulled the freshly toasted treat off the stick and rested it in the pie tin of melted butter. Jason had demonstrated how it was done, since his was finished before hers.

"There you go." Jason leaned in while watching her spin it to drench every side. "A nice dunk in the butter, now a roll in the sugar and cinnamon, and it's ready to go." He handed over a plate just in time and reached for his.

"Should we cheers?" Marlee asked as they each lifted their dough boys off the plates.

Jason gave her a sideways glance.

She grinned. "Like this." Marlee brought her treat close to his, gave it a small, muted tap, and said, "Cheers!"

A wide smile spread over his face, accented by the golden glow of dancing flames. "Cheers," he crooned in that low, sexy voice.

Marlee savored the blend of salty butter, warm biscuit, and the flavor of sweetened cinnamon. She licked the sugar granules off her fingertips and grinned. "That was amazing. I never thought anything could rival a toasted marshmallow," she said. "But that *totally* does."

She watched for that magnificent smile of his to appear once more. It did, as bright and warm as the flames. A burst of heat fluttered in her chest. She liked Jason. Was liking him more by the minute.

On their way to the anniversary party, Marlee had agreed to give him a chance. Inwardly, she'd decided to only be open to friendship, but after spending the day with a man who was proving to be more kind, generous, and down-to-earth than she could've imagined, Marlee had to admit she was interested in more than friendship.

The acknowledgment was as thrilling as it was terrifying, because what if this was just a different form of her? There was LA Jason and Phillipsburg Jason. What if he'd somehow discovered this whole other side of Marlee who loved the idea of finding love? She already knew the answer to that. Heck, it's not like she hadn't had crushes over the recent years. But nothing ever stuck. The truth was, whatever side of her had swam to the surface, it wouldn't last. Like Cinderella's magical spell, it would disappear at the stroke of midnight, or in this case, eleven.

"Should we do another one?" Jason asked.

"Definitely." Marlee reached for another piece of dough and began twisting it around the roasting stick. "So how long ago did you buy this place?" Marlee had been surprised to find that Jason now owned the Peterson's old ranch and farmhouse. A property they left behind when moving to Texas.

"I bought it a year and a half ago. I did a good six months' worth of remodeling before moving in." He lowered his roasting stick to the base of the flames, where spots of dark, ash-colored coal glowed with cracks of red.

"This is kind of a smaller ranch for Big Sky Country," she mused aloud.

"It is," Jason said with a nod. "It's basically big enough that I can live out my fantasy of owning my own ranch without having to employ a bunkhouse full of ranch hands year-round."

She glanced over at him. "But you *do* bring on a few, right?"

"I do," he said. "About three or four during the busy seasons."

A recollection was coming to mind. Marlee remembered hearing that Jason had given Billy Conner and his son jobs when the factory downtown was temporarily out of commission.

"You know," she said, hovering her roasting stick just above the flames. "A group of ladies at Sunday service were raving about you." She glanced over in time to see him raise a brow.

"They were, were they?" The deep rasp of Jason's voice was the perfect fusion of sandpaper rough and worn-leather smooth. Low, masculine, and one hundred percent cowboy.

"Mmm, hmm. About how you saved the Conner family when they were out of work for a while. I think one of the Weatherly twins even called you a saint."

Jason reached out, took a hold of her stick, and directed the tip to the spot his had been in moments ago. "Here's the best place," he said. "Give it a few slow spins, and before you know it, it'll be ready to go."

When he pulled his hand away, Marlee found herself leaning a little closer to close the gap.

Jason set his gaze back on the fire. "I wouldn't say there are a whole lot of saints walking around these days. And of the few there are, I'm definitely not among them."

Marlee considered that. "So in your mind, what keeps you from being a saint?"

He lifted an insinuative brow. "Aside from the not-so-pure thoughts I've been having about you?" he asked with a grin. "I did do *one* saintly deed not too long ago."

"Oh yeah?" she asked, intrigued.

"I stopped going to the eleven o'clock Sunday service and started going to the nine o'clock one instead."

Marlee tipped her head. "Okay..."

He grinned, as if he half expected her to know where this was leading; she didn't have a clue. "I didn't do it for me. I did it for a woman. One who was avoiding me so fiercely that I feared she might stop going to service altogether over it."

A recollection shot to her mind. "You offered me a seat," she said in a whisper.

"I did."

"And I didn't take it."

"You *ran*," he said with a laugh.

"I remember that now." A knot of guilt sank into her gut.

"I honestly feared you'd stop coming altogether if you ran into me there again."

Warmth danced around her heart as she took in what he said. "So even though you kind of liked me, and you wanted a chance to talk with me..."

"Very much," he said with a nod.

"Still you changed services so that you wouldn't scare me away from church?"

"Hey," he said, puffing out his chest. "Just trying to keep the man upstairs happy with me." He shrugged then and smiled. "That's probably the only saintly thing I've ever done."

Marlee held his gaze as more dancing heat circled her heart. "Somehow I doubt that." Heaven help her, she was crushing hard. All in one day. All on a man who'd had to coerce her into going out with him in front of half the townsfolk.

"So tell me what a day in the life of a ranch owner looks like." Sure, she was grasping for a topic change, but Marlee genuinely wanted to know.

Jason gave her a general outline of a typical spring day—which, he explained, was very different from a day in summer, winter, or fall where ranch chores were concerned.

He asked about her next. How she learned to gut the fish without cutting out excess meat. How old she'd been when she first learned. Along the way, he'd retrieved a plaid quilt and invited her to curl up with him on the patio swing by the fire.

"You mentioned," he said after a quiet moment, "that the folks at the trout farm know about your mom. I know who she is—Rachel Star, famous soap opera diva—but I got the impression I was missing something."

Marlee leaned her head on Jason's arm, inhaling the scent of his heavenly cologne. She hadn't let herself get so comfortable around the opposite sex since she was old enough to date men versus boys.

She tested the answer in her mind and was surprised to find that she felt safe sharing it with him. "If all you know about Rachel Star is that she's the scandalous man-eater on *The Wild and the Weary,* then you're definitely missing something." Marlee pinned the edge of the blanket between her finger and thumb, slid them along the silky edge as she thought back on the person her mother used to be.

"She and my dad hit it off at a mutual friend's wedding in California. She'd already changed her last name to Star—it used to be Connolly. She'd been working as an extra on movie sets and stuff. She did a few commercials too. In fact, she showed Britt and me this toothpaste commercial she shot years prior. I remembered being so proud.

"Anyway, Charlie said she quickly became enamored with the whole country life when she came out for a visit. She hadn't gotten the big breakthrough she always wanted, so she got a job out here helping with chores at a bunkhouse and, after dating my dad for just four months, the two got married. Rachel said she was done with Hollywood, ready to settle down and have a family."

Jason shifted a bit, closing the small gap between them.

The weight and warmth of him felt amazing. Marlee couldn't imagine how—after just one date—it felt natural to be so close, but it did. Close not only physically, but emotionally as well. Here she was, opening up about a topic she rarely talked to anyone about, yet it felt like she'd been confiding in him for years.

"According to my dad, Rachel got a call from her agent while she was expecting me. A TV executive was offering her a lead in a daytime drama—her dream job, basically—but they'd have to pick up and move to California, something my dad couldn't do. She talked about taking the job anyway and getting an apartment in LA, but as soon as the producer caught wind that she was expecting, he took the offer off the table."

She sighed, the feel of Jason so warm and close taking the sting out of the difficult memory.

"She never spoke another word about it," Marlee said. "Until Lilly was four years old. Britt was six. I was eight. It was like a switch. One day she was here playing devoted wife and mother to three, and the next she was packing up, telling my dad how much she resented him and *the girls* for entrapping her in a life she didn't want. And then she left."

The fire crackled louder in the absence of her words.

"Wow," Jason said. "No wonder you were leery about me."

Marlee shot him a surprised look.

"Or am I wrong?" he asked.

"No," she said. "You're right. I guess I just see this woman who'd come from a life of fame, or at least aspirations for it. She came, she tried the country life, and she left us all behind. We found out later that she'd been in touch with *The Wild and the Weary's* producer, Stan Wattley, who later married her, by the way. I guess Stan had already promised her the job."

Marlee shrugged, glad she'd been able to gloss over the story without sinking in. Like an ice skater on a frozen lake. Stay on the surface and avoid the stabbing pain of its frigid depths. But break through, and the darkness would penetrate, achingly thorough and bone deep.

"I'm sorry," Jason said in a whisper. "I can't imagine how a parent could leave their kids behind like that. It's against nature."

That comment surprised her too. Jason must have sensed it on her face, because his brown eyes widened. "Sorry if that's offensive," he said. "I mean, if you feel a sense of loyalty . . . " He died off there and gulped.

She didn't, but she couldn't exactly form the simple words. All she could think of was the fact that Jason was kind enough to worry about even that. She'd always felt that men were often oblivious to the tender needs and hurts of others. But Jason was proving her wrong. He was attentive, considerate, and seemed to be very aware of the sort of damage her mother might have caused.

"Where did you come from?" Marlee blurted, only halfway meaning to ask it.

Jason tipped his head to one side and inspected her, a mix of amusement and curiosity playing over his face.

A tug pulled at her heart then—subtle, but certain—as something began to occur to her. Slowly the realization trickled in as she tuned into the rhythm of Jason's steady breath, the hypnotizing rise and fall of his chest.

She wasn't the bull trout anymore, because—try as she might to deny it—Marlee had been snared by none other than Jason Keller.

She pulled away, just enough to take in the expression on his face, and recognized the wild thrashing of her heart. Trying in vain to resist the pull. Knowing—already—that it was too late. Jason Keller had caught her fair and square, and now she was simply along for the ride.

A trace of heat moved into her cheeks at the thought; could he see it on her face?

Jason's expression grew serious as he held her gaze. Slowly then, tentatively, he brought a hand to her cheek, traced the tips of his fingers along her jaw, and then down the side of her neck.

Marlee's heart hammered out an extra beat. She sighed out a shaky breath and tuned into the soft caress of his fingertips. Across her collarbone, then back up the side of her neck. Behind her ear. *So good.*

"I really like you, Marlee," he rasped.

She only nodded, too hypnotized by the bliss of his touch. His gaze dropped to her mouth, causing an entirely new thrill to spike through her.

Yes. Please, Jason, kiss me.

He lowered his head as if she'd spoken it aloud, stopping once he was a breath's space away. The sensation of his lips so close, his heated breath grazing her mouth as he sighed, all of it nearly set her skin ablaze.

Was he testing her? Giving her a chance to back out? Or perhaps he simply knew the moment of anticipation would make it even sweeter.

At last he came in, pressed his full, wonderful lips to hers in a slow, lingering kiss.

Yes. Marlee wrapped her arms around him, exploring the warmth of his neck, the contours of his shoulders, and the exquisite balance of push and pull as he kissed her in succession.

Bliss. There was no better word for the experience. She tipped her head, let out a small sigh of pleasure, and assured herself she'd stop things in just . . . a few . . . seconds.

After all, Marlee had never been one to kiss on the first date. And here she was—not even at the standard porch-step goodbye—and already she was wrapped in Jason's arms and enjoying the best kiss of her life.

May as well take advantage of the moment; it wasn't like it could last.

The thought, scissor-sharp as it was, sliced through her euphoria in a blink. She hadn't meant to think it, but Marlee could hardly ignore the truth. She knew herself all too well. She was the bull trout—the one that refused to get caught.

The reminder sank into her conscious thoughts like a heavy stone.

Regretting the action already, Marlee brought things to an end with one last kiss, but she wasn't ready to let go of Jason Keller just yet, of this new, delicious hope she'd found in just five hundred and forty minutes with him.

She rested her cheek against his, willing his handsome, spicy scent to memory. The feel of his short scruff on her skin.

Sure, she was seeing things differently now, while in the muscular arms of Jason Keller, but Marlee would fall back into her stubborn mindset by morning; she knew it.

"Uh-oh . . . hear that buzzing?" Jason asked softly. "That's my alarm." He pulled back enough to shoot her a heartbreaking smile.

Don't forget this, Marlee.
It's real. It's wonderful.
And you want it. You secretly really do.

Jason snatched his phone off the seat and tapped the screen until it stopped buzzing. "I did promise to get you home on time. Guess that means we'd better leave now."

"Oh," she squeaked. "You're right. I don't want to be late."

Lie—if she had it her way, Marlee would stay tucked in

Jason's embrace for the next hour and make up for all the kissing she'd missed out on over the years. She was entitled to that, right?

Especially since she knew how impossible it would be for her to get sucked into another moment like this. Even with the charming cowboy who was proving to be more magnificent than she could've imagined.

Knots of anxiety prodded deep in her gut as Jason helped her climb back into his truck. Marlee stretched the seatbelt over her chest and fastened the buckle with a final-sounding *click*.

It wasn't warm out by any means, but the spring night suddenly felt downright cold now that she wasn't cuddling into him. Especially as she considered that it would probably never happen again.

"What are you thinking over there?" Jason asked as he pulled onto the road. "You're awfully quiet. Payton always warned me that when a woman is quiet on the outside, there's a whole lot of talk happening on the inside."

Marlee glanced over and gave in to a smile. "Your sister's smart."

"So," he took one hand off the wheel and stretched it across the center console. "You going to tell me what kind of talk is happening in there right now?"

A dart of heat sunk into her chest as Marlee glanced down at his hand. She slipped her palm over his and laced their fingers together. It was an intimate act, one probably more fit for "official" couples, but the gesture didn't feel out of place. In fact, it felt perfect.

If only it could last. "I'm just thinking about how . . . " The bull trout inside her fought to use its voice, but Marlee wasn't ready to let it take over just yet. "I don't know."

"Uh-oh," he said with a groan. "It's my hair, huh? You hate my hair. It didn't pass the test."

She gave into a half smile. "No. I like your hair. A lot."

"Good," he said, "because I like *you* a lot. I'd like to get to know you."

That sentiment begged a response. A truthful one.

Her heart thundered a rapid stream of painful, protesting pumps.

"Here's the thing," she said. "I wasn't kidding when I said I don't mind being alone. In fact, I've made up my mind so completely, that . . . that even though I really like you, and I'd love to go out with you again—"

"That's great," Jason interjected. "That's what I want too."

"Yeah, but the problem is, I won't feel this way in the morning. See, when I wake up tomorrow, all of this . . . all these emotions I'm feeling will be gone. And I'll be right back in my don't-want-a-guy state of mind and convinced that what I felt tonight wasn't even real."

Her words seeped into the leather seats as she spoke, leaving nothing but the white noise of rubber tires on tar.

Well, at least she'd gotten that out of the way.

Now Jason knew that a relationship with Marlee Jenkins was impossible. And she'd probably come off just crazy enough that he wouldn't care any more. Whatever mystique she'd acquired by eluding him all this time had surely worn off, and now he could find someone normal to pursue.

Another, much deeper ache wiggled into that low corner of her heart. She wondered if the bull trout ever got lonely too. Watching all of his friends leave the pond one by one.

Jason slid a thumb over the back of her knuckles. "But what if you don't?"

She turned back to look at him, the cool gray light from the dashboard illuminating his face. "Huh?"

"You said you'd wake up and all your feelings for me

would be gone. Meaning, you *do* actually have feelings for me. So what if they're still there?"

If only that were possible. She'd had mini crushes since Charlie's diagnosis, but only fleeting ones. The bullheaded part of her was too stubborn to fall in love. "They won't be."

He chuckled under his breath. "So sure, are you?"

"Sadly, yes. It's not what I *want*. It's just what I *know*."

He nodded. "Okay."

Okay?

The white noise from their drive picked up again.

That was it, huh? That was weird. Why did she have to be so weird?

She blew out a pursed breath and turned to look out the window once more. Not that there was anything to see. Just a reflection of Jason as he gripped the wheel with one hand.

Marlee used *her* free hand to tug the tangerine lip balm from her pocket and smooth it over her lips. She inhaled the scent as she considered the conversation once more.

So he'd given up on her, then. That was for the best. When she got to her room tonight, Marlee would have a good cry over the loss of what might have been, and then she'd fall asleep, only to wake up and realize that her feelings for him were gone, along with this silly new Marlee who was just as enamored with Jason as the rest of the universe.

Probably more so, because she'd seen the real him. And *that's* who *she'd* fallen for.

"You won't dodge me any more at the fish farm, will you?" Jason rubbed his thumb over her hand once more.

"No," she promised. "I won't."

"And let's just say that we remain friends. Friends are good to have, right?"

Her heart did a leap in her chest. Geez, he was persistent. "Right."

"Well, let's say that you and I see each other from time to time, as friends, and the feelings—the ones that will vanish by morning—come back. Will you give me another chance?"

She considered that. "I'd probably be too proud to tell you they were back." She was only half kidding, but admitting it made her anxious for his reply.

"Then how about we use a code word? Or a code action? Like, let's say we're spending time together just as friends, and suddenly you're thinking of me as *more* than a friend, you could give my hand two fast squeezes." He demonstrated by squeezing her hand. "One, two. Just like that."

"Oh, cuz if we're hanging out as friends, we'll already be holding hands?" she asked through a grin.

He shot her a disapproving look. "Tsk, of course."

Marlee shook her head. "Fine. If all of those scenarios magically line up as you suggested, I'll . . . do what you said."

The look of triumph on Jason's face was priceless. It stayed in place as he pulled into her narrow drive, helped her out of the truck, and walked her up to the porch.

A wayward glance at a crack in the blinds said her sisters were watching from the front room window. Of course.

With the dark sky at his back, the illumination over his face, Jason Keller looked like an angel. A very gorgeous angel. The hickory scent from their fire blended with his heavenly cologne, reminding her of the moments they'd shared by the fire.

Jason fixed his brown eyes on hers. "So, are we already in just-friend mode? Or does that wait until morning?"

How was it that he could spark a fire in her chest with a simple question alone? Marlee rubbed her lips together as she considered. If things went how she figured they would, this would probably be her last chance to kiss him.

"Yes," she whispered. "I mean, *that* won't happen until morning."

The look on his face turned serious then, brooding almost, as he wrapped one, solid hand around her hip and squeezed.

Whoa. The fire moved, settling low in her tummy.

At last Jason lowered his head, tipped it just enough to come in for one soft, teasing kiss. "Goodnight, Marlee," he whispered against her mouth.

Her lids fluttered open. "Goodnight?" she squeaked, but it sounded more like a question since she was nowhere near done kissing him yet.

Jason straightened then, and placed the hat back on his head.

"Thank you for going out with me today." He pulled the door wide open for her. "I had a wonderful time."

"I did too," she whispered with a nod. Crickets chirped. A lone coyote howled in the distance, as if it, too, knew this would be her last taste of romance.

Marlee pushed past the ache in her heart and forced out a farewell. "Thank you again." She shuffled forward, one foot after the next. She was halfway inside the house when Jason spoke up one last time.

"Oh, and Marlee? Friends usually have one another's phone number. Mind if I get yours?"

Lord, thank you for sending someone persistent. "Sure." She recited the number for him while a celebration parade marched up and down her chest. The sound of barely stifled squeals from inside said Britt and Lilly were celebrating too.

A lazy grin pulled at one side of Jason's kissable lips. "Great," he said. "See you later."

"See you later." Marlee watched him for a bit, not wanting to step inside just yet. Not wanting to turn back into the woman she'd been before their date.

She had the sudden urge to holler at him from across the

yard, tell him that if he gets turned down in a day or two, it would be *that* woman who did it, not the one standing on the porch watching him leave. Not the one who ran her fingers through his hair. And definitely not the one who sank into the bliss of his kiss and felt it all the way to her toes.

Please, Lord, don't let this new woman vanish come morning.

SIX

TWO THINGS WERE clear to Jason after his anticipated date. First: he was crazy about Marlee Jenkins. Second: she liked him in return. As fleeting as she promised those feelings would be, Jason was determined to put them to the test.

With the citrus flavor of her magnetic kiss still lingering on his lips, he hurried inside, leaned against the couch, and tugged his phone from his pocket.

Earlier, Marlee had told him that her family sold the only two horses they had while her dad was in treatment. When he asked if she missed riding, she'd admitted that she did. She missed it very much. Perfect.

He typed out a quick text and read it over with a smile on his face.

You know what friends like to do together? Plant gardens. Mind if I come help you tomorrow after service? Maybe we can take the horses out when we're through.

Might as well get her roped into another date before dawn crept in. He hit *send*, tucked the phone into his pocket once more, and cleaned up the patio while Jepson neighed beyond the corral. Gypsy joined in too.

"I know," he assured them, hollering so his voice would carry. "You're sore at me for not riding you today. I'm sorry. I'll make up for it tomorrow. Hopefully."

With a stack of tins in one hand and a pile of empty

takeout boxes in the other, Jason made his way back inside. He hooked his elbow on the door handle and used it to slide the thing closed behind him.

He dropped the boxes in the waste bin and shuffled over to the sink, thoughts of Marlee on his mind. Her laugh—dang, how it tugged at his insides. So much he felt it might turn him inside out. She was funny too, and honest. To a fault, some might say, but at least he'd always know where he stood.

Getting along with his family—and Jason did consider the Bransons to be his second family—was important to him. Seeing Marlee joke around with Bob, laugh with Luke and Taylor, and give Mel and Pete rare, inside tips about snaring the biggest, most elusive fish in the bunch—all of it had lit some sort of fire in him. She was all he could have hoped in that department, and more.

He hadn't expected to explore the romantic side of things just yet, but the sparks had been fire hot and impossible to resist. Dang, he'd enjoyed her kiss, made all the sweeter by the taste of triumph.

Marlee wasn't just playing hard to get. Seemed the woman was, in truth, closer to impossible where love was concerned. But she'd given him a chance, just as she'd promised, and boy, had it paid off.

It had taken a whole lot of discipline to stop kissing that pretty mouth of hers at the doorstep, but he was a firm believer in taking things slowly. Besides, it wouldn't hurt to leave her wanting more.

Just as he set the tins into the sink, Jason's phone let out a buzz. His heart raced into new speeds as he tugged it from his pocket once more. His eyes shot to the one word she'd responded with. It felt as if that fire, the one he'd put out before taking Marlee home—had sparked back into full flame right inside his chest.

"Yes!" he cheered, throwing a fist into the air. He looked down at the screen once more, enjoying the look of those four small letters and the wonderful word they made.

Sure.

"Tomorrow it is, then." He recalled the time he'd gone to the amusement park with Payton years ago. They climbed onto a coaster that Jason had been dying to go on. Until he was strapped in and the thing took off at rocket speed. He'd encountered a shot of terror in those brief moments. A thrill mingled with fear of the unknown jerks and turns that awaited him.

One thing was clear where Marlee was concerned. This was sure to be one heck of a ride.

SEVEN

MARLEE'S EYES SHOT open to the sound of her alarm. She stared at her ceiling in the cool gray light and rested a hand over her heart. She'd keep it there just in case. If her feelings for him had vanished, there'd be a giant hole in their place.

Okay, Marlee. Time for the moment of truth: Jason Keller.

The very name caused a flare of heat to jump through her chest. Yes. Yes, yes, YES! She still liked him. She *like*-liked him. And he liked her too. Hope swelled within her like a life source of its own, something that might sustain her as well as any feast.

And feast on it she did. The whole time Marlee was getting ready, she allowed herself to play the part of a crushing teenager.

She'd hoped to see him at Sunday service, but it seemed he was still respecting that whole don't-chase-her-away-from-God rule of his.

Britt and Lilly stayed after for the single adult social, which left Marlee with the place all to herself. Perfect.

She stepped into Dad's old pair of denim coveralls, as she did every year while planting the spring garden. The oversized pair was covered in grease stains, but she loved them just the same. After pulling her hair back, Marlee tied a bandana around her ponytail and brushed on some blush.

She gave herself a glance over in the mirror and noticed Dad's old notebook tucked in the big front pocket. Marlee had forgotten all about it. What had started off as a few of Dad's musings in a notepad had turned out to be a journal she'd started to use to talk with her dad, tell him about what was new in her life. She'd missed it.

Tonight, she told herself as she set it on Dad's old dresser. She'd fill him in on everything after she and Jason spent another amazing day together. Already, she couldn't wait.

When a knock came to the door, it took everything in Marlee to hold in a squeal. She did, however, skip all the way to the door.

"Hi there," she said with a growing grin.

Jason looked her up and down. "Dang, you look cute."

She giggled, loving the compliment. "So do you." That was no joke. He had his cowboy hat and jeans on today, this time with a tight T-shirt that showed off the contours of his muscled chest.

"Shall we?" Jason asked.

"Yep. We can go through the house." Marlee motioned him inside. Once she had the door closed, she reached out, took hold of his hand, and led him through the kitchen.

"You weren't at the eleven o'clock service today," she said, glancing over her shoulder at him.

He locked eyes with her, seeming to search her face for a blink. "That's because I wasn't sure how you were going to feel when you woke up, remember?"

"Oh, that." Marlee couldn't believe she'd actually shared that with him. "Well, it was different this time."

"Oh yeah?" he asked in a singsong voice.

She nodded, knowing he'd need more of an answer than that. But it was too awkward to talk about. Besides, she didn't want to jinx it. But then a recollection came to her, and she knew just how she'd let him know.

Marlee softened her grip on his hand as they approached the sliding glass door. And then, quickly so he wouldn't mistake it, she gave it two squeezes.

Jason chuckled under his breath. "I was hoping you'd say that." He leaned in then, pressed a gentle kiss to her cheek, and spoke against her skin. "I feel the same way."

Dear Dad,

You'll be so glad to hear that I'm no longer the bull trout. I finally let myself fall for someone, and guess what? It's been ten whole days and my feelings for him are only getting stronger.

He helped plant the garden last week. He did all the tilling, and he even complimented your coveralls. We rode horses after that until sunset. Jepson and Gypsy. It was one of the most beautiful nights of my whole life. We've gone riding almost every night since then too.

Oh my gosh, I never thought I'd say this, but I'm actually falling in love! I think you'd like him too. He comes from Los Angeles, but he's a total cowboy at heart. He's not like Mom at all. When we're together, I can't stop smiling. He jokes with me about my obsession with making my own lip balm, and insists on "sampling" each flavor, which can only be done lip-to-lip. But don't worry—he's been a total gentleman so far.

Am I crazy for letting myself fall for him so fast? Britt and Lilly are thrilled about it, as you can imagine. And I am too, mostly. But there is just one thing I worry about. It's actually hard to even write about. It's just that a part of me does still worry, just a little bit, that something will lure him back to Los Angeles. That he'll leave me the way Mom left us.

It's almost like that bull trout is still inside somewhere, looking for a way to free itself. I'm sure if you were here, you'd have the perfect advice for me. You always knew how to slip your words of wisdom into any situation.

Tears ran off Marlee's cheek as she finished the thought:

I miss you so much it hurts. I wish I could go back in time, just for one night, and spend the evening with you. We'd watch that western TV series you loved. I'd make your favorite: garlic bread, Caesar salad, and lasagna with cheddar, not mozzarella. Britt would make those cookies you always liked, the no-bake ones. And Lilly . . . well, Lilly would set the table.

Marlee gave into a laugh as more tears came. She closed the book, pulled it to her chest, and gave into another round of sobs. "I miss you, Dad," she said. "I feel like I'm going to mess this up and blow it with him. Don't let me do that, okay?"

She reached over, flicked off her lamp, and stared into the darkness for a blink before closing her eyes. Things had been perfect with Jason, so much that she couldn't help but fear something might ruin it, even if that something was herself.

No. Don't think that way. She'd gotten past all that, and just in time too. Now she could really invest in the man of her dreams. Still, as she drifted off to sleep, Marlee found herself uttering the words once more.

Please, don't let me mess things up with him.

EIGHT

THE LAST SLIVER of sun had sunk into the horizon, leaving the small group in the cool glow of twilight.

"So let's do a little recap," Marlee said, tucking her lip balm back into her pocket. She eyed Payton and Luke. "I now know about Jason's passion for flossing his teeth."

"*Obsession* is more like it," Payton chimed. "Ten. Minutes. A night."

Marlee laughed. "And then the flossing session is often followed by a rummage through the kitchen for a late-night snack?"

Jason covered his face with one hand. "Yeah, yeah."

"I'm telling you," Luke said. "When Payton was staying there and she and I were getting . . . acquainted, we had to wait for that bedtime routine before our hookup by the fireplace. Felt like hours." The two chuckled, and Payton moved in to plant a kiss to Luke's cheek. Gunner had fallen asleep in Lilly's arms before dinner was even through, which explained why her youngest sister kept so quiet at the end of the table.

The gathering wasn't quite like the ones thrown by the Bransons, but it had still been a wonderful evening just the same. Payton and Luke hadn't been the only ones dishing the dirt on Jason. Taylor offered a few goodies as well, one about Jason's obsession with a lucky belt he wore for every rodeo.

Lilly and Britt were eager to share what they had on Marlee too, their main focus centered on her obsession with lip balm. "You should see how many nooks and crevices she sneaks them into," Britt said with wide eyes. "By the couch, in the kitchen, at the bathroom sink, in the study, by her bed, even in the car!"

Jason had come to her rescue, though, muttering something like, "So that's why she always tastes so good." It had been a fun evening, for sure. And as summer approached, there were sure to be a whole lot more. If all went well.

And there it was—that doubting voice in the back of her head. The one that tried to worm its way into every beautiful occasion.

"Oh, Jason," Payton said, pulling Marlee from her musings. "Dad was asking about the gala. He says you haven't committed to it yet. Why not?"

Marlee glanced over in time to see Jason shrug.

"Gala?" she asked, looking from him back to his sister.

"The Kellers host a massive gala dinner each year to raise funds for Operation Smile. My dad and a bunch of other plastic surgeons fly overseas and operate on babies who'd never stand a chance at getting the surgery otherwise."

"That's amazing," Marlee said.

"And Jason has gone with him the last few years to help out," Payton added.

Marlee set her gaze back on Jason. He lifted his chin, a thoughtful look in his eye. "I wasn't sure how you'd feel about me going back to LA for that, especially with . . . " He stopped there and shrugged again.

With everything that happened with her mom. Is that what he was going to say? The idea stung. "Of course I wouldn't want you to miss something like that, Jason."

"Would you come with me?" He asked it like the question had already been poised on his tongue.

"Yeah," Payton said. "That's a *great* idea. You'd love it, Marlee. Tons of food, a bunch of Hollywood's elite gathered in one place."

The idea planted a lump of fear deep in her chest. It sounded more like the last place on earth she'd want to go.

"The Hollywood crowd doesn't exactly appeal to her," Jason explained.

Guilt welled up in her gut. "I don't want you to miss it," she said.

"And *I* don't want to go without *you*."

The background chatter between Britt and Taylor died down. A chorus of crickets picked up in its place. This was definitely not the time to have a conversation like this, in front of a small crowd, family or not.

"We better get Gunner home," Payton said.

Luke came to a stand. "Right," he said. "Little stinker will want to eat once more before he hits the sack. Must get that from his Uncle Jay Jay," he razzed.

Marlee saw her guests out, trying her best to offer normal glad-you-came and thanks-for-the-fun-night greetings along the way, but her mind was stuck someplace else. Visions of champagne glasses clanking over a sea of evening gowns, tuxedos, and flashing bulbs. The very crowd that lured her mom away from them.

"Why don't you and Jason go out on the hammock?" Britt suggested as their company drove away. "Lilly and I can clean up the dinner mess, okay?"

"Yeah," Lilly agreed. "We'll clean up."

Bless Britt and Lilly. They'd obviously picked up on the unsettled tension in the air.

The far corner of their property hosted a small forest of trees. The Jenkins girls had hung several hammocks throughout the wooded property once spring began. It was the perfect place to enjoy a cup of morning coffee before the sun moved overhead enough for the branches to block it out.

And now, as dry pine needles crunched beneath the soles of her boots, Marlee couldn't help but think the light of their relationship was being threatened as well. Blocked out by the Hollywood-sized elephant from her past.

It took a while to settle into the hammock side by side, but once they were lying comfortably in place, the fabric nearly closing around them like a cocoon, Jason nuzzled his face into her hair and sighed.

"I don't want this to trigger you."

She didn't want it to either, but it already had. The aching thuds in her chest said it all. Not to mention the growing feeling in her gut that things between her and Jason couldn't possibly last. She clenched her eyes shut, fought the quiver of her lip as her fears shot from her heart to her lips.

"I'm scared you won't want to come back after."

"I know," he whispered. "But that won't happen. Ever."

She nodded, wanting very badly to believe it.

Jason found her hand, wove his fingers through hers, and sighed. "Listen, this has been the best two weeks of my life. I know what I want, and I know what I *don't* want. I don't have to do this event. I'm not even planning on it, I just . . . wish Payton hadn't brought it up."

Marlee remembered Gerald Tanner's baby, the one who'd been born with a severe cleft pallet. The surgery had been life altering. This was a good cause, and she didn't want to interfere in any way. Heaven knew if Jason could charm Marlee out of her determined mindset to fly solo the rest of her life, he could charm thousands of dollars from the Hollywood starlets at the event with that dimple alone.

The dread that had crept in lifted a bit. In fact, what had felt destined for an onslaught of outright despair only moments ago was beginning to fade. A flicker of hope sparked up next, mingled with a new flare of determination. Marlee had only enjoyed a taste of what being in love could be like, and she wasn't about to let it slip away so easily.

"When is it?" she asked. "The banquet."

Jason shifted in the hammock. "It doesn't matter. I'm not going."

"I want you to," Marlee said. "And if the invitation still stands, I'd like to come." It felt good to say it aloud. In fact, as Jason responded with things like *that would be awesome* and *are you sure about this?*, Marlee's level of certainty only grew. Yes, this was the right thing to do. And things would be just fine.

It wasn't until she pressed her lips against Jason's in a celebratory kiss that a wave of misgiving washed over her.

You're going to regret it, the inner voice warned. *This just might be how you lose him.* Perhaps that was true, but Marlee didn't want to live the rest of her life in fear. If she was destined to lose Jason to his old life, it'd be far better to have it happen now. She only hoped that this time the voice of doubt was wrong.

NINE

JASON EYED HIS reflection in the hotel mirror. It'd been a long time since he'd donned a tuxedo, and he couldn't say he'd missed it. He wondered how Marlee was doing on the other side of that door. He'd rented two rooms for the night, though he hoped they'd spend a decent amount of time cuddling on the sofa after tonight's event before parting ways.

A quick glance at his watch said it was time to head out; the limo would be there soon. He shot one last look at his reflection. He imagined what it might be like if he'd never broken free and pursued the life he'd always dreamed of. Would he be attending this party with a heart toward the kids they'd be helping, or with aspirations for reaching new levels of fame?

Or would he simply be plowing along like a neglected workhorse? Miserably chugging along, doing whatever it took to keep up the family image? He turned his attention to the door that separated his room from Marlee's. Three long strides took him close enough to knock, something he'd do once he calmed the sudden racing in his heart. The fact was, the evening could be another trigger for Marlee. The last thing he wanted is for doubts to creep back into that overactive mind of hers.

He straightened his arms to his sides, tugged on the sleeves of his coat, and let out a slow, paced breath. Time to see how this would play out.

Marlee could hardly believe her eyes. The woman staring back at her from the fancy hotel mirror looked a whole lot like the one and only Rachel Star. The pearl-colored gown Payton helped her pick out accented every curve Marlee had. The gorgeous, glittering piece made her look taller and bustier and... like a totally different person.

"I don't know if I can do this," she muttered under her breath. She smoothed a hand down the front of the gown and straightened her shoulders. *Poised, Marlee. Don't slouch.* Wow, she looked even more like Mom with the correct posture.

But as she stepped closer to the mirror in her matching stiletto heels, the resemblance started to fade. Marlee looked more like herself, a woman who—if she were honest—she'd grown to like over the years. Her mother might have rejected her, but Marlee had a whole lot of people who loved and cared about her. She had Jason now too.

The two hadn't exactly used the L word just yet. Heck, they'd only been dating for six weeks. But she'd known weeks ago that she was in love with him. Which must have been why she'd agreed to come to this thing despite her aversion to it.

A series of knocks sounded, and Marlee glanced at the door leading to Jason's room. A knot of nerves twisted inside her gut. She'd adapted a don't-ask-questions-she-didn't-want-the-answers-to policy where the evening was involved. If she weren't afraid of the answers, she might ask all sorts of things. Will the press be there? Will they snap pictures of us together? Would the picture end up in some magazine with a cruel title about the Keller Cowboy settling for a country bumpkin?

A new zing of nerves tingled up the back of her neck as

she grasped the lever to unlock the latch. A quick twist here, a turn of the knob there, and soon she was prying open the heavy oak door.

Whoa. Marlee had been so distracted by the thoughts in her head that she hadn't thought to prepare herself for what she might see on the other side of the door.

Jason blew out a whistle and tipped his head to eye her up and down. "Thank you, Lord in heaven, for this moment."

Marlee released a shallow laugh in response. "Ditto." She ran her gaze up his tall, magnificent frame, over those broad, angular shoulders, and up to that gorgeous face with the chiseled jaw and perfect grin. If he wanted to, Jason could make a living off of his ridiculously out-of-proportion good looks.

He extended an arm, turned his hand face up and lifted a brow. "Shall we?"

Marlee rested her hand in his. "We shall."

He led her to the limo next, and soon they were passing high-rises in the most crowded parts of Los Angeles. "Can't believe you used to live here," she said.

Jason kept his eyes pasted on her. "Neither can I."

She was glad they had brunch plans with Jason's parents and stepparents in the morning. It'd give her a chance to see the home he grew up in, since his mother had remained there after the divorce, and, of course, spend time getting to know each of them too, since tonight they'd be busy mingling.

A Spanish-style mansion with white brick and a red roof housed the event. Bold spotlights shone on a row of tall palm trees leading to a magnificent staircase. More floodlights illuminated the massive structure, causing it to glow against the dark night sky. Beyond the enormous windows, glowing chandeliers hung from vaulted ceilings, promising it would be just as grand on the inside.

A crowd of camera-carting paparazzi swarmed a man exiting one of those hummer limos a few yards ahead.

A tinted window separated them from their driver. Jason tapped it down an inch. "Jack, we'd like a few minutes before we exit, if you don't mind."

"Not at all," the man said.

Jason rolled the window up once more and shifted in his seat to face her.

A fresh round of nervous energy bubbled in Marlee's tummy.

Jason gave her hand a squeeze. "You nervous?"

She took in the kind concern she saw in those warm brown eyes and smiled. "Of course not." She laughed. "I mean, unless that shaky sound of my voice means I'm nervous. Or my hands. Do they feel clammy to you? And I think my heart stopped beating somewhere a few miles back. Should we be concerned about that?"

"Let me take a look. I *did* take some medical courses, you know." Jason brought a hand to her neck, traced the tips of his fingers down the delicate slope, and licked his lips. The furrow of his brow said he was focused in on her now, and that intense gaze was nearly as affecting as his touch.

He tipped his head to one side, brought his lips to the spot just beneath her earlobe, and kissed her there. He moved down an inch, and kissed again. And then again. The next kiss he planted was longer, slower, and enhanced by the gentle caress of his tongue. Goose bumps rippled over her arms.

"Ah, I can feel your pulse right here," he crooned. "It's going pretty fast, actually."

Yeah, thanks to him.

The damp heat of his breath caused an entirely new thrill to rise in her chest. Marlee reached out, steadied herself by gripping his shoulders. Thank heavens they were sitting down; her knees would have buckled beneath her at the bliss.

Jason pressed kisses along her jaw next, pausing when he made it to one corner of her lips. Slowly then, he traced the shape of her mouth with the gentle caress of his bottom lip, his heated breath only adding to the spell. And then all at once, he stilled. His movement, his breath, everything seemed to halt. Until she heard his next breath come at last, this one shaky, like hers.

She sensed he had something to say, yet she couldn't imagine what it might be.

He nodded subtly then, absently, as if he'd set his mind to whatever it was he was contemplating. And then it came. "I love you, Marlee," he mumbled against her skin.

If her heart *had* actually stopped a few miles back, it was making up for the missed beats now, pumping in excess as she tipped back to meet his gaze. Wave after glorious wave of warmth pulsed through her body. Jason loved her. And what a wonderful thing that was, because she felt the very same way.

She tipped back, took in the passion she saw in his brown eyes, and dared herself to speak. "I love you too," she whispered. Marlee had waited her whole life for this moment; she just hadn't known it until then.

That dimple sank into Jason's cheek again. At once he came in for another kiss—a celebration of the words they'd just shared. The confirmation that their tender love was, in fact, mutual.

And real.

And growing every day.

This time Jason skipped the gentle build up, the series of kisses that led to a deeper exchange, and started with a sense of passion she hadn't known in him yet, the urgent press and pull of his mouth coaxing her into new levels of surrender.

She melted into him, releasing a sigh of pleasure from low in her throat.

Yes. So good.

She belonged to Jason Keller, and she wanted nothing more.

Suddenly bulbs flashed from the other side of the tinted glass, causing a moment of awareness to strike. Still in a daze, Marlee willed herself to break from the kiss and speak.

"What was that?" she mumbled.

"Just the paparazzi," he said before kissing her again. "They can't see us through the tinted glass," he explained between kisses. "They just don't want to miss anything."

"Right," she said before giving in to one last kiss. She sighed, reminding herself of their shared affirmations of love, enjoying the fact that they had their whole lives to explore where it might lead. But tonight, they had a job to do. "We better get in there."

Jason groaned, tipped his head to catch her gaze once more, and gave her a brooding expression. "I can't tell you how badly I want to stay in here with you and blow off this event."

She grinned. "Me too."

Jason cleared his throat, reached for the lever on the console, and lowered the window that separated them from their driver. "Okay, Jack," he said.

Jack climbed out of the limo while Marlee refreshed her lip gloss and tucked the small purse back under her arm.

Jason straightened the collar of his suit coat and took hold of Marlee's hand. "You ready?"

Sure, she might have to deal with a few triggers among Hollywood's elite, but it was for a good cause, and she'd have the man she loved right by her side. It was time to make some money for those children.

With that, Marlee gave Jason's hand two squeezes. "Ready."

TEN

JASON SANK INTO a leather lounge chair and fixed his gaze on the glorious woman standing behind the donations desk. Marlee Jenkins had said it back—she loved him! A massive celebration broke out in his chest, the chambers of his heart ringing out like wedding bells in a chapel. If he were honest, that's exactly where he hoped they were headed. He wanted nothing more than to spend a lifetime with the Montana woman who'd captured his heart, and it seemed heaven's stars were aligning in his favor.

A smile crossed his lips as he watched the engaging manner in which Marlee spoke with the A-listers attending the party. She didn't intimidate easily, that was obvious, and Jason found that incredibly sexy. It proved all the more that she was the perfect woman for him, one not influenced by status or stardom.

He watched as she tipped her head back in laughter in response to something said among the small crowd gathered around her. There she was, that same, kind Montana Marlee no matter the circumstance. Forget the fact that she had deep wounds connected to the lifestyle led by her present company. She wasn't letting that stop her from being the generous woman he knew her to be.

A new flood of heat pooled into his chest. He hadn't been kidding when he thanked the Lord upon laying eyes on Marlee earlier. In that moment, Jason envisioned lifting the cowboy hat off his head, dropping to his knees, and offering the most sincere praise to his maker. Marlee truly was a gift, and he would do anything it took to do right by her.

A quick glance at the clock said they had more than an hour to go. In a moment, Jason would force himself to get back up and mingle. He couldn't help but dread it. He'd been back in LA for a total of nine hours, and already he was homesick. Bob Branson had a favorite saying; *your soul just knows when you're home.* Likewise, Jason's soul knew when he was *away* from home. As earnest as a few dozen of the attendees were, a heavy sense of arrogance and selfishness hung in the air. For many, it was about what the social gathering could do for them.

Ah well, at least they'd open their pocketbooks while they were there. Children from across the world would benefit from it, and that's what mattered.

Just then a woman across the way caught his eye. She was beautiful, no doubt, but that's not what got his attention. There was something familiar in the almond shape of her eyes and the high set of her cheekbones . . . The middle-aged woman looked like an older version of Marlee.

Oh, no. Dread punched him so hard it made his gut clench. Rachel Star had come, and if he wasn't mistaken, she seemed to be heading Marlee's way. A curse fell off his lips as he shot to his feet.

He eyed the crowds that separated Marlee from her mother. A cluster of tuxedos here, a mass of evening gowns there, and then it was Marlee, standing behind the tall donation booth, that wide grin weaving spells over one of the biggest Hollywood names there.

It would be foolish of Rachel Star to shine a light on the ugly truth of her past by addressing Marlee in such a public place, but if the woman were an opportunist, she'd risk it.

Jason couldn't have that. Marlee didn't need that sort of trigger reminding her of why she'd never wanted to give Jason a chance. He spun in place, looking for someone to replace Marlee at the booth.

Payton, Payton . . . where are you?

Before he came around full circle, a hand cupped his shoulder. He glanced back to see his sister standing there.

"Rachel Star is here," Payton said. "She says she wants to talk to you and Marlee, together."

ELEVEN

"WELL, IT HAS been a pleasure speaking with you tonight, Marlee from Montana," Kingston Conner said while taking Marlee's hand. He pulled it to his lips and planted a kiss on it. "Had I known you were going to be assisting on the service trip, I'd have signed up to go along as well."

Marlee laughed, sandwiched the man's hand, and sighed. Sure, he was pushing his late fifties, but the actor was as handsome and charming as ever. "Well, I only just decided last week. Perhaps it's not too late for you to join as well."

Morocco. Wow, what an adventure that would be. An eye-opening one, and Marlee welcomed it. Welcomed the chance to do some hands-on service with the man she loved.

The man who loved her in return!

A fresh thrill floated through her as she thought back on the way he'd said it. It had been such a whirlwind evening—her mind being pulled in so many directions—that Marlee kept reminding herself of the glorious moments she and Jason had shared in the limo. It was like discovering it was Christmas day again and again.

Her eyes wandered over the crowd. Where had he gone anyway?

"Didn't know this was your daughter. Of *course* that makes sense now that I see the two of you." The words, spoken by Kingston Conner, barely started to register when Jason appeared by her side.

His hand curved around her waist. "Payton's going to take over for you," he mumbled into her ear. "C'mon."

She felt the anxious energy in his touch, sensed that he wanted to usher her off as quickly as possible. As soon as she caught sight of the woman behind Kingston, Marlee realized why he was in such a hurry.

Chestnut hair streaked with gold highlights, blue eyes that sparkled like the diamonds at her throat, and the billion-dollar smile she used so well: Rachel Star.

The blood in Marlee's body turned to ice—rock hard and too frozen to move.

"My Marlee," Rachel chimed in a singsong voice. "How wonderful to see you."

TWELVE

MARLEE TRACED A finger along the rim of her glass, her eyes glued to the action.

"Patty Deveraux said you two were dating, which is why I told Stan we needed to come tonight, right darling?"

"Right, dear." Admiration rang thick on Stan Wattley's tone. Marlee could only imagine the way it beamed off the man's face. She just couldn't look at it for herself. It had been hard enough to agree to join the couple at the quiet table by the bar. If it weren't for Jason, she might not have agreed to it at all.

She glanced over at Jason in time to catch that reassuring wink he often gave. It provided a measure of comfort to know he was by her side. To know just how very much he wanted to be in that place. *You have him, Marlee. No matter what happens with your mother right now, you have Jason, Lilly, and Britt. That's all that matters.*

Marlee sensed that Jason hoped she'd find a measure of closure during the soirée. He'd suggested as much while encouraging her to agree to it. But Marlee wasn't so sure. It seemed more likely that she'd walk away from the meeting with an even deeper wound than before.

"Not that we wouldn't have come anyway," Rachel rambled. "We *love* to give to charity, but it just happened to provide an opportunity for Stan and I to propose something we think might be of interest to you both."

Marlee forced her gaze back to Rachel. The woman's blue eyes bounced between Marlee and Jason as a new, nervous energy filled the space. She was working up to something; Marlee could feel it.

"Go ahead," she finally urged. "What do you want to propose?" May as well cut to the chase.

Marlee braced herself by abandoning her glass and reaching for Jason's hand.

"Stan, why don't you tell them?" Rachel crooned.

Stan's goatee was peppered with gray, giving him that dignified appearance. And though his brown eyes seemed kind as he smiled at her, Marlee sensed a shrewdness behind them. "I've made Rachel co-producer of *The Wild and the Weary,* in case you haven't heard, and together, we'd like to offer Jason a role in the show."

"Not just *a* role," Rachel blurted over her husband. "It's the lead role. Like, you'll come onto the show in all your Keller Cowboy glory, and you'll be *The Wild and the Weary's* new main attraction. Your character will own a ranch of his own, just like you . . ."

If Marlee's blood had turned to ice moments ago, the couple's offer was a heat wave, causing the blood to melt and flow so quickly she felt her heart might drown. She stared at her mother in the moment of horror, bitterness sharp on her tongue, and fought to put order to the words in her head.

"I can't believe you're doing this," she blurted before she could stop herself. "It's not enough that you robbed me and the girls of a mom? Now you're trying to take the man I love away too?"

"Marlee," Jason mumbled, but Rachel was already rising to her feet.

The woman sucked in a dramatic gasp. "I can't believe you'd suggest such a thing. Do you not *know* that we sent money to help support you girls over the years?"

Stan was on his feet now too, resting a hand on Rachel's back. "It seems you've misunderstood our intentions," he said calmly. He urged Rachel to sit down with a nod toward her seat.

She did, and Stan lowered himself once more. "You would come to California with him, of course, Marlee. And your sisters too. Your mother would like to be a part of your lives. That's what she's *really* trying to say. All of you could move out here."

Rachel sniffed and dabbed the tip of her reddened nose. Tears welled up in her eyes, causing them to catch and reflect light, the way they did while the cameras rolled.

Fake. All of it was an act.

Marlee wanted to say so. To call them both liars, but Jason spoke up next. "I do appreciate the offer," he said, "but I don't have any interest. I chose the life I have because I love it. More than that, I love this woman by my side. You've really missed out on having her in your life. And that's a darn shame." He turned to Marlee then, took her by the hand, and gave the couple a curt nod. "Let's go, babe."

Marlee followed Jason's lead in a daze. Before she even realized what was happening, they were back in the limo.

It remained quiet on the way back to the hotel. Jason seemed to be digesting the situation as much as she was. Hopefully he wasn't regretting what he'd done by turning down the offer. The rational side of her said that was the last thing he was doing, but the wounded side of her couldn't help but worry. Perhaps the idea of *playing* a cowboy appealed to him. He could have the best of both worlds.

There was another worry too, this one attached to herself: would this make the feelings go away? Would she wake up in the morning and realize that the old bull trout had taken the reigns once more?

She and Jason parted ways at the hotel to change out of their evening wear, then met up at the couch in his hotel room to watch a movie. Still, the fear hadn't faded.

Jason ordered room service—chocolate-covered strawberries and a basket of fresh, hot rolls with raspberry butter—which was thoughtful, but Marlee couldn't help but think of how it reflected an entirely different life.

Please don't let my feelings for him die, she prayed inwardly. *Please help me stop freaking out.* Things were fine. She was sure of it. She just needed to get through the night, get back to Montana, and put her mind toward the trip to Morocco, which was just ten days away.

The idea was enough to put that spark of hope back into her chest. A spark she rode on throughout the rest of the night.

When morning came, Marlee walked over to the window and threw open the hotel drapes. While eyeing the cityscape—complete with manicured storefronts, swaying palm trees, and sunshine to spare—Marlee tested herself once more.

Yes. She was still very much in love with Jason.

A deep sigh passed through her lips. Thank heavens the old Marlee hadn't made a comeback. She thought back on the evening as she got ready for the day, recalling the way Jason had championed her in front of Rachel Star.

She replayed the incident once more as she rolled her carry-on toward the entryway of her hotel room. She was about to knock on the connecting door to Jason's room when an envelope slid onto the entryway tile from the hallway exit.

She glanced down at the cursive script penned onto the front: *Marlee, please read.*

The fear she'd fought off throughout the night came back full force.

Great. Just when she thought she'd survived the return of her mother, one more thing had to jump in her way.

A new knot of nerves built in her chest as she snatched the letter off the ground. She wouldn't read it yet.

She might not read it ever.

What Marlee *would* do was head home with Jason, prepare for the service trip to Morocco, and pray that her mother never bothered her or Jason again.

THIRTEEN

DEAR DAD,

We leave for Morocco tomorrow.

I still haven't read Rachel's letter. I'm not exactly sure of what I'm afraid of. I hate that I'm letting her have some sort of power over me again, but I can't help it. I'm terrified that whatever it says could drown this new, able-to-love-and-be-loved Marlee, and the old me will be left in her place. A coward, destined to be alone forever.

Marlee set her pen down and stared at the page, a new sort of determination bubbling within her. No. She wouldn't let her mother have that kind of power over her. She was going to read the dumb letter once and for all.

As soon as she was done, she'd come back and tell Dad all about it. It was too late to call Jason and tell him—being that it was one in the morning—but she'd tell him about it on the way to the airport. He'd be proud of her for reading it and for putting it behind her once and for all.

With that thought, Marlee scooted toward the edge of her bed. Her travel bag rested there, reminding her that she'd be spending the next twenty-six days with Jason. It wouldn't be a vacation, but it'd be so very rewarding—the photos Jason showed her from prior years said it all.

Stop delaying, Marlee. Go get the letter and read it.

A dart of determination sank all the way to her toes. "I'm doing it," she said, shooting to her feet and running over to her dresser. In one quick jerk, she tore open the drawer. A dive beyond the pile of mismatched socks in the corner, and the edge of the letter grazed her fingertips.

She snatched it into her grip and hurried back over to the bed. Quickly, Marlee tore the envelope open and plucked out a folded piece of lined paper. Excitement and dread clashed within her as she unfolded the page.

Handwritten.

Oh man, this was actually her mom's handwriting. The same mom who used to sing Mother Goose rhymes with her before bed.

She clenched her eyes shut as a flood of emotion gushed over her, but Marlee forced herself to choke it back quickly. She'd fantasized about what might be in here several times. An apology, perhaps. With a few words about how she hoped that she and her sisters had a good life. She might tell Marlee that she'd grown into a beautiful young woman, and that she could see that little girl inside somewhere.

Of course, it was possible the words in this letter weren't kind or tender at all. Which is why she'd waited nine whole days to open it.

With one last deep breath, Marlee forced herself to read it:

Marlee,

I regret that you and Jason did not see our offer for what it was: a chance for you and your sisters to get out of the dreaded life of running a trout farm.

I think it's only fair that I, as your mother, warn you about the danger your future holds. Jason Keller and I are made of the same cloth, whether you want to admit it or not. And if you hold him back now, he might stay for a little while—he might even stay long enough to marry you and father a few kids. But sooner or later, the nag for his old life will prevail, and Jason will eventually give in. He'll leave you, and by then, trust me, he will resent you and whatever kids you have for holding him back.

Don't say I never warned you.

The note slipped from Marlee's grip and onto the floor. She brought a hand to her mouth as a mounding rush of nausea rumbled through her. It was everything she did *not* want to hear from the very woman she did *not* want to hear it from—someone who knew firsthand what it was like to be Jason.

Stop, Marlee. They're not cut from the same cloth at all. They were complete opposites as far as Marlee could tell, but that didn't do much to reverse the train of imminent damage from plunging ahead.

Perhaps if she dived into the work in Morocco, Marlee would forget all about the letter and the warning and the overwhelming jaws of dread that were crushing her like a massive vise.

Jason will leave you. You'll be years into your marriage, raising kids and living life and thinking everything's perfect and wonderful, and suddenly he'll up and leave you forever.

The nausea rolled deeper, working its way up to her chest through her throbbing heart. Already, that new side of Marlee was shriveling.

She groaned, working to mentally fight it off. She wanted to hop off the bed, tear up the letter, and then set it ablaze in the backyard. Maybe she'd let the neighbor's dog pee on the ashes once she was done.

But she couldn't get herself to move. Already, the fear was having its way with her. It was inevitable, wasn't it?

Yes. She'd avoided it this long—the heart-to-heart with her old self. Maybe Old Marlee wasn't so bad after all. Maybe she was just trying to protect her.

Marlee would find out soon enough. May as well face this war now and see who would come out on the other side.

FOURTEEN

JASON HOISTED THE travel bag onto his shoulder and walked through the kitchen, taking one last glance at the horses in the corral. Taylor had agreed to come stay at his place while he was gone. To keep Jepson and Gypsy from getting lonely, he'd even volunteered to bring a date over each weekend to ride with him. Maybe even Britt.

Jason glanced at the horseshoe clock to see that he was forty minutes ahead of schedule. Which meant he could go help Marlee with any last-minute chores she had on her list.

A short, high-pitched chirp broke into his thoughts. His phone. He yanked it from his back pocket and grinned when he saw it was Marlee calling. He couldn't exactly explain it, but in the short second it took to bring the phone to his ear, a warning came to his mind.

Jason ignored it. "Howdy there, darling," he crooned. "I was just thinking about you."

The greeting was met with silence.

"Marlee?" His heart dropped in the quiet pause.

She sniffed on the other end of the line. "I can't go with you, Jason. I'm so sorry, but I just can't."

Sharp heat pricked his chest as he replayed the words in his head.

Please no.

His hand clenched into a tight, aching fist as a groan

snuck up his throat. It had happened, hadn't it? She'd talked herself out of loving him.

More sobs spilled through the line, seeming to confirm the fear.

And just like that, the heat in his chest exploded, shooting flames through his body in a blink. He scrambled for something to blame. Anything.

"Your mother's letter," he blurted, remembering how he'd encouraged her to read it and put it behind her once and for all. "Is that what this is about? What did she say?"

"That's not why—"

"The heck it isn't, Marlee. When did you read it?"

She sniffed again, then choked back a sob. "Last night."

He could only guess at the sort of moronic message the woman had left her. But really, how long could Marlee play the victim? She *knew* Jason well enough by now; she had to. So why would she let some stupid letter ruin everything?

Rage gripped hold of him at the question, thick and heavy. Bloating and swelling and begging him to pop off with things that would make Marlee sorry she'd ever loved him at all: *You did this to yourself. You were never going to be happy, were you? You were always going to be looking for an excuse to let me go, and now you think you've got one.*

He clenched his jaw shut over the words trying to form. *Help me, Lord. Give me the words, please.*

Another second ticked on. And then another.

This couldn't be happening. And what exactly *was* happening here anyway? Jason would go to Morocco while Marlee spent the twenty-six days erasing him from her memory? All so she could go back to ignoring him once he returned—was that it?

He punched a hard fist into the leather couch. This wasn't helping.

Think. Marlee was scared, he knew that much. But of what?

"What are you afraid of, Marlee? Because if you look at this from my perspective, I could spend a lifetime in fear too. I mean, look at this logically: *you've* been the bigger threat all along. I've known you might walk away from me from our very first date, but I loved you anyway because you're worth the risk."

No more, Jason. Leave it at that.

He glanced up at the clock. "Listen, I'm familiar enough with the butterfly concept. Letting it fly away and all that. I already know I love you. In fact, I'd like to spend the rest of my life with you. But if you don't feel the same, there's nothing I can say or do to change that. If there was, I'd be doing it."

The second hand ticked on. One quiet second after the next.

Another sniff came through the line, reminding him of just how deeply hurt Marlee had been. She'd loved the mother she once had, and the woman abandoned her. She'd loved her father too, and Charlie had passed away long before his time.

Jason guessed her troubles had more to do with her own loss than they did with him being an actual flight risk. But how could he help Marlee see the truth of it for herself?

The fact was, he couldn't.

He really would have to let her go.

At least for now.

His body went weak. Shoulders dropping. Fists loosening. Chest caving.

"Tell you what," he said softly. "If you're coming with me, I'll need to pick you up in thirty minutes. So decide during that time whether you're in or out. Once the thirty minutes is up, shoot me a text letting me know if you're going to come. Okay?"

"Jason—"

"Don't decide right now. Please, just . . . take the half hour, will you?" Jason would use the half hour himself, dropping to his knees and begging the Lord to pull this one final favor.

"Okay," she said in a whisper. "I will."

FIFTEEN

MARLEE SAT AGAINST her headboard, arms folded, as she stared at her luggage bag. Thirty minutes. She didn't want to wait thirty minutes. The truth was, the damage was already done.

It had taken more than half the night, but eventually, Marlee had finally seen reason. She'd had it right all along. She was simply too broken to be in a relationship with anyone.

She'd spent hours in tears and torment. So many that she was practically numb to it now. Her diary to Dad rested beside her on the bed, still open to the letter she'd been writing last night.

Her eyes shot to where she'd left off: *. . . terrified that whatever it says could drown this new, able-to-love-and-beloved Marlee, and the old me will be left in her place.*

She reached out and slammed the notebook closed, but that didn't stop her from reading the final words: *A coward, destined to be alone forever.*

Wow, her own words were already coming back to haunt her. She glanced at the book once more, squinting when she noticed something peeking from the plastic pocket on front. A paper with Charlie's new logo had been tucked into the space, but it seemed there was something just behind that.

Marlee tugged at the corner of a manila pouch, freeing it from the pocket completely, and saw Dad's writing on the front. Not the fast, sloppy print he'd scribbled onto the labels and boxes. This was his best penmanship in cursive lettering.

To my beautiful girls.

A gasp tore from her throat. Was it possible he'd left something behind for them? Something they hadn't yet discovered?

"Oh, please, please, please." Marlee flipped the pouch over and pinched the brass clip with a hurried hand. She opened the top fold and peeked inside to see three separate envelopes. She pulled them out and spread them over the bed. They were bulky, which meant they held more than simple paper.

One for Marlee, Brittany, and Lillian.

It felt as if her heart might stop at the sight of her name on that envelope. Carefully, she tucked her sisters' envelopes back into the pouch. Next, she lifted hers and pressed it against her heart while sobs of gratitude rocked through her body. How many times had she wished she could hear her father's voice just one more time? And this, in a way, was that very thing.

Surprised she had any tears left, Marlee wiped her face and sniffed, preparing herself to read the words he'd left behind.

Her hands trembled as she pulled the folded page from the envelope. Something silver and shiny rested in the deep folds, but Marlee would discover that after reading the letter. She pried it open and took in the wonderful sight of Dad's unique penmanship. What a treasure it was.

My Marlee girl,

Oh, how very badly I wish I could have fought a better fight. I wanted more than anything to be there for all those milestone marks. Lilly's graduation, your weddings, the birth of my grandbabies.

I'm not sure exactly how things run in the big place

upstairs, but I promise I'll be there on special days like that, walking down the aisle along your side and bawling like the big baby I am.

Marlee set the page on her lap, laughing and crying all at once. Oh, how she wanted to savor this. She slipped her hand into the envelope and retrieved a silver bracelet. She tipped her head to observe the charms linked onto the shiny chain. A soccer ball, a music note, and a tube of lipstick, which she assumed represented the chapsticks she made. Next was a rainbow trout, its body curved into an arch like the one on Charlie's logo. The final two charms were identical—matching crimson hearts.

She fisted the bracelet and read on.

I don't know what I would've done without you, Marlee. I remember how excited you were to get your driver's license when you turned sixteen. Not because you were dying to drive to the mall and meet a bunch of boys (well, maybe a little) but because you wanted to drive the girls to their soccer and choir practices.

I made your bracelet as if you were the girls' mother yourself, since you take pride in their accomplishments like any mother might. Thank you for that. Of course you know the fish represents your old man, and the trout farm too since it was such a great part of my life. I know you girls love that shop, but if you ever feel the need to let go of it and let some ornery old man take over, you have my blessing.

Lastly, I want to talk about those two hearts. No plugging your ears during this part. I know you better than you think, and I have a feeling you're gonna need to hear what I have to say.

A rush of tingly heat poured over Marlee's skin. Yes, she did need to hear it. She was so lost right now. Acting out in response to her mother's wicked words. Possibly letting go of the best thing she'd ever had.

One heart represents you. And if I'd have been able to make it match the love you give, kiddo, it'd be as big as our house. But the other heart is for the man you marry. Listen, I saw the way you closed off over the years. Went on fewer and fewer dates. Which is why I nicknamed you my little bull trout. But it occurred to me that you might be scared of letting someone in. So I want to share with you two things.

1. I loved Rachel, and I don't regret marrying her. How could I, when it brought me the three greatest gifts of my life?

2. The only regret I do have is letting hurt and fear keep me from marrying a second time. You remember Wanda—used to come over a lot. Bring us dinner. Stick around to read stories with you girls or help out with your math since I was terrible at it. She couldn't birth children of her own, and boy did she love you girls. She wanted to get married, but I kept putting her off. Eventually she gave me an ultimatum: agree to commit, or she'd accept a job offer in Wisconsin. I cried for months after she boarded that plane. But I never went and got her. I was too big of a coward. As you might have noticed, I stopped dating after that.

That's my greatest regret. And I won't be around long enough to undo it.

So here's where I turn things on you. I saw a similar fear in your eyes. A determination to keep your heart guarded with an army so strong that a guy wouldn't stand a chance.

Don't. Don't do that. Find the right man, and let him in. Let him bring you happiness and children and joy and love. It will feel like a risk, but love always is.

What your mother did already affected the past. Don't let it rob you of a future.

I love you forever and always, Marlee.

—Dad

A knock sounded from the front door, pulling Marlee from the daze she'd had on the letter. She shoved it to her chest once more and lifted her chin toward the ceiling. "Thank you," she breathed. "Thank you for saving me."

She hopped off her bed and raced to the door. Britt and Lilly were running the fish farm, and since Jason was supposed to be picking her up soon, Marlee could guess who it was. She flung it open with a flourish, ready to throw her arms around Jason and beg him to forgive her, but nobody was there.

Her eyes dropped to the porch step. A package of fish bait. A quick glance at the narrow drive said she'd just missed the UPS man.

She hurried back into her room to check the time. "Oh no." It'd been nearly an hour since she'd gotten off the phone with Jason. He'd be hopping on that flight any minute. And the only layover they had was in Paris. *Ten* hours away.

Marlee wiped her face with the back of her hands, shoved into her shoes, and shrugged her carry-on bag over her shoulder.

She'd caused Jason a whole lot of hurt and grief. This wasn't something she could undo over the phone. Hopefully she'd be able to make the flight on time. Just as she got to her doorway, the same place she'd removed her mother's necklace, Marlee remembered something she'd left behind. Quickly, she snatched the bracelet off her bed and dashed out of the house.

Please say he'll forgive me.

SIXTEEN

JASON KEPT HIS eyes pasted on his phone, willing it to do something. Anything.

That wasn't exactly true. What he wanted it to do is glow or buzz or beep with something from Marlee. Something that said she was sorry and she wished very badly that she'd have just gone with him. Maybe it would go on to say that she'd be thinking of him every minute of all twenty-six days and waiting to wrap her arms around him upon his return.

Announcements blared from the overhead speakers in French and English alike. Flight and boarding information, still nothing about their flight. But soon. Soon they'd ask the crew to line up and get ready to board.

It was maddening to think back on his conversation with Marlee. He'd spent the last fifteen hours doing that very thing. Ten on a flight to Paris. Five while stuck in the dreaded airport while the rest of his team toured a few nearby spots.

As devastated as he was and terrified that he might lose the woman he loved, Jason couldn't explain the occasional whispers of hope that came to his mind.

She's going to come back, Jason. Just wait.

The only thing that allowed him to believe this was the phrase he'd heard so many times. That if someone truly belonged to him and he let them go, they'd come back. Jason felt very confident that he and Marlee belonged to each other.

He only prayed she'd realize that for herself over the next few weeks.

"Son," his dad said from across the way. "Time to board."

Jason snapped out of his daze in time to see his dad and Mary waving him toward the lineup. He came to his feet, stretched out his legs and arms, and heard someone hollering from deep within the crowded airport corridor. His mind had to be playing tricks on him. There was no possible way for Marlee to be in this airport calling his name.

But he turned to look over the crowd just the same. Again it came. Someone was definitely shouting his name, and it sounded exactly like Marlee's voice. He scanned over the bustling passengers wheeling luggage as they broke off toward their gates.

His heart stopped short when he saw her. A pair of denim jeans and a pale gray sweater. The colors blended well enough with the crowd, but he'd spot that beautiful face anywhere. Her blue eyes locked on him across the way, and suddenly she bolted toward him, abandoning a shoulder bag on her arm and a carry-on at her feet. All blurred out of view as she wove past a woman with a stroller, an elderly couple squinting at the flight board, and what looked like an entire woman's soccer team.

"I'm so glad you didn't leave yet," she breathed.

He was too. But before he could say so, Marlee pressed a kiss to his lips.

Fellow passengers broke into whistles and cheers. A deep thrill poured into him, filling every empty, hurting space with warmth and hope.

"I'm so sorry for panicking like I did. I love you." She kissed him again, and then again. "I love you so much."

Jason kissed her in return, echoing the sentiment between jagged breaths of his own.

A sharp whistle sounded from the boarding area, gaining both Marlee and Jason's attention at once. He looked over to see his father waving them toward the gate. "We've got Marlee's bags. Now come get on this flight before we have to take off without you. Good to see you, by the way," he said, nodding toward Marlee.

Jason rested a hand at her lower back. "Let's go to Morocco."

More waves of joy, peace, and hope poured over him as they took their seats on the flight.

Marlee was here. That was a start.

As soon as they were seated, Marlee lifted the armrest between them and snuggled into him. During the flight, she shared details of the notes to her dad. She told him about her mother's letter next, and the panic it caused.

Lastly, Marlee described the precious letter from her dad. She explained how his words had saved her this time, but said she didn't want to risk losing Jason again. That's when she told him about her plan to see a counselor when they got back; it was time she put her fear of abandonment behind her once and for all.

Boy, was Jason glad to hear that. In fact, he could feel a barrier of his own whittling down at the idea of Marlee shedding the fear that had haunted her for so long.

Once she drifted off to sleep, Jason took some time to let it all sink in. It was hard to believe she was really there with him. Thank the heavens.

He leaned down to kiss her head, relishing the warmth of having her close once more. He considered the trip they were on, the healing and hope they'd help bring to so many, and realized he and Marlee had been blessed with a large dose of those very things.

Some might say Jason Keller had lived a charmed life. In

a lot of ways, they'd be right. But he'd known times of hardship too. And he could honestly say that there, with Marlee Jenkins by his side, he had enough hope to keep the plane afloat, and his future, now that she might very well be a part of it, had never looked brighter.

EPILOGUE

MARLEE GRINNED AS she watched Gunner tear down the hallway in a Big Wheel. Never had she seen a family welcome outdoor play toys in the halls of their very own home, but that's what made the Branson family so unique. Bob and Dee had gone so far as to knock out walls and remodel their home, all so it could accommodate large gatherings such as this, even in the winter months.

While cradling a bundle of logs, Jason stepped over Mel and Pete, who'd gathered around the fireplace to string popcorn onto a Christmas garland for the tree. "Got more wood," he announced as he lowered himself beside the mantel.

Carols played in the background as Bob crooned out a few lines of his own.

"How's the hollandaise sauce coming along, dear?" Dee asked, scurrying beside Marlee with a pan of oven fresh rolls.

Marlee whisked the yolks a bit more. "Think we're ready for the melted butter."

"Looks like it," Dee said before glancing toward the family room. She hollered to Jason's parents, inviting them and their spouses to help themselves at the snack bar. "That goes for you too, Britt and Lilly," she added.

Marlee's sisters, who'd declared the Branson home their new favorite place, hovered over a ball of dough on the floured counter. "Thanks," Lilly said. "Should we make the next batch first?"

"No, you two go ahead. Rachel and Payton can take care of the next dozen. I think you're in more demand over there by the ranch hands."

Marlee glanced over to see Taylor, Lincoln, and Brody by the chips and dip. Britt and Lilly wasted no time heading to that end of the snack table as well. Joy swelled thick in her heart as she recalled the months that had passed since she first came to the Bransons' place for their anniversary party.

Marlee might have freaked out for a bit when she'd read her mother's threat, but fear hadn't won. In fact, with her angel father's help, she'd defeated that fear in the very same day. Of course it took longer than that to rebuild trust with Jason. She'd likely frightened him by panicking the way she had, but they'd come a very long way since then. Especially with the help of the very wise counselor she'd been seeing.

Now when Marlee mused on a future with Jason, she was no longer riddled with voices of doubts and fear. Hope had filled the void completely, and Marlee couldn't remember being so happy.

"Can I have everyone's attention?" Jason hollered from the front room. He dusted off his hands and motioned toward Marlee, giving that playful smile as soon as their eyes met. "Mind coming on in here for a minute, babe?"

Was it just her, or had the music died down along with the chatter? Excited whispers rose from Britt and Lilly's corner of the room.

Marlee rested the whisk and dusted her hands on her apron.

"Here, hon," Dee said. "Let me get that for you." She untied the apron and shimmied it up and over Marlee's head, then gave her a playful spank on the butt. "Go ahead now, dear."

Marlee let out a laugh. "Thanks." She pasted her eyes on

the travertine floor as she wove through the loved ones gathered there, and soon she was standing beside Jason, the yummy scent of his aftershave toying with her senses already.

"I've been thinking about the best way to ask you this," he said in that low, raspy voice, "and when I started questioning our family and friends about it, they all said they wanted to help."

Marlee furrowed her brows. "Help?"

Jason grinned and waved a hand to the group. Marlee spun around to see a new addition—a large banner stretched across the room. Flag-shaped cards held bright red letters, each spelling out one very important question.

Will you marry me?

A deep thrill shot straight into her heart. Hot and cold all at once. She spun back around to face Jason.

Jason lowered himself onto one knee and looked up at her through his dark lashes. "Marlee Jenkins, from the first time I picked up a pole and hit the pond at Charlie's Trout Farm, you caught my attention. You didn't exactly make it easy for me, but eventually, you gave me a chance. And since then, you've captured nearly every thought that passes through my mind. More than that, you've captured my heart."

He tugged a small box from his pocket and held it in his fist. "I want to spend the rest of my life with you, Marlee. I want to spend year after year making amazing memories together." He cracked open the box to reveal a glistening diamond ring. "Will you be my wife?"

Marlee could hardly see him through the tears. It went pin-drop quiet as she stared at the ring, the sight of it a promise all its own. She moved her gaze back to those gorgeous brown eyes of his.

"Yes," Marlee cheered. "Of course I'll marry you."

Hoots, hollers, whistles, and cheers rang throughout the

home. Mel and Pete broke into some sort of victory dance while making rap noises.

Jason shot to his feet. "She said yes!" He plucked the ring from the box with shaky hands and slid it onto her finger, then came in for a celebratory kiss. "I love you," he mumbled between kisses.

"I love you too," she assured.

"Lucky thing she said yes," Taylor said. "It would have really ruined dinner if she'd said no."

Luke tossed a pillow at him.

"Let's see the ring," Britt and Lilly hollered in unison.

Jason wrapped his arm around Marlee as she held out her hand for all to see. The beautiful diamond ring earned a round of oohs and ahs. Other comments filtered over the room. *It's perfect. Gorgeous. So happy for them . . .*

In a moment of quiet pause, time seeming to slow for a blink, Marlee's bracelet caught a splash of light from the Christmas tree, causing one of the charms to glow: Charlie's trout. Her heart leaped at the sight. He'd promised to be there for special days, hadn't he?

Yes. The waves of warmth rippling through her said that he was, in fact, celebrating with them too. Tonight, she'd taken an important step toward fulfilling the wish Charlie had for her. Her eyes drifted down to the two crimson hearts.

Jason might have joked about her capturing his heart, but in Marlee's case, the statement rang true.

He'd hooked her from their very first date. And now, together, life was sure to be one heck of a ride!

Award-winning author **Kimberly Krey** has always been a fan of good, clean romance, so she decided to specialize in writing 'Romance That's Clean without Losing the Steam'. She's a fervent lover of God, family, and cheese platters, as well as the ultimate hater of laundry.

To stay connected, and receive a FREE book, subscribe to her newsletter: https://bit.ly/2A2nu31
Confirm to receive your freebie.

To follow her author page on FB @: Kimberly Krey Author

For a printable PDF of her work (listed by series) see her website @ https://www.kimberlykrey.com/

SELLING HER RANCH, STEALING HIS HEART

Annette Lyon

ONE

How do you go on when everything that used to be right was now wrong?

Teresa didn't have any answer to that.

What she did know was that thirty-eight horses needed to be fed and watered this morning, as they did every morning, and that if she didn't do it, no one would. Which was why, when her alarm had gone off at five o'clock, she'd fought her pillow's gravitational pull, thrown on her jeans and a sweatshirt, and headed down from the bunkhouse to care for the horses boarded at J-Bar-D Ranch.

No matter that tears streaked her face as she shoveled loose hay by the light of her headlamp. No matter that Dorothy, the owner, had been buried two days before.

Teresa hefted two bales onto a cart and then two more on top of those. Then she headed down the alley between the outdoor stalls. At the far end, she pulled a pocket knife from her jeans and cut the twine on a bale. It separated naturally into "flakes" of roughly five pounds. Apricot, one of the older horses, walked over, knowing her breakfast was coming.

"Here you go, girl," Teresa said, throwing two flakes over the metal bars right at Apricot's feet. The other horses were now at attention and moving toward her. "I'll get to you all," she promised, throwing two more flakes to the next horse and the next. Each bale fed about five horses, so on the sixth, she cut the next bale and continued working.

The morning lightened considerably, though the sun had yet to appear above the mountaintops. Teresa turned off the headlamp, and a few minutes later, took off her beanie; she was getting hot. She left both on a stump and then returned to the cart of hay to finish up the feeding.

By the time she returned, the last three horses were pawing and snorting their discontent, wanting their breakfast already. She fed Hank, then moved to the last two horses: her very own Epione and Asclepius. She stroked their noses and patted their necks. Epione nuzzled Teresa and pawed, but Asclepius made an impatient sound and stomped his foot on the hard earth.

"You're next, you two," she promised. "I never forget you."

Asclepius stepped closer and edged his nose over the bar, waiting to be stroked, so Teresa obliged. Trust the pair to bring a smile to her face even on a day like this.

She threw the last of the hay into their stalls, and after her horses began eating, she headed for the hay barn, where she'd return the cart. Out of habit, she glanced at the main house to her left, expecting to see the bedroom light on in the main house and Dorothy coming out with a mug of herbal tea to help Teresa warm up. She'd done that every morning for years.

But Dorothy wasn't in the main house any longer. No one was. The sweet old woman had enjoyed a remarkably healthy senior life. Which was why, though she'd been closing in on ninety, her death from a pulmonary embolism came as such a shock.

Teresa settled the cart in its place and wiped the sleeve of her sweatshirt across her eyes to clear the blurriness created by tears threatening to fall. How many more mornings would she instinctively look at the main house, only to be reminded that she'd never again see Dorothy?

But Teresa had to keep going, so she did. Someone had to care for the horses at J-Bar-D. That's what Dorothy would have wanted, and what she'd put into her will as well. Dorothy's only child, Joan, would inherit the land, but Teresa was to stay on as sole manager of the boarding facility.

At least there's that, Teresa thought. Without her position here, she couldn't afford to board her horses elsewhere. Her job gave her free rent in the modest studio bunkhouse above the stable, and it gave her two horses free boarding. She got paid a small wage on top of that. Nothing she'd ever get rich on, but enough to get by comfortably. It was surprising, really, how little money you needed when housing was covered for both you and your horses.

Her next job would be grooming the arena for riding and lessons. She removed pieces of manure with a stall fork, which looked like a rake held with the tines up. The job was a bit like scooping a giant kitty litter box. That done, she removed items from yesterday's lessons: orange cones, mounting blocks, and trot poles.

All of that prepped the arena to be dragged. She always loved that part of her morning; driving in concentric circles, creating a comb-like design behind her, felt like a morning meditation, like raking a Japanese Zen garden. From the time she finished and before patrons arrived and lessons began for the day, the arena looked pristine.

She started the little tractor, then drove over to the frame near the arena. Or she intended to, but she stopped on the way because in the distance, she spotted a man in a suit, someone she didn't recognize, exiting a shiny black car parked along the unpaved drive that ran by the main house. Teresa hit the brake and squinted to see him more clearly.

The guy held a sign, which could have been a campaign sign or yard sale sign; she couldn't read it from there. The man stopped, looked about, and, seemingly satisfied, gripped the sides of the sign and pushed its two wire ends into the ground.

"What the . . . "

A protective feeling swept over Teresa. What did this guy think he was doing? If he hoped to be hired as a Realtor, he'd have another thing coming. What nerve to show up with his own sign!

She killed the engine and hopped off the tractor, attention entirely on figuring out who this interloper was. As she drew closer, she could make out the red text at the top: FOR SALE.

The bottom had a photo and white text—likely a head shot and a phone number.

She wanted to leap over the fence, tear his sign out of the ground, and demand he get off the land and never come back. That would be an overreaction, so she tamped down her loyalty-based anger as she approached. As she drew closer and could see him better, she thought he looked relatively young—no more than thirty. The right age to have a beginner's ego, but not old enough to know better than to trespass.

That was the kindest thought she could come up with as she faced the prospect of someone trying to sell Dorothy's land, Teresa's home. She'd give him an education.

"Excuse me," she called as she pulled off her gloves. She tucked them into her back pocket, still walking, and when he didn't respond, she repeated herself, louder, still closing the distance between them. "Excuse me!"

This time his head came up, and he looked around. When he spotted her, he offered a wave and a wide, overly friendly smile, as if they knew each other. The gesture made her step come up short for a second. She grunted in annoyance and picked up her pace, heading for him like a bull toward a matador. He took a step back from the sign and eyed it before stepping forward and pushing one side deeper to level it out. He wiped his palms together as if even a little dirt was unacceptable.

Teresa glanced down at her hay- and dust-covered clothes, including her boots, which had as much manure as dirt caked to their bottoms. Maybe he'd think she was a walking ball of disease. She resisted rolling her eyes, but only just.

Once she was close enough to read the white text, however, her nostrils flared. Sure enough, this was a Realtor, and his picture was as fake as any she'd seen. He had a canned smile, slicked-back hair, and wore what looked like the same suit he had on now, or perhaps its twin. Men like him probably had a closet full of variations on a suit theme, much as she had jeans and flannel shirts filling her closet. She couldn't imagine willfully choosing a life in which you'd have to wear a suit every day.

She glanced at the picture again. Yep. It was definitely the same guy, but in person, he looked better, his hair combed but not with a helmet of gel. His smile looked relaxed and natural, not awkwardly wide as if the photographer had told him to say cheese and hold it. The sign had a plastic holder hanging off it, which he surely planned to fill with fliers. Not if she had anything to say about it.

"The ranch isn't for sale," she said, her voice still raised as she crossed the last few feet. Up close, the guy—Derek Walters, the sign said—looked tanned, which fit right in with her life here, but she was willing to bet that his tan was of the spray-on variety. He belonged on the cover of some men's health magazine, not on a ranch, where his Italian leather shoes would get dusty and scratched up in the gravel. This was no place for anyone afraid of dirty.

Derek nodded toward the sign. "Actually, it *is* for sale."

"No, it *isn't*," Teresa said, her voice stiff. "I don't know who you are, but you're going to toss your sign into your fancy car and get out of here, or I'll call the cops." She pulled her phone out of her back pocket to show that she was serious. "Do you want to be arrested?"

He smiled, amused rather than worried. "On what charges?"

"Trespassing."

"Yeah, that's not going to happen."

How exactly did he manage to speak while smiling? Teresa wanted to hate him, but his air wasn't one of arrogance or ego, only confidence mixed with a bit of confusion. She folded her arms.

"You think I don't dare call the cops?" She dialed 911, then paused to see if she needed to hit send.

He didn't withdraw, raise his hands in surrender, or apologize. Instead, he stepped forward, arm extended, to shake hands. "Derek Walters."

She gave a pointed look at the sign. "I already figured out that much."

When it was clear she wasn't about to shake hands, he lowered his arm. "My mother owns this land. Joan Walters. Joan *Dixon* Walters."

"Oh," Teresa said, taken aback on hearing his mother's maiden name. This was Dorothy's only grandchild.

"Yes, and I'm—"

"Trying to *sell* the ranch."

"Well, yes, but—"

"You can't. You have no right. I know what Dorothy's will said." Teresa wasn't about to let this guy get a word in edgewise. "Your grandmother was barely buried, and you're already trying to sell the place? What does your mother think of that, or are you doing it without telling her? You should be ashamed of yourself." This was supposed to remain her home, hers in all but name. "You can't do that. If you don't own it, you can't sell it."

Derek Walters looked hurt and confused and overwhelmed all at once. His jaw worked for a few seconds as he seemed to try to figure out what to say. He was speechless. Good.

She wouldn't talk first. Let him feel the weight of the awkward silence. Let him feel guilty over betraying his grandmother's wishes. She kept her arms folded and brows raised in challenge, glad that anger kept her tears at bay.

At last, he leveled his gaze at her. "Not that I have to justify anything to you, but legally, I actually do have the right to sell."

"How? Dorothy's will hasn't even gone to probate yet," Teresa said. She didn't know much about wills and the law, but she was pretty sure that settling an estate in court took months, maybe years.

He held up a finger to stop her from speaking as he opened the sleek leather bag hanging from his shoulder. She closed her mouth, her curiosity—and suspicion—piqued. He pulled a folder out of his bag, opened it, and slipped out a stack of papers bound with a thick clip. He held them out for her to see. "First of all, my grandparents didn't have a will; they had a trust. That means no probate. According to the trust, when both of my grandparents have passed away, my mother becomes the executor. But she's not able to act in that capacity right now." He held out the papers further, encouraging her to look at them. "As you can see, I have power of attorney for my mother."

Teresa cocked her head, as curious as she was suspicious—or wanting to be. He seemed to know way more than she did about this stuff. Was he a lawyer? What was a trust, anyway? She didn't want him to realize just how little she understood, so she hoped her bearing would show him that she was a force to be reckoned with. "Why does your mother need a power of attorney?" She knew what one of those was, at least.

He cleared his throat as if trying to hide a rising emotion. "She's in a care center . . . due to a medical condition that makes her unable to make these kinds of decisions. It's up to me to carry out my grandmother's wishes."

"How convenient." Teresa looked at the document briefly, then back at him, though she couldn't help but feel a pang of sympathy for the guy, *if* what he said was true. For all she knew, though, Joan was in great health, and her son was trying to make a buck. "Dorothy never said anything about her daughter being in a care center." Only that her daughter hadn't visited in a couple of years, which made Dorothy sad.

"That's because Grandma didn't know about it," Derek said. "When my mom was diagnosed, she made me promise to never breathe a word to Grandma. See, *her* mother lost her mind at a young age, and losing her own memory was one of Grandma's greatest fears. Knowing that her daughter was dealing with the same thing?" He shook his head. "That would've devastated her."

Dang it all. Teresa didn't want to believe the guy, but he seemed sincere—as if he'd really cared about Dorothy.

On the other hand, so what if he had power of attorney? That didn't mean that selling the ranch was the right thing to do.

"Do you really think your grandmother would approve of selling J-Bar-D?" Teresa asked. He opened his mouth to speak, but she raised her own finger to cut him off. "No. Don't you try to defend this. Dorothy told me what she wanted. I saw her will, and she confirmed her wishes only a month ago.

Her plans were for me to stay on as manager, and the ranch was *not* to be sold. I don't care how much money you think you can get from selling the place. What do you plan to do, build a bunch of condos or a strip mall? The last thing Big Fir needs is a Walmart."

His shoulder slumped slightly. "That's not what I want at all."

Emboldened, Teresa stepped closer. "Why haven't I met you before? I can understand why your mother might not have come, if she was trying to hide her condition, but why haven't *you* visited? Why weren't you at the funeral?" Teresa could feel her tone getting ready to rise to dog-whistle levels, so she bit off the rest of her speech and tried to breathe calmly, though the air came out unevenly.

Derek stood before her for several seconds before answering. He slipped his hands into his pockets and looked at the ground, his eyes a bit glassy. He had a heart, a tender one. And she'd been attacking him. Teresa felt a twinge of guilt.

At last he looked up. "I was stuck in Hawaii. All flights were canceled because of a volcano erupting. You're right that Grandma wanted her manager—you—to stay on." He shook his head sadly. "But that applies only if the ranch remains unsold. Now if you'll excuse me, I'd like to visit the house."

"No." She stepped in front of him, blocking his way. The house was sacred to Teresa. She wouldn't let this guy inside—someone who hadn't seen his grandmother in years and who'd even missed her funeral because of a vacation.

"What?" Derek asked, brow furrowed.

"Leave. Now." She pointed to his car with one hand and held up her phone in the other. "Or I *will* call the cops."

He raised his arms in surrender. "Okay. I'll go. This time. But I'll be back."

As he headed for his car, Teresa called after him. "And I'll be waiting!"

Without another word, Derek got in his car and drove off, tires kicking up a dust cloud behind him. She watched him retreat, confused, scared, and oh-so-worried.

TWO

DEREK LOOKED IN the rearview mirror to see the dim shape of the woman, which was obscured by the thickening cloud of dust kicked up by his Lexus. He tried to remember the name listed on the will as the ranch manager but came up blank. Should have asked for her name, introduced himself properly.

Except he'd tried to, and she wouldn't shake his hand. Thanks to the sign with his grinning mug on it, she knew exactly who he was, but beyond "manager," he couldn't pull up her name. Maybe it started with a *T*?

She was an interesting one for sure. Passionate, loyal, a hard worker. Pretty, too. Not that her name or qualities mattered when it came to his decisions about the ranch. He loved the place as much or more than anyone, including her. Tina? Tori?

A text came in, which he ignored. Another came in, and another, and another, until his phone seemed to be blowing up with incoming messages. Next came an incoming call. Chances were that they were all from the same person trying to reach him, and Derek had a suspicion who it was: his business partner, Jake.

Derek drove around a bend until the ranch—and the woman—were out of sight. He went another half mile for good measure before pulling over. By then, he'd gotten three more texts and a voice message notification.

On the shoulder of the old highway, he shifted to park

and checked his notifications with dread. Sure enough, every message was from Jake.

The H deal doesn't look good. Call me.

The next was similar: *Yo. Call me now.*

So was the third: *It's important.*

His stomach turning sour, Derek scrolled past a few more texts that said variations of the same thing, then listened to Jake's voice message.

"Hey, it's me. I gotta talk to you, stat. Robbins is threatening to . . . just call, okay?"

Derek's thumb hovered over the words *call back*. Without hearing it, Derek knew that the hotel and convention center deal that he and Jake had worked on for the last two years had fallen through. He'd had a suspicion about it before he left the Big Island, when Robbins seemed aloof and evaded Derek's questions, pussyfooting around details they'd agreed to months ago.

The multi-million-dollar deal would have torn down an existing, rundown hotel and rebuilt it into a modern one, with an attached convention center with all the modern amenities. Several conventions and weddings had already asked to be put on a tentative waiting list, pending the completion.

As if Robbins's sudden wishy-washy behavior hadn't been enough, the volcano eruption spelled the end. Building anything in Hawaii meant building on a volcano, and therefore a potential danger. But the entire archipelago took that chance, and an eruption had never threatened that particular seaside property. Until now.

To Robbins, the whole thing was too big a risk, and no amount of talking about Hawaii as a destination for millions of tourists and businesspeople would sway him. Without him as the lead investor, the others would pull out one by one.

Derek managed to get over the sick feeling in his stomach enough to call Jake.

After one ring, he answered. "Hey."

"Robbins is out, isn't he?" Derek asked.

"Yeah."

Derek propped his elbow on the car door and rested his forehead in his palm; a headache threatened to shoot through his temples. He needed to get some Excedrin soon. "I think the final nail in the coffin was when he found out I couldn't get back to my grandma's funeral because of the eruption."

"But that's crazy! The place would make money without trying."

"I know. I told him all of it," Derek said.

"I know." Jake swore on the other end. "You're the best, and if the best can't convince Robbins, no one can."

The compliment wasn't enough to pull Derek out of the glum rut. "I'm heading back to my hotel from the ranch. I'll call you later, okay?"

"That's right . . ." Jake's voice trailed off with a tone of pity. Derek cringed, wishing he hadn't mentioned the ranch. "Robbins pulling out makes the ranch situation even worse, doesn't it?"

"Yeah." Derek couldn't say more than that and didn't want to. "I'll call you later."

"When will you be back in the office?" Jake asked.

Through the windshield, Derek looked over the landscape that felt so much like home, a view that some people said was ugly because it was supposedly colorless and dead. The land wasn't either of those things. He saw thousands of shades of brown soil and white clouds, red rocks and green shrubs. He heard and noticed animals, from lizards to eagles to bison, all over. And the deep, deep blue skies. Too bad he couldn't throw his problems into the wind and stay here in Montana.

He tore his gaze from the view. "I'll be a few days, probably. I'll let you know. We'll talk soon."

"All right. Hang in there," Jake said, then hung up.

Derek returned his phone to the holder, then breathed out heavily. Grandma had gotten the ranch into deep debt, and with his mother in a full-time care facility—expensive in and of itself—the job of paying off his grandparents' debt had landed squarely on his shoulders.

He couldn't help but remember the pain on the manager's face. Teresa. *That* was her name. The ache in her eyes had reflected the pain he felt in the center of his chest. He didn't *want* to sell the place, but he had no choice.

It's not my fault. It's not anyone's fault, he wanted to tell her.

The Hawaii deal was his last shot at saving the place. Yet he knew that even if it had gone through, it would probably have merely served to delay the inevitable by a few years. That was assuming that his portion of the profits was enough to pay his mother's past and ongoing medical bills on top of the ranch's debts.

He'd spent the happiest days of his childhood on the ranch with his mom and grandparents, mostly when he was pretty young and later, in his teens, during summer breaks. He regretted not coming more when he got older, letting friends and sports and college life become more important.

When had he last ridden a horse? He couldn't remember for sure.

He looked out the car window in the direction of the ranch, toward the blue and purple mountain range beyond. This place wasn't supposed to be "tamed" and filled with people. The idea of selling it—likely to a developer who would, as Teresa predicted, build condos or a strip mall on it—was his definition of a nightmare. But what else could he do? If he didn't sell, the government would seize the land, he'd have to declare bankruptcy, and his mother would no longer receive adequate care.

Grandpa didn't have life insurance. The small savings he'd had Grandma spent on his funeral and final expenses. Since then, Grandma had run the place into the ground. Unknowingly, but no less seriously.

Add to that his mother's care, which would likely go on twenty years or more, and it was all too much.

Family comes first. That's what his grandparents and mother had always taught him. That's what he was doing. So why did he feel like a traitor?

He had no siblings, and neither did his mother, who'd raised him alone—or at least, with his grandparents' help. His father died before he was born, so he'd never known him. Derek would've given a lot right then to have more family. Any family he could turn to, really. A father would have been nice. Or a brother or sister—older or younger, he didn't care which. Just someone he could turn to, to ask advice of, to counsel with about his mother and how to handle everything.

He found some Excedrin in his bag and tossed back two caplets with a drink from his water bottle. Then, with a sigh, he plugged the hotel's address into his navigation app, put the car into gear, and hoped that by the end of the forty-five-minute drive, he'd feel better.

Last night, after a closing on a single-family home in Mesa, he'd gone straight to the airport, and after landing in Billings, he'd driven straight to the ranch. Now he wished he'd changed clothes somewhere along the way. His suit, which he'd worn overnight, felt all wrong here, and his tie seemed to be actively trying to suffocate him.

With one hand, he loosened his tie and undid the top button of his shirt. That helped. At an abandoned two-way stop, he took the tie off altogether and tossed it onto the passenger seat before going through the intersection.

The constant feeling that he was betraying his grandmother wouldn't leave him. It felt like a loaded backpack that was heavy and off-kilter, pulling on his shoulders and weighing him down.

Every so often as the car ate up the miles, the image of Teresa, flaming mad, flickered into his mind. At first, it was a nice distraction. She was pretty, with brown hair over one shoulder in a braid, a figure toned from hard work, and skin touched by the sun just enough to leave a smattering of freckles across her nose. She was fiery—exactly the kind of woman Grandma would have been drawn to. But soon, thinking of Teresa only intensified the weight on his shoulders because he felt guilty for hurting her too. Soon she'd be out of a job and a home.

I don't even know her, he reminded himself. *Her opinion shouldn't matter.*

Yet Grandma had known her, trusted her, and had to have loved her if she wanted Teresa to live on the ranch. That said volumes about who Teresa was, which meant that in a way, Derek *did* know her. Plus, she loved the ranch and her work. He understood that feeling. Oh, how well he understood.

Teresa clearly knew nothing of the financial realities, and therefore saw him as a city-slicker villain. If he'd shown up in jeans, she probably wouldn't have been so quick to assume he was an outsider and a jerk.

At last he reached the hotel, where he lucked out by being able to check in early. He found his room and sat heavily on the bed. Taking off his suit felt like work, and he wished he could wear his flannel lounge pants and a T-shirt without having to make the effort to unpack them.

He lay back on the bed, both hands raking through his hair as he debated the future of the ranch and paying for his mother's care. Of Teresa, and not wanting to hurt her.

After a few unsuccessful minutes, he grunted and sat up.

If a forty-five-minute drive while pondering the problems hadn't shown him any options, staring at the ceiling from a hotel mattress wouldn't either. Especially when he had low blood sugar and a headache.

He slipped his phone out of his pocket to find someplace to eat that wasn't McDonald's or Subway. As tempting as room service would be, he couldn't justify the splurge. *It's probably time I downgrade the car, too,* he thought. Not unhappily, as he hadn't bought the Lexus because he cared about luxury cars. Rather, he'd bought it because appearances mattered in his business. Unfortunately, meeting clients at properties didn't go as well when you arrived in a beat-up Camry.

As he scrolled through the area's limited dining options, his phone buzzed with a new call: the Shady Acres care facility. But the call wasn't coming from his mother's room or from the front desk. The call came from the main office. What was wrong? Teresa and the ranch forgotten, he answered.

"Hello?" he asked tensely. He stood and began pacing the room, bracing himself for bad news, and annoyed at himself for not stopping to visit his mother before he left town. He usually did, just in case. He didn't want to be one of those adult children who missed their last chance to see a parent. Not that she ever remembered his visits, but *he* did, every one. They were all about the same, like various shades of taupe—technically different but hard for an outsider to distinguish between. He kept going, holding to the belief that the feelings she had when he visited lasted longer than the memory of his presence did.

"Is that you, honey?"

Mom. Not the facility coordinator or a nurse. He breathed out relief and tried not to let emotion leak into his reply. "Hey." She'd never called from a number besides her own in her room, and calls from the main office generally weren't good news.

"When are you taking me home?" She sounded like her old self from years ago.

"As soon as I can." That was Derek's generic answer every time she asked the question, which was pretty much every time they spoke, in person or over the phone.

When she'd first moved into the facility, he'd tried to be totally transparent with her. All that did was upset her, sending her into scared fits over never going home again. The idea of being permanently in this facility left her shaking and crying, and she'd ask what would happen to her six-year-old son, Derek. How would their apartment's rent be paid? Worse, ten minutes after calming down, she'd ask the same question, and the cycle repeated.

The nurses explained that when she felt fear, she regressed into the past, to Derek's childhood or even earlier—sometimes to her own youth. Eventually, his favorite nurse, Shanese, had advised him to answer her in a way that wouldn't upset her. She wouldn't remember the answer anyway. Just don't make her afraid. He tried to follow that advice while making his answers as true as he could.

"Nurse Dandridge thinks I should go lie down," she went on. "But I insisted that you're coming for me any minute now, and I demanded that she let me call from the office. She tried to say I could call from my room or the front desk, but I wouldn't have it. I'll wait right here for you. I have no intention of lying down." She scoffed. "Nurse Dandridge will simply have to be disappointed."

That's what she called Shanese, who reminded his mother of Dorothy Dandridge, the famous black actress and singer from the fifties and early sixties. Grandma Dorothy had loved the celebrity, and Derek had a sneaking suspicion that part of her fascination was due to Grandma and the singer sharing the same first name. He didn't remember Shanese's last name, but it wasn't Dandridge.

"A nap sounds like a great idea," Derek said. "I won't be there right away." Understatement, seeing as he wasn't even in the same state.

"Oh, but Daddy, why? What's taking you so long?"

And there it was: she'd forgotten that she'd called her son and thought she was speaking to her father, Grandpa Joe. That happened most often when they spoke on the phone and she got it into her head that he was still a grade-school-aged kid. The adult voice of her son threw her.

Derek settled on the hotel room couch, leaning forward on his legs. "You know how it is," he said carefully. He'd never get used to playing along, pretending to be his grandfather. Shanese was right; trying to reason with someone who had Alzheimer's only upset them. If he went along with her belief, she'd remain happy. His primary goal was caring for his mother, and keeping her content during this phone call was the best he could do today.

"Are you coming in time for us to get home for dinner? Mama's making chicken dumplings and peach crumble. You know how much I love those."

"Yes, I know." That answer was totally honest. His eyes threatened to mist up, so he blinked a few times and pinched his index finger and thumb across the corners, pulling away any moisture that might turn into tears.

His mother went on. "I suppose it's all right if you're a little late; Mama will save me some. What time do you think?"

He tried to channel what his loving grandfather would have said in this situation that Derek could use as a partial truth. "I'm not sure, but you'll have time for a nap."

By the time she woke up, she'd have forgotten this

conversation. "How about you go ahead and let Shan—Nurse Dandridge—take care of you for a bit, okay? You sure deserve it. What do you say?"

The silence while waiting for her to speak stretched. Was she okay? Did he need to speak loudly to get a staff member's attention through the line? A slightly deeper female voice sounded in the background, and his mother responded to it, but her voice was muffled, as if she'd covered the receiver.

"That'll be just fine, Daddy," she said, the tone clear again.

Daddy. The single word made his heart ache. Too bad her father had died years ago and couldn't visit or comfort her. Too bad that her only child was hundreds of miles away, getting ready to sell off her childhood home. Too bad that she had no idea about her mother's death.

The love in his mother's voice both warmed him and pained him. He never could figure out how such two opposing emotions could fit inside a person simultaneously.

Mom chatted a bit longer until another voice called to her and said that they needed the phone. His mother grunted at them. "Sorry. Looks like I need to go. Love you."

"Love you too," Derek said, struggling to leave off *Mom.* "And I'll be there soon."

Just not today.

The line went silent, but Derek didn't remove the phone from his ear for a few seconds. He had to be sure she'd hung up. His phone buzzed against the side of his face, so he pulled it away and looked at the screen. The call had ended, and a text had arrived from a number he didn't recognize, but which had the same area code as the J-Bar-D. Someone local.

I apologize for being rude this afternoon. Seeing the sign was a shock. Please stop by the ranch to visit sometime soon so I can show you why it shouldn't be sold. —Teresa

As olive branches went, this was a good one. She didn't know that he didn't need convincing, or that the issue was actually that he *couldn't avoid* selling rather than he shouldn't.

He reread the text a few times before deciding how to reply. He didn't need to go visit the ranch again on this trip, but for some reason, he wanted to. A visit to his old childhood play spots might be good for him—he could take a long stroll through some of the fields in the distance. He could sit below the gnarled apple trees that were too old to produce anymore but had been perfect for a kid to climb into and pretend to be a soldier in a lookout. He especially wanted to visit the lookout spot he'd long ago nicknamed the Watchtower.

Oddly enough, the idea of Teresa, a virtual stranger, coming along didn't bother him. She'd appreciate his need to say goodbye.

Goodbye, he thought again. The word echoed in his head. Every moment the reality of selling the ranch drew closer, the invisible backpack of betrayal felt heavier, as if someone were loading more rocks into it. He felt ready to collapse altogether under the weight.

Derek typed a reply. *How's tomorrow morning?*

THREE

WHEN TERESA HEADED down from the bunkhouse the following morning, she felt a little guilty for telling Derek to show up at five o'clock. Emphasis on *a little*. Coming in the morning had been *his* idea not hers, and that's when she started working. He had no clue what he was getting himself into. While the purpose of his visit was to show how important the ranch was, she couldn't entirely dismiss the satisfaction that giving him a bit of comeuppance would bring.

She flicked the switch at the base of the wooden stairs, turning on the single bulb hanging from the middle of the ceiling of the stable. She grabbed her regular supplies, adding an extra headlamp and pair of work gloves for Derek. Before she stepped outside, she checked the clock on the wall—5:02. Time to see how long it would take for the pretty city boy to show up. He'd help with the work even if he foolishly came wearing a three-piece Armani suit.

She closed the door as she stepped outside and glanced toward the unpaved drive where she'd first seen Derek and his sign. In the predawn darkness, she could barely make out the circular drive in front of the main house, where she expected him to park again. No car yet. Her gaze slid over to the for-sale sign a few feet away. She gripped his pair of gloves in one hand and headed for the hay barn.

Four steps later, a large figure appeared and blocked her way. She yelped in surprise.

"Good morning," Derek said.

Teresa gathered herself. "Whoa. I didn't see you." Her eyes were starting to adjust to the darkness, though she wished she'd put on her headlamp before leaving the stable.

"You did say five o'clock?" he asked.

"Yeah." Not that she'd expected him to be punctual. His car wasn't by the sign, so he must have parked in the patron lot closer to the arena. She held out the gloves. "Here. Time to feed the horses."

Derek took the shovel, but as she walked past him, he called, "Teresa, hold up."

She turned around. "Yeah?"

"Are the old black cowboy boots still in the stable? I don't own any others right now, and I'm pretty sure my grandpa's brown ones are too small."

That was unexpected. She'd wondered about those boots since being hired and assumed they belonged to a neighbor or ranch hand. "I'm pretty sure they're in the closet by—"

"The tack. Thanks."

Without another word, he headed for the stable. Teresa strapped on her headlamp and turned it on in time to see him briefly before he slipped inside. He wore old sneakers, equally worn jeans, and a long-sleeved, plaid shirt. Add cowboy boots and a matching hat, and he'd fit right in. Had he bought that shirt in town, or had he packed it in his luggage? She had an odd hankering to know.

A few minutes later, he reappeared wearing the boots, which suddenly made him look very much *not* of the city. His morning stubble only added to the image of a strong cowboy. If she hadn't known better, she would have assumed that his filled-out chest was a result of lots of physical farm work, like stacking heavy bales of hay and wrangling cattle to be branded. But any muscles he had were the result of using machines in a gym.

Sure, he knew how to dress the part on the ranch, but he was still an outsider.

"Do you have one of those for me?" he asked, gesturing toward her headlamp as he approached.

"Yeah." She fumbled a bit, nerves suddenly getting the better of her now that she saw just how good-looking he was up close. She nearly took off her own headlamp to hand over. The straps of his headlamp had tangled around her wrist, but she finally succeeded in extricating the thing. "Here you go."

"Great. Thanks." Derek put on the headlamp as he walked. He eyed the eastern horizon. "We'll get sunlight in what, about an hour?"

"Yeah," Teresa said. "Almost exactly." He could tell?

"Let's go haul some hay." He hadn't called it straw. Most people from the city didn't know the difference between hay and straw. He'd probably learned the difference when he was a kid. But the impressive part was that he *remembered.* He strode confidently for the hay barn.

Teresa followed, keeping up despite his longer stride, so they arrived at the same time. She meant to start explaining how she did the feedings, but Derek quickly grabbed the cart. Without a word, he hefted a bale of hay onto it as easily as if it weighed no more than a gallon of milk.

He adjusted the bale's position on the cart and glanced up at her. "We need how many, about four?"

"Y-yeah," Teresa said, surprise tying her tongue for a second. "And two flakes per horse."

"Just like the old days," he said. He settled a second bale next to the first as easy as anything.

She should have helped him with the last two bales, but

she was curious to see if stacking those on top of the first ones would be any harder for him. They were for her, but maybe that was because she was shorter than he was.

He grabbed the twine on one bale, stacked it perfectly atop another, and did the same with the fourth and final bale. He moved so smoothly, effortlessly, that she half wished she had the guts to go up and check his pulse, pressing her fingers to his neck, to see if it had gone up at all. If that wouldn't have been beyond weird, she totally would have done it, as much an excuse to touch his skin as anything.

When he finished stacking the last bale, he looked at her expectantly. "That look okay?"

"Oh, *yes*," she said, then blushed, realizing that she'd just blurted out her thoughts—that *he* looked *great*. Good thing her reply made sense with his actual question too. She coughed nervously and smiled, hoping it didn't look too awkward. "Let's go."

She turned, and he followed, pulling the cart. With every step, she was aware that his eyes were behind her. Watching her? She totally would have watched him and checked him out if their positions had been reversed. Those kind of thoughts had to stop, or she'd be blushing all day and ready to pass out from her own racing pulse.

He brought the cart to the exact spot she always did, and he waited as she cut the twine from the bale, but no longer; he needed no instructions, instead grabbing a flake in each hand and tossing them to the next horse before moving on. She looked down at her hands, which weren't big enough to hold a single flake each. She usually grabbed one flake with two hands, tossed it in, and then grabbed another for the same horse.

But Derek's hands were plenty big enough to grab a five-pound flake in each, and he easily tossed them over the edge into the stall, exactly where they belonged. He aimed away from the water troughs, too, something she'd been ready to warn him about.

He returned to the cart, grabbed two more flakes, and repeated the process. She didn't move with nearly the speed he did.

He turned around from tossing another set of flakes into a stall and headed back to the cart, but she stopped in his tracks when he noticed her staring at him. She detected a slight quirk of his lips in his mischievous glance before he grabbed more hay, as if he knew she'd been expecting a novice. As if he found a sense of satisfaction in surprising her.

"Am I doing it right?" he asked from the cart. A glint in his eye told her that he knew full well that he was doing it right.

"Pretty much," she said, unwilling to give him credit for a perfect job done. She wasn't one to stroke a guy's ego for the sake of stroking it.

Derek was key to her future and that of the ranch. He was the enemy. On the other hand, a little voice in her head whispered that getting on his good side might be wise; alienating him wouldn't convince him to keep the place. She softened her approach and admitted what she'd been thinking, though not with any adjectives approaching *perfect*. "You've clearly done this before."

He shrugged modestly. "This used to be my job in the summers, when my mom and I stayed here during summer breaks. It's been a few years, but I guess it's like riding a bike."

She studied him, trying to figure out what made him tick. Every time she learned something about him, it contradicted something else. He was one big ball of paradoxes that she couldn't figure out, not the least of which were the conflicting facts that she hated the guy and really liked him at the same time.

Without much more conversation, they were about to finish the feeding in about a third of the usual time. That's why she let herself slow down at the end to give some extra attention to Epione and Asclepius. In turn, they nuzzled her neck. They filled her up in a way nothing else could. To think that if the ranch did sell, she wouldn't be able to care for them. Oh, her heart just ached.

She patted their necks then turned to get back to work. The sun was about to crest the mountains, so she took off the headlamp and beanie—she could see just fine now and was getting a bit warm. She set both on a stump, then combed through her matted hair with one hand. Derek wasn't wearing a beanie but ran his fingers through his hair, too. So help her, when he shook it out, he looked like a shampoo commercial.

He clapped his gloved hands, sending bits of hay into the air, and asked, "What's next?"

Teresa quickly thought through the rest of her tasks for the day: make sure the water tanks, which were fed by a nearby spring, weren't clogged. Groom the arena. Treat the wood in the stall that Hope kept gnawing on, and more. At last she landed on the perfect job for him.

"Can you drive a tractor?"

No doubt he'd pretend bravado, saying that yes, of course he could handle anything with a gear shift and a steering wheel. Men liked to show off, and working things with engines seemed to be a modern equivalent to a caveman beating his chest.

"Pretty comfortable," he said. "Depends on what it is." He wasn't exaggerating his abilities. Why couldn't he have been arrogant? That would have made hating him so much easier.

She suddenly felt quite sure that he could manage the small tractor just fine, but she wouldn't have him groom the arena; that needed to be done in a specific way to look right. She'd give him the job of tidying the pile of manure out back, a pile that, to the untrained eye, looked like dirt. Would he recognize it?

"Come this way," she said, gesturing for him to follow as she led him to the shed. She opened the attached garage door, which rose with a lot of metallic clanking to reveal the old machine. She felt like the cowboy version of the women on *The Price Is Right*, showing off what a contestant had won.

"Know how to drive one of these?" she asked, half hoping he'd ask for tips or—better yet—bravado would get in the way, and he'd make a fool of himself. She was still hoping for *something* to counter her respect for him, which was steadily creeping upward.

"Old Ellie is still running?" He walked into the garage and ran a hand over the dusty side. In a single swooping movement, he climbed into the driver's seat, as if he'd done it a thousand times. He probably had. He eyed the controls for a second, then nodded. "Looks good."

"Okay . . . great." Teresa said, again taken off guard. "Don't turn it on yet, or you won't be able to hear me, but I need you to take it around back. You'll see a big mound that's started to spread out a bit. It needs to be more compacted before it gets hauled off."

"Gotcha," he said. "Clean up manure hill."

She felt a strange mix of emotions at knowing he'd figured out the chore before seeing the pile at all. First a slice of disappointment went through her that he knew what it was and didn't seem the slightest bit fazed by it. Second came even more of that annoying respect. She had to guard against that. Having warm feelings for the man who planned to sell off the closest thing he had to a childhood home—and her livelihood—would be dangerous.

"I'll be checking the water tanks if you need anything."

"Sounds good," he said, then started the engine. Over the roar, he called, "If some of the pipes are clogged, be sure you insert the bladder all the way before filling it, or it'll burst."

"I know," Teresa yelled over the loud engine. She was the manager of the place. Of *course* she knew how to clear a clog in the pipes. She also knew that Dorothy, child of the Depression, had always gotten on edge whenever a bladder attachment failed, which was inevitable. Dorothy's biggest concern? They were "expensive" to replace at a whopping twenty-five dollars a pop.

Granted, the first few Teresa had broken didn't burst from wear and tear, but from exactly what Derek had warned her against: she hadn't inserted the bladder all the way into a pipe, so the water pressure made it bulge out of the pipe, and instead of clearing the clog, the bladder kept expanding until it burst. She'd ruined three bladder attachments before Dorothy gently gave her a talking to about not wasting resources and explained how to clear the pipes properly. Since then, Teresa had lost only one bladder, and that had been due to basic wear and tear.

She walked over to the spigot and watched Derek expertly guide the tractor forward. He steered around one corner, headed along the way to the outdoor stables, and then turned left again to where the manure was collected. The pile butted up against a concrete wall, so compressing it and piling it higher was simple if you just knew how to maneuver the tractor.

She watched him the whole way, telling herself she did it to be sure he was okay. But if she was being totally honest with herself, it was also to watch him in action, and she was quickly impressed with how easily he maneuvered the tractor and the arm that raised and lowered the bucket. He seemed at ease in the seat, reaching for the gear shift without looking for it, as if he did it all with muscle memory. The first rays of dawn were hitting his hair just so and lighting up one side of his face.

Teresa found herself staring like some mesmerized schoolgirl. She shook her head to clear it of any admiration or attraction. This man was the enemy. The fact that he could wield a shovel and drive a tractor didn't change that. He was still about to take away her home, her job, and her horses.

FOUR

TERESA TURNED HER back to Derek, knowing he'd be fine with the manure pile, but wishing she could justify standing there and watching him longer. She headed to the wood crate that held an assortment of tools she might need on any given day. She fished out an old sieve. Though bent and rusting on the edges, the sieve helped clear clogs of hay and other debris that were hard to reach by hand. Every so often a clog appeared that the sieve couldn't clear, and that's when she pulled out the rubber bladder attachment on the hose. Hopefully her arm and the sieve would be enough today.

Before she could head for the water tanks, the tractor sputtered to a stop.

"Teresa!"

She turned around to find Derek turned in his seat, looking back at her. "Yeah?"

"In case Grandma never told you, she had a box of about twenty bladder attachments in the house, so don't worry too much about busting one now and again."

"There are *what*?" Teresa felt her mouth hanging open slightly. "You've *got* to be kidding me."

He chuckled. "I guessed she never told you. I bought a whole case a few years ago because she seemed to worry about them all the time. She was generous with helping others but tended to be a bit thrifty otherwise."

Thrifty was an understatement.

"Where in the world are they?" She would have noticed them in the stable, hay barn, shed, or bunkhouse, and Dorothy couldn't have gotten anything into the storage attic above the bunkhouse without help.

"In her bedroom closet."

Teresa laughed at the ridiculousness of the situation. "She gave me a talking to every time one broke about how expensive they were." She'd been in that very bedroom dozens of times, never knowing that several years' worth of clog-clearing bladders with perfectly good brass fittings sat behind the closet doors. In hindsight, it did sound like frugal Dorothy. "I'm going to find them," she declared, dropping the sieve back into the crate and tossing her gloves on top.

Behind her, Derek's laughter rang out, followed by the tractor engine starting up again.

When she reached the front door, Teresa punched in the key code, which she'd done thousands of times. She knew the code better than her own cell number. She pushed the door open, assuming she'd walk inside, find the box, and take it right out to the stable for when she needed a new bladder.

But with her first step across the threshold since the funeral, the sights and smells of Dorothy's house enveloped Teresa along with its emptiness. The floral scent from Dorothy's obsession with air fresheners, the mustiness from the old walls, and the hint of bacon grease, which must have soaked into the plaster over the decades.

All of it said *home.* All of it said *Dorothy.* All of it released a torrent of emotion that hit Teresa like a punch in the chest.

She stood there in the entry for several minutes, looking around. The front room had an old china hutch filled with tchotchkes. The bookcase beside it—which housed books that hadn't been opened in a decade or two, like the full set of the *Encyclopedia Britannica* on the bottom shelf in the living room—dated from 1973, if Teresa recalled correctly. The popcorn ceiling screamed the same era. If the entry brought back memories and emotions this powerfully, what would the rest of the house do to her?

Teresa ran a finger along the wallpaper to her left, tracing the raised black velvet design on the gold, something Dorothy had had a love-hate relationship with. Dorothy had thought the wallpaper was ugly, but some of her neighbors viewed it as fancy and a status symbol. Dorothy hadn't cared about impressing people for the sake of impressing them, but she certainly was aware that some people treated her better simply because they assumed she had money. Ergo, the hideous wallpaper remained.

After a few minutes, Teresa made her way a bit farther into the house, but instead of heading straight to Dorothy's room, she took a moment to pay her respects to each area of the house—first the kitchen, then the guest room, then the hall bath—seeing them all with new eyes, remembering the time she'd spent in the house and grieving for her friend.

Now that she knew how the ghosts of the past affected her, she didn't want to go into the master bedroom to find the case that Derek had bought, not without preparing herself first. She returned to the front room and sat on the blue and pink floral couch, still covered in clear plastic to protect the fabric. She ran a finger along the plastic, tracing the design, one she used to think was ugly but that now looked beautiful because Dorothy had picked it out as a young wife. On this couch, she'd read to her young daughter, opened Christmas presents, taken naps, and who knew what else.

Teresa was suddenly aware of tears streaming down her cheeks. The house felt both full of Dorothy and utterly devoid of her at the same time. Teresa wiped her face with both hands and took a deep breath. She stared at the popcorn ceiling and hoped her eyes were dry, knowing she needed to get herself together to finish the morning chores. When her gaze lowered to the far wall, she noticed a collage of pictures beside the window, one she'd been aware of but hadn't ever looked at. The pictures were of Dorothy's only grandchild. That meant Derek.

After wiping her cheeks again, Teresa dried her fingers on her jeans and crossed to the pictures to really see them for the first time. They weren't in any chronological order. A baby picture was somewhere near the middle, and one of a little boy by a ladder on the top right. Several others showed a young boy.

One showed Derek at a distance, astride a horse. His cowboy hat shaded all of his face except for his grin. That boy, on that day, had been utterly happy.

Beside the collage was an eight-by-ten of a teenage Derek with acne, braces, and bad hair. She let out a hint of a laugh. She'd had an intensely awkward stage of her own; seeing another person's awkward photos was a bit of a validation. In Derek's case, that picture, paired with one from today, could be passed around junior high schools as a comfort to teen boys that they, too, might be able to emerge from those awful times and be as hot as Derek was now. She felt her face flush at the thought.

"At least I didn't have my headgear on in that one."

Teresa nearly yelped for the second time that morning. Instead, she swallowed the gasp and whirled around to see Derek standing in the entryway. The magic of the house, with whatever hold it had held over her earlier, evaporated in that moment. She once more stood in a dated living room with a floral couch that clashed with the entry's garish wallpaper.

"Sorry," Derek said, taking a step farther. "I didn't mean to startle you."

"No, I'm fine," she stammered. "It's—I—"

"I finished with the manure and drove the tractor out by the arena. Figured it needed to be there next to groom it." He'd saved her from trying to find words; her brain didn't seem to be working. "When I couldn't find you, I saw that the front door here was still open, and worried that . . . " He cleared his throat. "Anyway. Glad to see you're okay."

Once more, she couldn't find words, and once more, now that the shock of seeing him had passed, the sadness from before returned. Dorothy's laughter would never again ring in these walls. Her cooking would never again waft amazing smells to the bunkhouse. She'd never again walk through these rooms.

"I miss her," Teresa finally managed, so quiet that she wasn't sure he'd hear.

He must have, because he closed some of the distance between them. When he was an arm's length away, he said, "So do I."

She looked around the room, out the window to the mountains in the distance. "I love this whole place."

"So do I," he said again, following her gaze. "Did you know that the place was named after my grandparents? The *J* is for Joseph, and the *D* is for Dorothy." He smiled at a memory. "They liked to pretend that the *D* really stood for Derek. I really do care about this place, more than you can know."

"Then *why* are you selling it?"

His face fell, and his shoulders followed. He looked at the sculpted brown carpet for several seconds before raising his face to hers, his eyes glassy with unshed tears. "Because I have no other choice."

FIVE

"I'M IN A no-win situation," Derek said. He looked around the room—at the china hutch, the stack of crocheted afghans, the pictures covering the walls. "Can we talk about it somewhere else?"

"Yeah, okay. Not right now; I have to finish the morning chores before classes start." She wasn't about to have that conversation on a restricted amount of time. Discussing the future sale of his grandparents' home, his mother's childhood home, would be difficult enough for her. Yes, he was selling it, but if he had half a heart—which she was quite sure he did—talking about it here would be hard for him, too.

They lapsed into silence for a few moments, and then she added, "She used to call this the parlor."

"I remember." Derek chuckled quietly. "As if it were a formal receiving room in some English aristocrat's house."

Of course, the place looked about as opposite from a fancy British parlor as it could. Dorothy had filled it with things she loved because of the memories they evoked. Some of them were downright tacky, and her taste would never in a million years grace a design magazine. Teresa loved the room anyway; it was a microcosm of a life well lived, a summary of the things and people Dorothy had loved.

Derek broke the silence next. "How about I clear the tank pipes while you groom the arena? Or the other way around, if you'd prefer. Or if there's something else you'd like me to help with, say the word."

"You do know that I'll hold you to explaining the sale," Teresa said.

"I don't think I'm getting out of anything," he said. "If Grandma liked you as much as I think she did, then you're two peas in a pod when it comes to . . . " His voice trailed off as if he knew he'd been about to say something that would get him into trouble.

When he didn't finish his sentence, Teresa tilted her head and asked, "When it comes to what?"

He licked his lips as if he didn't quite trust the words about to come out of his mouth. "Well, Grandpa called it Grandma's *spunk*, but . . . " He lifted one eyebrow and grinned sheepishly. "Others called it *stubbornness*."

Teresa folded her arms and gave him a half-smile that held a challenge. "What do *you* call it?"

"Tenacity."

"Huh," she said with half a nod. "I can get on board with that. Just remember that with my *tenacity*, I'll badger you until you finally spill the secrets of selling the ranch."

"There are no secrets, Miss . . . "

"I'll hold you to that." Teresa headed for the door, where she turned around and looked back at him. "Call me Teresa. None of that 'miss' stuff."

"Will do," Derek said, tipping his head and touching the edge of his cowboy hat. The gesture gave her an unsettling yet delicious thrill.

Was he flirting? He seemed smart. Kind. Too good, if that was a thing. None of those adjectives matched the image in her head of a villain with a mustache that curled on the ends, which was basically how she pictured anyone who'd sell the ranch.

She headed out the door, but again, he called her back. "Do you want me to grab a new bladder and clear the pipes?"

Goodness, she wasn't thinking clearly at all. "That would be great, thanks." She looked out to the arena, where the tractor waited for her. "And thanks for leaving the tractor by the gate."

He smiled then, a gentle, sincere one. "You're welcome."

For a split second, Teresa felt as if he were saying something more with that phrase, but then she mentally scoffed at herself, thinking, *What, do you think you're Buttercup, and "You're welcome" means "As you wish"?* Feeling herself blush so hard that her cheeks felt on fire, she turned and walked to the tractor, sensing him watch her retreat.

She reached the tractor only to note that he'd parked it in the perfect spot to attach the heavy frame that dragged the arena smooth. She looked back up and saw Derek striding away from the house, toward the outdoor stables. She chided herself for assuming Derek Walters was a villain of any stripe. He was a genuinely nice guy. An extraordinarily *handsome* nice guy.

But for some reason, he believed he had to sell the ranch.

After she got the frame attached to the tractor, she turned to the arena, where she'd need to move the cones and other training gear before grooming it all. That's when she noticed all of it—the cones, the stairs, the posts, all of it—was already cleared. So was the manure.

He even did the kitty litter cleanup. She couldn't hate him anymore, but he sure wasn't making it easy to even mildly dislike him.

She returned to the tractor and drove it through the open gate. As she groomed the arena in the same concentric circles she made every morning, her mind wandered, of course, to Derek and his insistence on selling. She couldn't help thinking through possibilities of why he couldn't find a way to keep the place.

Did he think he'd have to abandon his city life and relocate to the ranch permanently? She could quite capably manage the place herself, and she'd tell him so. She had plans to increase the number of lessons and offer other services too. With some updating of a few structures, the J-Bar-D could board more horses.

She wasn't afraid of hard work. She could make many of those improvements herself. After all, she could handle a circular saw, electric drill, and nail gun as well as any man. Very little would need to be hired out, only a few things like replacing some of the wiring in the main house.

Dragging the arena seemed to take half the time it usually did, though whether that was because he'd prepped it for her, or because she'd been preoccupied by her thoughts, that time flew by, she didn't know.

She unhitched the frame and returned the tractor to the garage. When the garage door squeaked shut, she checked the open-air stalls but didn't see Derek near any of the tanks. He had to be nearby; she didn't think he'd have left without telling her.

"Derek?" she called, ducking through the low door to get into the indoor stables. She figured he'd be inside, and even if he wasn't, she needed to treat the wood in old Hope's stall with motor oil so the horse would stop gnawing it. No sign of Derek.

She fetched the small can of motor oil from a nearby shelf, along with a paint brush, but before she applied any, she heard a footfall behind her and turned.

Derek held out a bar of soap. "Rub this on it."

Teresa looked at the pink bar. "I'm not trying to make the place smell like a flower patch."

He stepped past, his arm brushing hers, which sent goose bumps up one arm and down the other. She tried to process the feeling—a flurry of emotions had erupted, ranging from strong attraction to deep admiration. He rubbed the soap across the gnawed wooden edges, seemingly unaware—thank heavens—of his effect on her.

"Soap works better than oil. Unscented probably works better, but this is all I could find."

"Yeah, that was Dorothy's favorite," Teresa said. "Why does soap work better?"

"One theory is that an application lasts longer because soap doesn't soak into the wood like oil does." He thoroughly rubbed the chewed areas he could reach from the concrete floor of the stable, then opened the half-door gate and stepped inside the stall, where he rubbed the bar in a few more spots. He found a few she hadn't noticed yet.

All morning, her view of Derek had been improving, and once again, he went up a few degrees. And, once again, she tamped down the admiration and respect developing inside her. This wasn't her friend. This was the guy selling away Dorothy's home.

He stroked Hope a few times and then came back into the main area, locking the gate behind him. "Anything else we need to do?" He stood close, something not quite necessary in the wide aisle. She wanted him to touch her arm again.

"Um . . ." For a second, Teresa couldn't remember what she was responding to. "Nothing that can't be done later. We can go talk now, if you're up to it." Not that she was sure *she* was up to it.

"Don't you teach soon?" he asked, checking the clock on the wall.

"I don't teach many lessons. Our main instructor is Amber, and she'll be here soon. She handles it all on her own."

"Then let's pack ourselves a lunch. We can walk around the ranch and talk."

"Great idea," she said. If he wanted to walk the entire perimeter of the ranch, they would. He might remember why the place meant so much.

At the same time, her stomach seemed to buzz with the thrill of spending time alone with Derek when they weren't working. They might walk side by side, brush arms again. Maybe hold hands... or kiss...

What am I thinking? She nipped those thoughts in the bud. She needed to stop it with thoughts of his being so near, so strong, so kind, such a hard worker. And best of all, not in the least intimidated by her own strength and abilities. Not to mention the morning shadow on his jaw, his kind eyes, his broad shoulders...

She returned the oil and paintbrush to the shelf a few feet away, hoping that a little physical space would help get her emotions in check and her thoughts back on track. Her recent lack of any dating life was making her imagination go wild. *I've been watching a few too many romantic comedies alone in the bunkhouse on Friday nights.*

She found herself returning to stand as close to Derek as she had before. She looked up—their faces only inches apart—and said, "A picnic sounds perfect."

"Great," Derek said. "It's a date."

Another zing went through Teresa, muddling her thoughts into something resembling oatmeal.

"Let's go make a lunch and then saddle up my horses. I don't think I introduced you to them, Asclepius and Epione."

"The gods of medicine and soothing pain? Nice."

"Yeah. Wow, I've never met anyone who knew what their names refer to."

"What can I say?" Derek said with a mock-humble shrug.

"I was one of those geniuses who got a degree in the utterly useless field of humanities."

"Mmm, not so useless," she said, grinning. His degree was proving quite good at impressing her. "Come on up. We can pack a lunch in the bunkhouse." She led the way to the stairs and trotted part of the way up when she heard a *thunk* and turned around.

Derek was holding a hand against the side of his forehead. "Forgot about the low clearance of that beam. That, or I was shorter last time I went upstairs."

"Let's get you some ice for that."

"Lead on." He held out an arm, and his smile revealed perfect teeth. Man, he really should pass around before and after pictures to give hope to awkward young teens. She wouldn't mind having a current picture of him on her phone to enjoy.

When they reached the bunkhouse door, she fished for her key in her pocket. The butterflies in her stomach went into a flurry, as if this were a doorstep moment after a date. Most recently, she'd had to strategically dodge a guy's advances when he expected a kiss that she had no intention of giving him.

This time, Derek Walters stood beside her, not at the end of a date, but, arguably, at the beginning of one. Depending on one's definition of *date*. Whether this would count as a date, she couldn't help but imagine what it might be like to kiss Derek Walters.

And how, if he ever tried to kiss her, she absolutely would *not* duck.

SIX

DEREK MADE SANDWICHES with items from Teresa's fridge as she cut up apples for them, ones harvested from the family orchard, no doubt.

He heard the freezer spitting out crushed ice, and a minute later, he felt a cool plastic bag gently pressed against the side of his forehead. He'd forgotten about the bump altogether, thanks to the effective distraction of Teresa. Now, as she held the bag of ice, she stood so close that he could smell her perfume. Or maybe it was lotion, or shampoo. Whatever it was, breathing in the scent and having her touch him in such a tender way all gave him a heady feeling, as if he'd had one too many drinks.

"You all right?" Teresa asked suddenly.

"Right as rain," he said and zipped up a sandwich bag, hoping to sound normal when he was having a hard time breathing slowly with her so close. He noticed that his knees were locked and quickly relaxed them. The last thing he needed was to pass out in front of the woman he was about to discuss something important with. What would he attribute it to? Certainly not to smelling her perfume or the fact that such a beautiful woman was touching his face and hair.

"Here, you hold it in place," she said, taking his free hand and lifting it so it covered the bag. "I'll finish up the lunches."

He wanted to reach up and take not the bag, but her hand, and entwine their fingers. He imagined them walking the perimeter of the ranch that way. He resisted the impulse. Looking like a creep would be even worse than fainting. He held the bag, and she gently pushed him toward the table.

"Go sit down. I'll be right over."

"I'm fine. I—"

"We'd better make sure you're not light-headed or anything before you try to ride."

She had a point, so he went to the table and took a seat. Teresa fished a canvas backpack from the coat closet and set it on the counter, then loaded it: the apples first, followed by the sandwiches. She added a couple of cheese sticks, a bag of mixed nuts, and a few rolls of fruit leather made by Grandma—he could tell by how they were rolled and wrapped.

By the time she'd filled two CamelBaks, he felt much better, though he couldn't promise that he wouldn't end up light-headed if Teresa got close to him again. That wouldn't happen while riding, though. He debated whether to suggest they hike instead.

He was starting to get muddled thinking when he was close to Teresa, enough that he found himself stumbling over words and, apparently, smacking his head into ceiling beams. If he couldn't get a grip—if he couldn't remember his own address after an intoxicating whiff of her perfume, he'd need Jake to help him with the sale. No way would he remember everything required in closing on a property when she was near.

"You okay to walk down the stairs?" Teresa asked, lifting the backpack off the counter.

"Absolutely." He stood and crossed to the sink, where he left the ice bag. "Let's go."

He insisted on wearing the backpack, and they each carried a CamelBak. Downstairs in the stable, he followed her to where she kept the tack for her horses, and they each carried a saddle and blanket outside. The sun was up now. Some cars were in the guest lot, and some people milled about. Teresa greeted several by name, including Amber and a few students.

He and Teresa made quick work of saddling her horses, something that surprised him—muscle memory was an amazing thing. He hadn't saddled a horse in years. He mounted Asclepius and watched in admiration as Teresa mounted Epione in what looked like a single, smooth motion.

"Where to?" he asked.

She seemed to ponder for a moment, and then she just said, "This way." She clicked her tongue and led the way through an old junk area that held old parts for various machines, most of which were rusty and choked with weeds.

Grandpa Joe had called it Treasure Alley. *Ya never know solutions you might find in there,* he'd say.

Derek guessed where they were headed, and a minute later, when she turned onto a narrow path toward the foothills, his suspicion was confirmed—the overlook that as a kid he'd called the Watchtower. He'd loved *The Lord of the Rings* movies and loved the idea of the place being a station where you could see miles and miles into the distance and warn of incoming Uruk-hai. The view from up the overlook was amazing, and although he hadn't thought of it in a long time, he couldn't wait to see it again.

The Watchtower was where Grandpa Joe had brought him when Derek was maybe eight. They'd looked out over the valley and made wishes together. Grandpa had said their wishes would be carried away to the Fates on the wind. When Derek had asked what the *Fates* were, Grandpa began the first of many storytelling sessions Derek would later learn were about various world mythologies: Greek, Roman, Egyptian, Norse, Finnish. He'd loved them all.

The incline increased, and they lapsed into an easy silence save for the rhythmic *clop-clop* of the horse's feet.

After nearly forty-five minutes, they reached a fork, and Teresa guided Epione to the right, just as he'd known she would, to the Watchtower. The overlook had been his happy place as a kid, almost a hideout that, ironically, was open to the valley, though it was hard to see from below.

He used to sit on a flat stone a couple of yards from the edge, where the sun warmed the rock. He lay there, staring at the clouds. Sometimes, when Grandma and Grandpa said he could and his mom wasn't home, he came up and stared at the night sky and the swath of stars sweeping across the darkness like the magical sparks behind a wizard's wand. He studied the constellations and learned every story associated with them.

For a second, he felt a pinch of possessiveness over the Watchtower, but he bit it back. Teresa must have found the overgrown fork and the Watchtower on her own. She didn't know his history with it. She clearly appreciated the place, and that said volumes.

This would probably be one of the last times he'd ever visit the Watchtower, and while he'd pictured himself returning alone, he realized he didn't mind having Teresa there. Not when he knew how much she loved the J-Bar-D.

Soon they'd gone up the final, steep stretch and had reached the top. The place looked as if it had been planned, cut from the mountain with plenty of space for horses to rest and eat grass against the mountainside and with the flat outcropping extending outward.

The hours he'd spent here were some of the most sacred of his life. He'd lain here as a ten-year-old, praying for answers. He'd sat there in stillness, reveling in the majesty and reverence of nature. If he hiked up, the only sounds besides the wind riffling through tall grasses were his own breathing and movements. If he rode up, the silence might be also broken by the occasional click of a horseshoe on the rocky ledge. Many times, he'd felt certain that an answer to prayer had returned to him on the wind.

Life had been much simpler then. Now he was faced with a problem far bigger than a whisper on the wind could fix.

Grandma hadn't meant to mishandle the money. She'd always been kind and generous—now, he knew, to a fault. Grandpa hadn't ever showed her the books or explained how he managed them. And the combination meant losing the ranch. At least that hadn't happened while Grandma was alive. Her sudden passing was a blessing in that regard; she'd been only weeks—at best months—away from losing everything.

Teresa headed for a half-dead tree, the very one Derek had used as a hitching post so long ago.

Great minds, he thought as she gently tied Epione to a branch and he did the same with Asclepius to another. She stroked Epione's neck and murmured to her in a pleasant tone, then did the same with Asclepius before she faced the valley and walked to the flat stone. He joined her, feeling oddly comfortable with this virtual stranger at his side. He felt home again, largely, of course, from simply being at the J-Bar-D and now being at the Watchtower. But everything seemed right, including wearing his old boots again, which had molded to fit his feet over years of work and still fit perfectly.

Their boot steps became a rhythm in the otherwise still day. At the edge of the stone lip, which was like a single stair, Teresa closed her eyes, took a deep breath, and let it out. Her face reflected contentment and awe—a mixture of emotions he understood completely. She looked lost in thought as she opened her eyes and gazed across the sweeping land, the broad sky enveloping it in its blue embrace.

"Isn't it beautiful?" she said, so quietly that he wasn't sure if she expected a reply.

He decided to err on the side of answering. "Sure is." He

meant her as much as the view below. He'd met his share of rich, beautiful women, and while they looked to be near perfection in an airbrushed kind of way, Teresa had a fresh, clean beauty about her that seemed . . . real. She didn't have fake lash extensions, which seemed so popular, and her hair wasn't streaked with what he'd recently learned was an ombre dye job. She wore no makeup that he could tell. If she were to add makeup to her already stunning looks, she'd turn the head of every man in the state. She'd already turned his head in worn jeans and a flannel shirt.

She rested on one leg—the one closest to him—which shifted her weight just enough that their arms brushed. Even through sleeves, the contact sent a pleasant zap through him, a feeling he hadn't felt in a long, long time, and never from something as brief as a touch on the arm. From the corner of his eye, he tried to see if she'd noticed the contact, but he couldn't tell. She hadn't shifted away, though. He took that as a good sign.

He decided to do the same thing: shift his weight toward her. Their arms touched again, this time not as a brush. They came to rest against each other. She didn't pull away then, either, a fact that sent his heart racing.

"When I stand here," she said softly, wistfully, "anything feels possible. I can leave all my cares and worries on the valley floor."

"Exactly," he whispered, his throat tightening with emotion. "That's exactly it."

Suddenly, she sniffed and wiped her eyes. His brow furrowed, and he turned to look at her. "Hey, you okay?"

With a sad shrug, she shook her head. "I'm not so good at leaving my cares on the valley floor today. They've followed me." She wiped some tears again. "Dorothy treated me as if I were her own granddaughter. I'm going to miss her so much." She folded her arms and hugged herself.

Derek briefly debated what to do. He didn't want to overstep his bounds, but he also didn't want to be a jerk who didn't do something about a woman who was crying. He turned toward her and put his arms out in invitation, hoping to offer some comfort. He half expected her to pull away. Instead, she stepped into his embrace and relaxed there, resting her face in the hollow below his shoulder. She seemed to fit there like a puzzle piece made for that spot.

After a bit, her crying ebbed, but she didn't withdraw. With her head still resting on his chest, she whispered, "Thank you."

"Of course."

"And . . . I'm sorry."

"For what?" Baffled, he tilted his head to the side and down, trying to see her face. *He* was the one selling the ranch. She had every reason to hate him.

"For how I've treated you." Her voice was soft but not shaky, as he would have expected after a cry. "Dorothy wouldn't have approved, and that alone tells me that I was way out of line. I judged you, and then I got afraid and angry. I took all of that out on you." She sighed. He couldn't see her face from that angle, so he shifted, trying to make eye contact. She sniffed. "I assumed you were a city slicker and a jerk, and I'm so, so . . . "

She lifted her head and looked right at him. Their faces were so close, he could hardly breathe. The slightest movement toward her, and . . .

Suddenly they were kissing. Who'd closed the gap, he didn't know, and he didn't care. But he was sure of three things. First, that Teresa was in his arms. Second, that she was kissing him just as intently as he was kissing her.

And third, that he didn't want it to ever end.

SEVEN

TERESA PULLED BACK from the kiss and caught her breath. She looked up at Derek, then down at his shirt, feeling self-conscious now that the moment had passed.

Such an unexpected moment.

A really good unexpected moment.

His cheeks had taken on a pink cast, which made her a little less embarrassed. They stood there, neither sure how to break the silence. Derek reached down and entwined his fingers through hers. She looked at their clasped hands and then up, meeting his gaze.

She smiled, then stepped to the side, tugging for him to follow. When they reached her favorite spot—a slightly raised, stair-like ledge—she sat and tugged again. He took the spot next to her. The rock stair was plenty wide for them both, so he sat at her side, which was fine as far as she was concerned.

The stone was cool, not having been warmed by the sun yet. The chill sent a shiver through her, and Derek responded by putting his arm around her shoulders, which was just as good as, or better than, holding his hand.

They had yet to say a word since their kiss. Or was that *kisses*, plural? What exactly counted as *one* kiss? Maybe she should think of it as their *kissing*, not *a* kiss or multiple kisses . . .

She rested her head against his shoulder; Derek was the

perfect height for that. *Too bad he's going to make me homeless and unemployed. This would be almost perfect if not for that.*

"I, uh . . . I'm sorry for back there," he said.

Oh no. He thought her silence meant she didn't want the kiss. The kisses. Their kissing. Warm butterflies swooped through her.

"No, don't apologize," she insisted.

His arm and chest noticeably relaxed. "Really?" Then he turned his face to the side to look at her straight on. She lifted her head from his shoulder and looked at him. As before, their faces—and their lips—were very close. She wanted to kiss him again—*really* wanted to—but didn't have the guts to initiate so soon.

"Really," Teresa said. "No reason to apologize . . . " She nodded toward the spot they'd been standing during all the awesome, toe-curling kissing. "For that."

He tensed slightly. "Should I be apologizing for something else?" His tone said that he already knew the answer, but that wouldn't stop her from trying to change his mind about the sale.

Teresa wrapped her arms around her raised knees. "Look out there," she said, staring into the distance ahead. "The land. The ranch. The nature. The beauty. The animals. All of it."

For several seconds, he didn't turn to look. She could feel his stare, so she waited for him to change his focus. Eventually, he acquiesced, slowly turning to look forward. But at the same time, his arm dropped from her shoulders. She immediately felt the absence, and for more reasons than the warmth it had provided.

Derek rested his forearms on his knees. "I can't count the number of times I've looked out there," he said finally. "At everything you said. It's home to me more than any other place has been. It's priceless."

She blinked, and a tear trickled down one cheek. "But you *are* putting a price on it." Her voice held a sting of accusation. She rested her feet atop the stair and hugged her knees to her chest.

"I *have* to sell it," he said, but with a voice that sounded sad, not insistent.

"I can't believe that." The warmth that had coursed through her moments before was gone. She felt a chill, and she leaned the slightest bit away from him.

Derek groaned and scrubbed a hand down his face. "Trust me, I wish there were another way."

"There *has* to be," she insisted.

If he insisted on selling, despite his claim of loving the ranch...

She shouldn't have kissed him. That just made the whole situation more confusing. She and Derek met barely over twenty-four hours ago. She *felt* as if she'd known him for longer, but that wasn't the same as actually knowing a person. And if he wanted to sell the place, she certainly wanted nothing to do with him.

How stupid could she have been to kiss the guy selling the J-Bar-D?

But part of her wished she could have met Derek in a different way and at a different time. That in that alternate reality, they could pursue this seedling of attraction, see if it might lead somewhere. But so long as he was the person threatening everything she held dear, that was an impossibility.

"You won't have to manage the place," Teresa said intensely. Her emotions were spinning, her words tumbling out like water over stones. "I'm happy to live in the bunkhouse and take care of the whole ranch myself. I've been managing it for years—the basic work and maintenance end, anyway.

Dorothy handled the finances after Joe passed. You can take that on, or, if that's too much work—because I know you're busy—you could hire it out to a local accountant; I imagine that would be cheaper than getting someone from Hawaii or wherever you live."

"Arizona."

"Yeah. So an accountant wouldn't cost much." She paused long enough to take a breath, just long enough for him to shake his head and try to cut in.

"Teresa—"

"No," she insisted. "Nothing has to change."

"It's not that simple—"

She stood quickly, cutting him off. She *couldn't* let him speak, not unless it was to agree with her. To create some distance, she took a few steps away, then folded her arms protectively again. "Tell me why you have to sell. Are you in some trouble and need a tidy profit or a big tax break to make up for some other bankrupt business?"

"No," Derek said firmly. He got to his feet as well. "Would you please let me explain?"

Teresa reluctantly nodded, her lips pressed tight so she wouldn't interrupt again.

"I have no intention of doing anything to line my pockets. I'd never do that to my grandparents or their legacy. I hate that selling the ranch means upending your life. Really. You don't deserve that." He spoke with regret and with such love for his family that it took her off guard. She'd expected him to match her anger, be indignant. That would have made arguing back much easier. Instead, he'd gone all kind and understanding.

She found the storm of emotions spinning inside her slowing down. After swallowing against a knot in her throat, she licked her lips and challenged him. "So what, then?"

"I'm going to do the best I can with the cards I've been dealt."

Throwing her hands into the air, she cried, "What does that even mean?"

Teresa paced away from him and stopped near the edge of the overlook. From here, she could make out the roof of the bunkhouse. She heard Derek's footsteps approach from behind, but she didn't turn around. She wanted him to touch her shoulder *and* to keep his distance. The conflicting emotions were driving her crazy.

Couldn't Derek have been that slimy villain from a melodrama, with the twirly mustache? Instead, he was a kind guy near her age who happened to be exactly the type she found attractive.

"Do you believe that I love the ranch?" Derek asked.

"Yes," Teresa grudgingly admitted. "Which is why I can't understand how you can even *think* of selling it." She wished her words would stoke her inner anger, making it grow white-hot, but all she could feel was sadness and something like resignation.

"The ranch is in deep financial trouble."

She turned at that, her forehead creased with skepticism. "It is?"

"It hasn't made much money in at least fifteen years. For most of their lives, my grandparents scrimped to get by. They never had much savings." Derek tilted his head to one side. "Rather, they were overly generous helping other people, so they dipped into their savings constantly, and it never grew."

Once more, Teresa had to grudgingly admit that what Derek said sounded accurate. "That sounds like them."

"Everyone in Big Fir knows to come to the J-Bar-D if they ever need help," Derek said. "That's how it's always been. They were too kind for their own good."

Teresa had heard that from townspeople too—several times just at Brewed, the local coffee shop. Sort of a shop. It was attached to the gas station "downtown," which amounted to a few businesses near the freeway entrance.

No matter what your trouble was, the people of Big Fir said, Joe and Dorothy Dixon would never turn you away without doing their all to help. She'd admired them for it, never suspecting that their generosity might have caused any trouble.

But it had—so much trouble that their grandson thought he had to sell the ranch. Teresa's anger receded gradually, like a tide, leaving sorrow in its wake. She dreaded hearing whatever Derek would say next.

He stepped beside her and stretched out an arm, pointing. "Their land used to reach to that red fence in the distance."

"The *Steadmans'* property line?" she asked in surprise.

"Yep. They bought that strip about fifteen years ago." He rotated and pointed a bit to the right of the Steadman land. "The J-Bar-D also used to include the whole area on the left there, all the way to the river."

She turned to him, eyes wide. "Not the Watsons' alfalfa fields too."

"Yep. Every few years, they sold off some acreage to make ends meet. It was originally about six hundred acres."

"Six hundred? But the J-Bar-D isn't even sixty acres anymore." She knew they'd sold off some land, but more than ninety percent?

"Grandpa wasn't great with business," Derek said. "Grandma was worse. But they both loved their neighbors. They just gave and gave. They both lived through the Great Depression, so their mindset was always to buy the least expensive equipment possible and then run it into the ground before replacing it. They'd grown up knowing hunger and their families' unemployment. Grandma's family was even homeless for a spell. So when they had a roof over their heads and food to eat, they simply gave to others." He paused as if gauging her reaction, or maybe letting the facts sink in.

In her bones, she knew he spoke the truth. She'd been right; she had every reason to dread this story. But she needed all of it. "Go on."

"When Grandpa died, they had no life insurance, and just a little bit of savings to go toward funeral expenses."

"Was she able to pay for the funeral?" she asked, head coming around.

"Depends on how you look at it. Grandma had to put four thousand onto a credit card. She wanted a nicer casket, but she didn't have enough left on the card. The basic expenses maxed it out."

"I had no idea."

When would the sun warm the overlook? She ran her hands up and down her sleeve-covered arms, trying to warm up. How much of her chill was due to Derek's story, and how much from the actual cool morning air?

"The ranch hasn't had any real income since Grandpa died. No more crops at all."

That didn't make sense, and Teresa called him on it. "Hold on. We currently board thirty-six horses, if you don't count my two, which get free boarding as part of my pay. Then there are riding lessons six days a week, and those aren't cheap. The ranch *has* to bring in a decent income."

"It *should*," Derek said.

"It doesn't?" Teresa's stomach dropped.

"Almost everyone gets boarding discounts. Several horses—at least nine that I know of—haven't been charged a dime in three years, ever since the oil fields had to lay off a bunch of workers. Same with riding lessons: most of the students enrolled are on what Grandma called 'scholarships.' She didn't have the heart to charge full price if someone's parents couldn't afford the lessons. That happened a lot—she'd start out meaning to give a scholarship for a month or two to help the family between tough times but then never charged tuition again, even years later."

"What was her monthly income?" She braced herself for the answer.

"About three thousand . . . in the red."

The ranch *lost* three thousand every month? Teresa felt as if the wind had been knocked right out of her. Any swirling emotions now dropped heavy in her middle, like a pile of wet concrete.

Derek continued, probably glad to be unburdening himself. "She had two lines of home equity credit, both of which are maxed out. In the last few months, she started using credit cards to pay for groceries, utilities, gas . . ."

"My paycheck . . . " Teresa shook her head, the backs of her eyes pricking. "That's awful."

"If I can't pay the back taxes, the government will seize the land—unless the bank does first because both equity lines are months overdue. We aren't looking at just making regular monthly payments going forward. To prevent losing the ranch altogether, very soon, we have to pay off everything that's currently overdue too."

"You have no choice," Teresa said flatly, finally understanding.

"I can sell it and pay off the debts, or I can have the ranch taken from me. Either way, I lose it. Better to sell and pay off the debts so that hopefully—"

"You can go back to Hawaii?" She immediately regretted her words, especially when she saw the pained look on his face. "I'm sorry, I—"

"I was in Hawaii for business. And I want to pay off my grandparents' debts honorably."

"I'm sorry," she said again. "I suppose a profit would be nice, though."

He straightened his back as if getting ready for a debate. "Yes, but not for a selfish reason." He folded his arms and looked her in the eye. "I intend to use the profits to pay for my mother's care and medical expenses." This was the first time his voice had gotten remotely testy. She couldn't blame him, not after how defensive and angry *she'd* been, how quickly she'd judged him.

Her face crumpled in shame. "You're doing the best you can to take care of your family, while I'm apparently a freeloading jerk."

"No, you're not," Derek countered. "You're not either of those things."

Teresa thought back over the last few years to how doting and kind Dorothy had been, giving free boarding for Teresa's horses, a generous salary, and even cooking for her regularly. Dorothy hadn't had money for any of it. "But she couldn't afford to pay me."

"You couldn't have known that." Derek said, his tone softening. "None of this is your fault."

"I guess." She didn't trust herself to say more.

If she'd been aware of the situation, maybe she could have helped Dorothy with the books, found places to cut back on expenses, started paying off debts before the finances grew dire.

Had Dorothy known that the ranch was in trouble? *Really* known how bad things had gotten? Teresa doubted it, but the point was moot. The ranch was stuck, with no way out. It had to be sold to pay debts and to provide for Derek's mother. If he didn't sell it, the debts would remain, with no way to pay them, and what would happen to his mother?

The whole thing was awful. But to make things worse, the attraction she felt toward Derek, and the amazing kisses they'd shared, had made her want to date him. No way could she date the man who would sell the J-Bar-D and leave her and her horses homeless, even when he had solid reasons for doing so. She just couldn't.

Yet attraction still zipped between them like static electricity. If she was going to have a fighting chance of controlling her emotions toward this guy, she had to leave. Now.

"I have to go." She turned on her heel and headed to the horses.

"What about lunch?" Derek called as he followed her.

"I'm not hungry anymore," Teresa said as she untied Epione's reins, only to tangle them with the nervous energy in her hands. She couldn't bear to look him in the eye. She wanted another kiss, but that would be about as smart as throwing herself off the overlook and expecting a parachute to appear.

Derek touched her arm, startling her into looking up. When their eyes locked, her cheeks went hot. She swallowed and tried to look away but couldn't. He looked deeply into her eyes and said, "Are we good?"

She tried—failed—to find enough moisture in her dirt-dry mouth to answer. Her eyes burned, but they, too, had dried up.

"Are we good?" he asked again, still with his warm, strong hand holding her arm firmly, protectively. In any other circumstance, she would have felt comfort from such a gesture. Now, she needed to get away from it; her attraction toward him was getting too intertwined with her loyalty to the ranch. She couldn't think clearly.

"I understand why you're selling," she said slowly. His face lightened with relief, but then she added, "Goodbye, Mr. Walters," and his face fell. "I'll move out of the bunkhouse right away. I'll continue to care for the horses until they're relocated, but don't worry about paying me. They need to be cared for one way or another, and I'm happy to do it in the interim."

With that, she mounted Epione, clicked her tongue, and trotted for the trailhead.

"Teresa," Derek said. "Wait."

She stopped the horse for a moment but kept her back to Derek so he couldn't see that her eyes had released their grief. Tears streamed down her face. He was calling her, but she *couldn't* turn around and let him see her tears. Besides, turning back would do no good, change no facts. "I understand why you're selling. I do. But you need to understand that I *cannot* speak to the person who sells the ranch ever again. I just . . . I *can't*."

"Teresa, please."

With her heels, she nudged the horse forward faster. Soon the wind whipped through her hair as she and Epione galloped away, leaving Derek, and her hopes, behind her on the overlook.

EIGHT

DEREK WANTED TO go after Teresa, but he had a feeling that if he did, it would be asking for trouble. Maybe he could just send her a text. He pulled out his phone and confirmed that he had service at the Watchtower.

Leave her alone for now, he told himself. *She needs some space.*

He needed a little time too, to cool off from the moment they'd had . . . one he felt quite sure had been mutually enjoyed, and one of the most amazing kisses he'd ever had. Maybe any kiss with a pretty girl at the Watchtower would have been amazing.

But he didn't believe that. Teresa had something about her, something different and special. She was nothing like the other women he'd dated. None of them in their seemingly airbrushed beauty held a candle to Teresa's natural beauty and candor. She didn't hide her thoughts and feelings or pretend to be someone she wasn't. She had strength and kindness—two qualities that surely helped her manage the ranch.

Teresa seemed to have been close to Grandma, which meant that she was also generous, helpful, and probably shared Grandma's wacky sense of humor. He knew one thing for sure about her, though: she loved the J-Bar-D as much as he did.

Any one of those would have been enough to make him want to get to know her better. Together, those qualities lit up a path in his heart leading straight toward her—one so clear that even a beginner tracker could follow it. He wanted to explore that path—explore it *with* her. Not possible, at least not today. Maybe not ever, unless she'd be able to somehow overlook the part he had to play in her career and home.

He'd give her some space. No calls or texts today. He'd go back to the house, look over Grandma's file cabinet and computer to gather any information he didn't already have: receipts or bills that hadn't been recorded in spreadsheets, property deeds, contracts, and anything else he might find. He hoped he'd uncover assets Grandpa had forgotten to tell Grandma about.

The search should occupy him for the day—and keep him from reaching out to Teresa. He suspected that laying eyes on him would upset her, and the last thing he wanted was to cause her more pain.

Derek tied Asclepius to the old tree again then returned to the stair step. He'd wait there so Teresa would have time to get Epione taken care of before he showed up. He couldn't see the outdoor stalls from here, so he'd have to guess when she arrived, but the trip back, all downhill, took quite a bit less time than the trip up. He checked his watch—five after noon. He'd wait until half past to leave, and then he'd go slowly.

The view, which typically held his attention and let his mind wander to fantastical, happy places, only made him think of Teresa and the kiss they'd shared. He grunted and turned his back to the view, even though sitting on flat stone without the step in front of him wasn't as comfortable. Now his view consisted of the old tree, where two horses had been hitched. Where Teresa had ridden away from him.

Great. No matter where he sat or looked while he waited, Teresa and the ranch would be in his mind. He needed a distraction. *Cell phone to the rescue,* he thought, clicking the screen on.

He did the typical mindless checking of various social media accounts, but as he scrolled, he could still feel her lips on his. He checked his email—a mistake, because a bunch of work-related messages were gathering inbox dust, and some were likely important. They'd have to wait.

Maybe blasting some music of classic rock groups—ones his mother had made sure he learned to appreciate—would help. But without earbuds, he'd end up playing Def Leppard or Rush at full volume. He'd done that during his teen years and was quickly informed by his grandparents that the music echoed off the rock and carried for miles. He checked news headlines instead, hoping to fall down a journalistic rabbit hole with clickbait articles leading him deeper into the interwebs until he'd forgotten what time it was and about Teresa altogether.

After reading a political piece, he moved to crime reports, including a story about a Marine veteran who'd bilked several hundred thousand dollars out of people through a fundraising website, claiming he'd lost his wife and children in a fire and now had mounting medical bills of his own.

Turned out that the man wasn't a veteran at all. Worse, he had three former wives, hadn't been married in years, and he had no children. Derek shook his head, wondering what kind of lowlife would do such a thing. He needed something more positive to read about. Something to lift his spirits. He checked his watch: twenty after.

Ten more minutes, and he'd head back. He swiped and clicked until he felt quite certain, based on the picture of three bald children, that he'd found a feel-good article. Sure enough, the feature was about a summer camp for children with cancer, giving them the chance to have a "normal" camp experience where they weren't the only sick ones, and where they could participate in activities that they normally couldn't, due to extra accommodations they needed, from wheelchair ramps and oxygen pumps to chemo treatments.

While he scrolled past an ad, the screen changed to show an incoming call from Phoebe Lambert, a sweet lady who'd been a client for years. She was also a chatterbox who excelled at taking up time without saying much. He'd been on the receiving end of her conversations and phone calls many times, and he'd never escaped one without spending a minimum of half an hour on a call. Sometimes she called just to chat, with nothing on her mind about real estate at all.

Jake had often told Derek to make up an excuse and hang up; it wasn't as if the agency was made up of a bunch of therapists. But Derek never had the heart to cut her off. He'd known Mrs. Lambert longer than Jake had and knew that she hadn't always been this way.

Before her husband's death, the couple bought and sold all kinds of properties, often flipping them, though they didn't do the remodeling themselves. They paid their grandsons modest wages to do the work, which went into their college funds. Since Mr. Lambert's death about a year ago, she'd closed on one deal and hadn't committed to any new ones, but she called regularly.

Jake was right in that investing time in Mrs. Lambert right now didn't help them from a financial standpoint. Every minute Derek spent talking with her was lost money, or so Jake said. Derek didn't mind the time; some things were worth more than money.

His thumb hovered over the button that would send the call to voicemail. If he ever had a moment when he could justify avoiding a lengthy conversation with a lonely widow, this was it. But in his mind's eye, he saw Grandma Dorothy's face shaking her head at him and tsking. She'd been a widow too, and she'd raised him better than that.

He moved his thumb to the side about an inch and pressed the green icon instead. "Derek Walters."

"Derek, dear, it's Phoebe Lambert. How are you? I heard you were stuck in Hawaii, what with those lava flows and who knows what else. I heard that islands were in danger of typhoons again or some such. Typhoons—in Hawaii! Can you imagine? Of course you can; you were there, and even if you hadn't been, it's all over the news. Are you back on the mainland again, or are you stuck on the island, dodging red-lava rivers and getting rained on by volcanic ash like in some movie? What do they call that kind of show, again . . . let's see . . . dystopian, was it? Apocalyptic? I don't remember. I can't keep up with the young people anymore. I'm too old for that."

She finally paused long enough for Derek to answer. "I am back," he said quickly, unsure if she was actually waiting for an answer, or if she'd paused only to inhale.

"Oh, that's so good to hear. Were you able to fly home? I wondered if you'd have to take a boat, and if so, I sure hoped it would be a cruise ship rather than some rickety ferry because can you *imagine* what crossing hundreds of miles of the Atlantic Ocean would be like in a *ferry*? Oh, wait. That's the *Pacific* Ocean, isn't it?" She chuckled. "Oh, my. Facts and figures sure get twisted up in my white-haired head. At my age, it's a wonder I don't wear my nightgown to the grocery store."

This from a woman who had a standing appointment with her hairdresser every Monday and Thursday. Derek had never seen her remotely unkempt. He wouldn't be surprised to learn that she wore something to bed that would be fitting for a social call, just in case.

After another chuckle, she added, "Did you?"

Derek had to rewind her last spiel to remember what she'd asked. Right—how had he returned? "I was able to fly out eventually, but I'm not in the office. I'm in Montana on business, so if you need something done soon, you might want to call Jake—"

"Oh, that won't be necessary," Mrs. Lambert cooed. "I'm patient. I'm getting old, but I'm in no rush. Granted, I probably should be in a rush; my parents both lived to ninety, and that's only three years away for me. Plus my dear Wallace is already gone, so I really could go any time. Even with all that, I can't seem to make myself hurry." Phoebe Lambert had a way of making him smile, and he sure needed a reason to smile today. Derek was glad he'd answered.

"That's a good way to live, Mrs. Lambert," he said, walking over to a log and sitting on it. "We hurry too much in the modern world."

"Isn't that the truth! I don't know how you young people do it, keeping up with the intelligent phones and those application things. I don't understand it, and I never will." As evidenced by the fact that she had only a landline and vowed to never get a cell phone, not even a "dumb" one.

"Slowing down is one reason I'm glad to be in Montana right now, actually," Derek said. "I spent a lot of time here growing up with my grandparents and my mom. I learned to get up early, work hard, and then enjoy a sunset with a cool glass of lemonade."

"Sounds downright dee-lightful," Mrs. Lambert said. "I try to follow the example of my grandson Gary. He enjoys things in the moment in a way most of us spend a lifetime trying to learn. I've told you about Gary, haven't I?"

Amazingly enough, she hadn't. "I don't think so."

"He's on what they call the 'spectrum,' if you're familiar with that."

"Not terribly, but a little," he said.

"He's got a lot of challenges, Gary does," Mrs. Lambert continued. "He struggles with making friends and getting along with other children. And he's not so good at sports or things like that—he's a bit uncoordinated. His mom used to say it was just his long legs and big puppy-like feet, and that the rest of him would catch up, but he never did get over the awkward stage. And he's still as difficult to predict as ever—he gets angry and frustrated at things most children wouldn't."

"How old is he?" Derek asked, trying to do the math. Phoebe was pretty old to have a grandchild who was still a child.

"He just had his twentieth birthday, but he's more like a six-year-old. You should see him when he's with his dog. Or my cats. Or any animal, really. He becomes a different boy. Normally, he's really sensitive to things—loud sounds, bright lights. He can't *stand* being hugged or touched at all, but he loves it when my cats curl up on his lap and lick his face. He lets them *lick* him! This is a boy who has to wear shirts without tags because they're too scratchy. *Amazing.* He reads books while using his dog as a pillow. They sleep together every night."

The young man really did sound like a child. Derek felt for Gary's parents and the challenges they'd faced in raising him.

Phoebe sighed wistfully. "He's come a long way since they figured out that animals help him, but he'd be much better off today if they'd figured that out when he was little. The earlier children like him get therapy and what they call *interventions*, the better they are when they grow up. I've had a bit of a dream that—" She cut off suddenly. Something very un-Phoebe-like.

"You have a dream that . . . what?" Derek prompted.

"Oh, it's silly, really. I wouldn't know the first thing about it . . . but all right. Here's my dream. I'd love to put together a place where children—and maybe even struggling adults like

Gary—could spend time with animals and get the kind of therapy they need."

Derek's mind was suddenly going in a thousand directions at once. He tried to run through scenarios and calculations. Pieces of a possible solution floated around him, and he tried to grab them and click them into place.

Mrs. Lambert was extremely wealthy. She literally had millions to spend on any cause she thought worthwhile. To date, those causes, after paying for her grandchildren's college educations, had been spent improving neighborhoods, donating scholarships for disadvantaged students, and remodeling soup kitchens. Unlike many people, Phoebe didn't restrict her philanthropic ventures to ones that would eventually generate money. She genuinely wanted to help make the world a better place.

Suddenly, Phoebe had become a beacon of hope. Derek stood and paced the Watchtower with nervous, excited energy. "I have an idea that could make your dream a reality," he said, slowly and cautiously. "Maybe."

"Oh my. Truly? What is your idea? Do tell."

He turned and paced the other direction. "I need to do some research before I say more, but I'll look into it and call you tonight, okay?"

"Will this idea of yours help children like Gary?"

"If I can pull it off, it will help Gary and hundreds—maybe thousands—of others."

"Then go do your research," Mrs. Lambert said. "Go ahead and rush on this one. If it's something that could help Gary, I want to be alive to see it happen, and I don't have years and years anymore. I'm the last living member of my high school graduating class, you know."

A smile spread across his face—and it felt good. "I promise to hurry. I'll call you tonight."

NINE

THAT NIGHT AFTER a few hours of research and many calls to friends he knew in charities and legal work, Derek felt confident that his idea of transforming the J-Bar-D into a therapeutic, nonprofit ranch was viable. He called Phoebe to explain, and he didn't get more than a few sentences out before she jumped aboard.

His initial excitement and relief were tempered by the realities of how dire the ranch's situation was. Phoebe could single-handedly pay the taxes and other debts, but the additional money a therapy ranch would require to get running—starting with cabins for attendees, a medical facility, insurance, and a dining hall, just for starters—would require even more money. And there went any profit. Not even Phoebe could pay for all of those improvements *and* a significant profit for Derek to use for his mom.

The paperwork wasn't done, but he felt confident that he'd saved the ranch. Yes, he was technically still selling it, but the J-Bar-D would continue to exist even after Phoebe passed. Best of all, it would help hundreds upon hundreds of children and young adults.

And yet.

He faced the other reality: not selling the whole thing to an investor meant saying goodbye to money that would secure the cost of years of care for his mother.

He usually liked his career, but the downside—the really big, yawning, gaping hole of a downside—was not having a steady paycheck. He got paid only after a sale was finalized. He'd lost track of how many times he'd counted on a commission to pay for the next few months of his mother's care, only to have a sale fall through right before closing.

Real estate income was feast or famine—not a big deal for a bachelor with no significant responsibilities, but a burden ever since his mother's health declined. Now he desperately wanted a stable sum that he could count on to provide for her. He'd made do, somehow, before Grandma's death, and he'd make do going forward, somehow.

The morning after his call with Phoebe, Derek flew back to Gilbert. He wanted to send Teresa a text so she'd know he was gone but would return soon, but he closed the app instead. She didn't want to speak to him ever again, and though she hadn't mentioned texting, she surely meant it.

His first stop back in Arizona was the Shady Acres care facility—a ridiculous name for a blazing hot Arizona location, though when he stepped inside, the air conditioning felt like welcome shade. He found his mom in good spirits, though she warned him to watch the icy step on the back stoop, probably thinking she was back on the ranch in winter.

"Be sure you take cookies for the road," she told him, patting his hand. "I made a fresh batch this morning."

Of course, she had no access to a kitchen, but Derek nodded. "Will do," he said. "Are they raisin?"

"Of course," she said with a laugh. "Those are my specialty."

After an hour's visit, he kissed her cheek, getting ready to leave.

She held his face with both hands, kissed his nose, and said, "I love you, Buddy Boy." That's what she'd called him when he was little, but not since he was about fourteen and got embarrassed easily in front of friends. She'd returned to the term only after her mind had started to fade.

He looked into her starry eyes, which weren't entirely present, and said, "I love you too, Mom." He left with glassy eyes. When he got into his car, he imagined introducing Teresa to her. She'd be kind to his mom in a way many people weren't, getting impatient with someone losing their memory.

That wouldn't be happening. Teresa said she couldn't date the man who sold the ranch, so that was that.

He spent the better part of a week putting together the paperwork to arrange the sale with Phoebe and help her set up a nonprofit, which required hours on the phone with a good lawyer in Montana for many of the details. Phoebe was the one client who'd never dropped a sale on him; he could always count on a commission from her. Judging by her excitement over this deal, she'd have to be bound in a straitjacket to avoid closing this deal.

When everything was set, he flew back to Montana and closed the deal at a title company with Phoebe and her lawyer. Then he drove out to the J-Bar-D to let Teresa know about the sale, and, if he was being honest with himself, to say goodbye to the ranch, and likely to Teresa. The place wouldn't belong to him or his family anymore. He hoped that Teresa would be glad about what he'd done with it and that she'd continue to be managing it. But the fact remained that he was the guy who'd sold the ranch, and she refused to speak to him.

She *couldn't*, she'd said. And he understood. He hated the situation, but he understood.

Derek pulled up in front of the main house, parking in the same spot he had the day he'd put up the for-sale sign. He killed the engine and stared ahead at the arena and stable, and the bunkhouse above that. Teresa was somewhere over there.

He'd thought of her constantly over the last week. He wanted to see her again, hold her again, kiss her again.

How was it that he'd barely known her for a couple of days before he'd left the ranch? He'd lost track of how many times he'd reached for his phone to text her. Each time it had felt natural, as if they'd known each other for years instead of days, as if they hadn't been in separate states for most of that time. As if they'd had months of time to get to know each other before she'd said she could never speak to him again.

Each time he'd reached for his phone, he'd put it away with the image of her riding away from the Watchtower. If he were to call, she'd hang up. If he texted, she'd ignore it or insist he never contact her again.

He was moments away from seeing her again. Yes, he'd be violating her wishes, but he had to tell her how the sale was happening and what it meant. He thought of the Watchtower and sent a prayer into the winds that she'd give him a chance to explain before telling him to leave—just as she had the first time they met right here.

He'd thought through the possible conversation a dozen times but still had no clue how to begin it—and that would be the most important part: Teresa listening long enough for him to get the information out about Phoebe and the nonprofit.

He rounded his car from the back, clicking the key fob to open the trunk, where he would put the for-sale sign before seeking out Teresa. When he grabbed the sides of the sign and pulled, it wouldn't budge. Big Fir had had its first freeze of the season, and the ground seemed to be holding tight to the metal.

He brushed his palms together and walked to the trunk, where he found the work gloves he kept there for things like this. He put them on and returned to the sign. He'd just leaned down to grab the sides when he heard a familiar voice.

"I can't call the cops to say you're trespassing," Teresa called. She walked his direction from the arena. "But I thought I made it pretty clear that I didn't want to see you again. I said I'd move out as soon as I can."

The sight of her made his heart leap. Even at a distance, she was gorgeous—her hair was down under a cowboy hat, spilling around her shoulders onto her red and blue flannel shirt. There was something magnetic about a woman walking confidently in cowboy boots. Walking to him. He straightened, smiling until he made out the tense set of her face. Then he braced himself.

She stopped a couple of yards away, seemingly to register just now what he was doing by removing the sign. "I don't suppose you're taking that out because you've changed your mind about selling." Her voice was flat, full of pain.

"No, but—"

"Then you already sold it?" She cupped her mouth with one hand, and tears sprang to her eyes.

"It's not what you think," Derek said quickly.

"That was fast." Teresa shook her head and turned away from him.

"It *was* fast, and for a good reason—"

"I'm sure it was. I'm glad you'll have enough money for your mom. I . . . I really am." Her voice was high and strained. Before he could answer, she strode away, trying to end the conversation.

He wasn't about to let that happen. "I have to explain, and I need you to hear me out."

She kept walking. Derek yanked the sign out of the ground, tossed it and the gloves into the trunk, then grabbed a file folder from the passenger seat. He jogged after her, keeping an eye on Teresa the whole time, which meant inadvertently stepping in half-frozen puddles and piles of manure, and once landing on hardened, uneven mud and twisting his ankle. Too bad he was wearing sneakers instead of his boots. He made a mental note to grab them from the stable before he left.

Teresa rounded a corner, and he lost sight of her. He looked but found no sign of her in the arena, the hay barn, or along the row of outdoor stalls. He hurried into the stable in time to catch Teresa taking the last two stairs to the bunkhouse.

He followed, taking the steps two at a time. When she went into her apartment, he prayed she'd open the door to him. Only a few seconds after the door clicked shut, he knocked several times. He waited, but the door didn't open.

"Teresa," he called, "it's good news." He waited a good thirty seconds before trying again. "You get to stay on as the manager. And there's even more good news."

After what felt like an eternity, the handle slowly turned, and the hinges creaked open. Derek held his breath, eager to see her face again.

At last, there she stood. She'd taken off the hat, though her hair still hung about her face—a face that held pain. She leaned against the doorjamb and sighed. "Look, I understand. Really. Of course your mom needs to be cared for. I just . . . I can't . . ." She closed her eyes, and tears fell down both cheeks.

"You get to stay on," he said again, feeling urgency to get the whole thing out. "The J-Bar-D will continue as a ranch."

"For how long?" Teresa asked. "What if the new owner decides to raze the place, pave it over, and build a Walmart?"

"That can't happen. I made sure of it."

Teresa's face shifted from suspicious to unsure. "What?"

"The buyer is creating a charity that will keep the J-Bar-D running for decades. It'll outlive both of us."

She sniffed and stared at him as if he were speaking Greek. "I don't understand."

"You have my word. That's what is going to happen." He gestured toward the bunkhouse behind her. "Can I come in to tell you the rest?"

Teresa sniffed again, wiped her eyes with both hands, and stepped back, gesturing for him to enter. She still didn't speak.

A moment later, he and Teresa sat across from each other at the round kitchen table. Derek slipped into Realtor mode. "The woman who is buying the place will be putting it under a 501," he began. Teresa looked confused, so he added, "That's a nonprofit organization—the charity I mentioned. She's setting it up so that the place will be able to run indefinitely."

"How? What about the debts?" Teresa's voice still sounded quiet and unsure, but a layer of curiosity had appeared as well.

"She has the capital to pay off *all* of the ranch's debts."

Relief and awe washed over Teresa's face. "Really?"

"Really," Derek said. "And that's not all. She's turning the ranch into a therapy camp for children and young adults with special needs."

"That's the charity," Teresa clarified.

"Yep."

She sat back in her chair, looking as if long-held tension were draining out of her. "That's . . . wow. That's *fantastic.*"

He tried to memorize every second of this moment so he could remember it later: the wonder in her voice, the joy in her eyes, the smile that made her even prettier than before, if that was possible.

"What happens now?" Teresa asked.

"The owner has a grandchild on the autism spectrum, so autism is where she wants the camp's focus to be at first. But eventually, she wants to have sessions that focus on those with other special needs—Down syndrome, cancer, and so on. The options are endless." He paused for effect and then grinned. "The manager gets to make those calls."

She covered her mouth with both hands, still smiling. "I can't believe it."

A sliver of guilt wormed inside him. He hadn't found the money to guarantee his mother's care. Derek wouldn't let that guilt surface—not here, not now, anyway. Yes, he could have gotten the money if he'd sold the place to a big developer. But at least the burden of Grandma's debt was gone. He'd figure out his mom's care somehow.

"*You* get to manage the whole thing while living in the main house. After Grandma Dorothy's personal effects are removed, you'll live there. The owner will remodel the bunkhouse into dorms as the first step for campers and eventually build a cabin or two for more. Of course, Epione and Asclepius have a home here regardless of whether they're part of the therapy program."

"And the other horses?"

"The buyer is looking into that. She'll help relocate some, talk to some owners about buying their horses for the program or getting a discount on boarding if their horses are part of it. It'll work out. No one wants to see any homeless horses."

Teresa stared at the table as if avoiding his gaze. Her eyes were red-rimmed, but she radiated happiness. "I don't know what to say. It's all so amazing. Thank you."

"I couldn't live with myself if I'd allowed the place to turn into a Walmart." Derek had dropped his gaze to the tabletop too. As if on command, they both raised their heads, and their eyes met. She looked so happy.

What he wanted to do right then was scoot his chair around the table and kiss her again, but that would have been stupid. Would he ever kiss her again?

He didn't kiss women often or easily—their previous kiss notwithstanding. He sensed that she didn't hate him anymore, that she wouldn't mind if he talked to her again in the future, but *talking* and *pursuing a relationship* were two very different things.

Just because she wouldn't mind a text didn't mean she'd want to enter a long-distance relationship. Those rarely worked anyway.

And that's what they'd be facing, because after selling to Phoebe, he would have to work harder than ever to care for his mom. He'd have to venture into selling larger and more expensive properties to make up for the money he lost by not seeking a bigger investor.

He wouldn't have time to devote to any kind of relationship, long-distance or otherwise. Best to leave on a good note.

He had a feeling that he wouldn't be visiting the ranch again. Phoebe would turn the place into something amazing, and she promised to keep the name. But even as the J-Bar-D, the ranch would be different. It would never again belong to his family. In a couple of years, no one would remember that the ranch was named after Joseph and Dorothy Dixon. Remodeling and new construction would mean that the place wouldn't look or feel like the original.

He slid the folder across the table. "Here are the details, including contact information for the new owner, Phoebe Lambert. I think you'll like her. She has your info too. I trust her. She'll do right by the ranch."

A tear trickled down Teresa's cheek, but judging by her smile, it was a happy tear. "I can't believe you managed to save the ranch and get enough money for your mom."

In lieu of an answer, Derek cleared his throat and pushed away from the table. "I'd better go. You wouldn't believe how much paperwork this kind of thing involves. I swear, a forest dies every time a property closes." He headed for the door. Behind him, he heard Teresa follow and hoped their goodbye would be brief and pleasant.

"Thank you again," she said as he got to the door. "I can't thank you enough." She reached for the handle, but when she didn't turn it, Derek looked at her.

Suddenly, Teresa stepped forward, went on tiptoe, and gave him a soft, slow kiss. It was a simple one, but therein lay the power. His insides turned to gelatin. She pulled back and looked up at him. "You have no idea what this means to me."

He had some idea. But her nearness—and her kiss—were muddling his brain and he couldn't get any coherent words out along those lines. He went with the automatic, "You're welcome," followed by the equally generic, "I'm glad it worked out."

Still standing close, she went on. "Things are set with your mom, then?"

She'd noticed his dodge. Wishing he had control of the door handle and could slip out before answering, he tried to moisten his mouth enough to speak. What should he say? "Getting there," he managed. "I'll figure it out. I, um, better go."

"Right," she said. "All that paperwork."

"Yeah." Their eyes locked for a moment. She released the handle and stepped a little closer, as if she might kiss him again. He wanted her to—oh, how he wanted her to.

He opened the door himself and stepped through. "See you later," he said, though that was probably a lie. He hurried down the stairs, out the stable door, and to his car. The whole way, he was unsure whether he wanted her to call him back or whether he was relieved when she didn't.

He drove off as fast as he could, realizing twenty-five minutes later that he'd left without his boots.

TEN

TERESA STOOD IN the doorway of the bunkhouse until the outside stable door thumped shut. Only then did she go back inside. She crossed to the kitchen window and watched Derek head to his car and tried to read his body language. He'd seemed distracted, unsure of himself.

Maybe she shouldn't have kissed him. He hadn't reacted at all how she'd hoped, though could she blame him? It was a wonder he was still civil. He'd sacrificed so much to save the ranch. He didn't have to come all the way to the ranch to tell her.

But he had.

After believing that the J-Bar-D would soon be gone, her wish was realized: Dorothy's house would remain standing, the stable would continue to board horses, and lessons would continue. All of it with changes, but good ones. And if her projected salary on the paperwork was accurate—a number she'd spotted near the back of the folder and nearly gasped at—she'd be making three times her former salary.

For several minutes after the dust from his car had settled, she stared out the window, pondering what he'd done. Though he'd dodged the question, she knew that he hadn't secured the money for his mother, Dorothy's daughter. That needed to be fixed. But how?

Her mind wandered to the past, to times with Dorothy, to thoughts of how beloved she and Joe had been to Big Fir.

An idea suddenly sprang to mind. Teresa raced to her laptop on the coffee table. She spent the next two hours setting it all up. Heart pounding in her chest, she created a campaign on a fundraising site. She wrote up a description:

To care for one of Big Fir's own. Following the death of Dorothy and Joe, to provide long-term care for Joan Dixon Walter, their only child.

Below that, she added what few details she knew about Joan's needs, mentioned Derek, and finished with the history of the J-Bar-D and how much the Dixons had given others. Nervously, and second-guessing herself, she finished the campaign and set it to live.

Of course, that's when her work really began; she had to spread awareness. She stayed up late into the night, designing a flier to hang in all of the local hangouts, especially Brewed, and to deliver in person to long-time residents. That meant driving dozens, if not hundreds, of miles, but she was determined to spread the word.

She printed out the flier on her own printer, using a ream of plain white paper, the only kind she had on hand. Ordering something colorful online would take too long, and she didn't want to drive an hour to the nearest city of any size for something that probably didn't matter anyway.

Bleary-eyed, she went to bed around four in the morning, collapsing into a deep sleep of contentment, but got up only two hours later to feed the horses. After the morning chores, she toyed with the idea of going back to bed, but the sight of the fliers in a neat stack on her kitchen table, sitting beside the folder Derek had brought over the day before, changed her mind.

She got herself a bite to eat, then called the arena teachers so they'd know she'd be away and why. She hung up a flier on the bulletin board next to the lesson schedule, using two tacks to be sure: one on top, and another on bottom.

Then she climbed into her Dodge truck and headed to town.

She didn't hear from Derek for several days, something that was both a relief and a disappointment. On the one hand, the next time she saw him, she wanted to tell him about the campaign. On the other, she couldn't do that until it had results. That took time.

She missed him, though, and wanted to ride with him again. To sit at the overlook and talk with him. Reminisce about the ranch with someone who knew it and loved it. She wanted to spend an evening here in the bunkhouse, leaning against his shoulder with his arm around her, and watch old movies with him. She'd apologized for how she'd treated him, but that wasn't enough.

On top of everything else, she wanted to kiss him again. For a really long time.

As good as he'd looked in the suit when they'd first met—what man didn't look good in a suit?—something about him in jeans and cowboy boots made her knees weak. Sure, a Realtor had clout and money, but a man who did physical work, who was as emotionally strong as he was physically tough, was something else. Derek was a man secure enough in his manhood to show a more sensitive side. And that was the most attractive thing of all.

His five o'clock shadow did come in a close second.

She purposely avoided looking at the campaign, terrified it wouldn't earn anything. A few hundred dollars coming from relatively poor townsfolk would mean a lot to Derek, but it wouldn't be enough.

One afternoon, her cell had a call from an unfamiliar area code. She let it go to voicemail, figuring it was a telemarketer.

But the message that was left revealed the caller to be a reporter from a big New York paper. She wanted an interview with Teresa about the campaign. Why would anyone outside of Big Fir—outside of Montana—know or care about it?

Teresa cracked open her laptop. As the page loaded, she closed her eyes and braced herself to see a few hundred dollars. Everyone she'd talked to loved the idea, but the townspeople had struggled through recessions. Many were Boomers without the first clue about online donations.

She slowly opened her eyes. Nearly half a million dollars. Her mouth agape, Teresa scrolled to the history of donors. Initial pledges were, as expected, from locals in small increments—twenty dollars here, fifteen dollars there, with notes about Joe and Dorothy helping them in their time of need.

But the more recent donors had names she didn't recognize, and they included larger sums, sometimes hundreds of dollars, and in a few cases, a thousand or more. Several were anonymous, and others came from cities all over the States, Canada, and parts of Europe.

The campaign had been shared on Twitter and Facebook thousands of times. It had gone viral with a couple of hashtags: #HelptheJBarD and #CareForJoan.

Nervous, and thinking this was all too good to be true, Teresa called the reporter back and gave the interview. An hour later, she got another call, this one from California. She hesitated only a second. A glance at the computer screen was enough of a reminder that the more she talked, the more word would spread.

After the second interview, she set her phone down and paced the bunkhouse, shaking with mixed gratitude and utter disbelief. She grabbed her phone and somehow typed out a message to Derek.

If you're still in Montana, can you come out to the ranch? I need to give you something. A text wasn't the place to say that he would soon receive half a million dollars for his mother.

Her usual self would have worried over every word, especially after kissing him yesterday. Gratitude and excitement overrode nerves, and she sent the message. A few seconds later, the little bubble of three dots appeared, showing that Derek was replying. She held her breath as she waited.

I came by to pick up my boots. Thanks, though.

Not what she meant. But wait, he'd been at the ranch?

Right before the first interview, she saw his boots in the stable. Sock-footed, she left the bunkhouse and ran down the stairs. His boots were gone. She ran back up and looked out her kitchen window. His car was parked in front of the house. He was still at the ranch.

Instead of replying, she slipped her phone into her jeans pocket and headed down to the stables. She put on her own boots, then went in search of him. He wasn't in the stable or by the outdoor stalls. She ran to the house and hurried through the rooms. He wasn't there, either.

She went back outside. His car was still here. So where was he?

That's when it hit her: he'd gone to the lookout. She would have noticed any horses missing, which meant he'd gone by foot. She saddled Epione as fast as she'd ever saddled a horse. Without looking back, she headed up the trail to the lookout, heart pounding in her chest.

The usual forty-five-minute, leisurely walk took her just over ten on horseback. At the final incline, she urged Epione forward, and soon they were at the top.

Derek sat on the rock stair, forearms resting on his thighs as he looked over the valley. At the sound of her arrival, he turned to look at her. Teresa tied her horse to the old tree, sure that when she got closer to him, Derek would hear her heartbeat. It throbbed in her ears, and her heart seemed ready to leap from her chest.

"Hey," he said, standing. His tone was inscrutable, melancholy mixed with something else.

He came up here to be alone, she thought with dismay.

She pulled out her phone and unlocked it, then brought up a browser tab where she'd brought up the campaign. As it reloaded, she said, "I, uh, needed to show you something."

"Oh?" Again, she couldn't read his tone.

"Yeah." She reminded herself that she was bearing good news. Then she'd leave so he could have his private moment.

The pledge number was higher, by ten thousand. Unable to hold back a grin, she held out her phone. "Look." He stood below the step, and she stood on it so they were at eye level.

Curious, he took the phone. For her part, Teresa couldn't keep herself from bobbing with pent-up energy.

"I don't understand," Derek said. "Someone's trying to profit from my mom's situation?"

"Oh, no, not that," Teresa rushed to assure him. "You're Big Fir's George Bailey."

"I don't follow."

"From *It's a Wonderful Life*. George Bailey helped his town all his life, and then, when he needed help, they helped him."

"I didn't help the town."

"Your grandparents did. And those returning the favor go way beyond the Big Fir."

Derek looked at her phone again. Now his eyes were wide as he registered the dollar amount. "You mean . . ."

She nodded. "Everyone who knew your grandparents and was helped by them has given what they could to help you and your mom. They love your family. Word spread all over the state and beyond."

"Half a million dollars," Derek said in nearly a whisper.

"Almost. Turns out that the site takes a small percentage, but the total you get should still be—"

"Wait, *you* did this?"

"Yeah."

"Why?" He sounded sincerely baffled.

"You saved your grandparents' ranch even though it meant you didn't have the money for your mom."

He wiped a hand down his face. "I can't believe it."

"Your grandparents did it. And you. And your mother. People wouldn't have responded like this unless they loved you because of who you are."

Derek lowered the phone, and his jaw worked as he seemed to try to get hold of his emotions. "*You* made it happen. Thank you."

Had he stepped a little closer, or was that her imagination? The stone stair was between them, so he couldn't have moved far. Maybe she'd drawn nearer.

He ran a hand through his hair and blushed. "You know, I, uh, have wanted to return to Montana. I'm tired of the hot desert heat. I've wanted to move my mom up here, where she grew up and would probably be happier. I had to stay in Arizona to work for my mom, but with this... I can take care of my mom and not work so hard—maybe work with the charity instead. Or do a little real estate when I feel like it; I'm licensed here." He reached out and touched her arm, sending an electric thrill into her chest. "If you're not entirely opposed to the idea, after I move up, maybe we could get to know each other a bit better?"

"I'd like that," Teresa said, then grinned. "But only because you're no longer the bad guy turning the J-Bar-D into a parking lot."

"Fair," Derek said with a grin. His hand was still on her arm, and now his thumb gently moved back and forth—a delicious feeling. "I've wanted to ask you out since we first met, but..."

She cringed a bit at the memory of what she thought of him. "I was pretty awful."

"No, you were loyal. I knew that first day by the stupid sign that you were beautiful, but more than that, you had something special about you." He held up the phone. "I was right. You're basically Wonder Woman."

"Not hardly," Teresa said, taking her phone from him and feeling her cheeks grow hot.

"You know, I've always had a thing for women who save the day."

"Oh, really?" Teresa leaned toward him in what she hoped he'd know was an invitation. "That's a bit of an exaggeration, don't you think?"

"Not even a little." Derek noted the horse behind her and nodded toward it. "But maybe I can call you something else. Epione—soother of my pain."

If only Derek knew how much he'd soothed *her* pain by saving the ranch and how much joy he'd brought her in a short time. Now they'd have time to get to really know each other—and she couldn't wait.

"If you're into superhero women or Greek goddesses or whatever, does that mean you're cool with women who are a bit... forward?"

He leaned in, and now their faces were so close that she could feel his breath on her cheek. "Oh, yeah," he said. "But see, if you don't start a kiss, I'll correct the oversight and do it myself." His eyes were playful, and the look of desire in them made her stomach tumble.

"Please do," she said.

And he did.

Annette Lyon is a *USA Today* bestselling author, a four-time recipient of Utah's Best of State medal for fiction, a Whitney Award winner, and a five-time publication award winner from the League of Utah Writers. She's the author of more than a dozen novels, even more novellas, and several nonfiction books. When she's not writing, knitting, or eating chocolate, she can be found mothering and avoiding housework. Annette is a member of the Women's Fiction Writers Association and is represented by Heather Karpas at ICM Partners.

Find Annette online:
Blog: http://blog.AnnetteLyon.com
Twitter: @AnnetteLyon
Facebook: http://Facebook.com/AnnetteLyon
Instagram: https://www.instagram.com/annette.lyon/
Pinterest: http://Pinterest.com/AnnetteLyon
Newsletter: http://bit.ly/1n3I87y

THE COWBOY'S SECOND GO

CINDY ROLAND ANDERSON

ONE

BEING FAMOUS... NOT infamous had been Callie Stewart's goal when she'd left Montana and moved to Nashville seven years earlier. She'd wanted to make something of herself and prove her critics wrong. But things hadn't gone as she'd planned. Instead of achieving notoriety for her singing and songwriting, people knew her as the girl who had accused the rising country super-star Laney Loveland of stealing her song.

She hadn't actually accused Laney... just her slimy manager, Boone Redford. He was the real thief. He'd stolen Callie's new song she'd written and then passed it off as his own work. At least he hadn't stolen her heart. She'd known better than to believe in any kind of romantic love. Her ex had taught her that lesson quite thoroughly.

"Mama, are we there yet?" a little voice asked from the back seat. "I'm hungry."

She glanced in the child safety mirror and smiled at her adorable son with sleep-tousled, light brown hair. His twin brother was still sleeping soundly next to him. The only love she believed in now was for her two boys.

"Almost, pumpkin," she said, noting the mile marker on the side of the road. Only five more miles until the exit. "Do you want some apple slices?"

"Can I have licorice instead?" Max asked.

"Only one piece," she said, handing him a piece of the strawberry flavored candy. "Aunt Joy will have supper waiting for us." And hopefully something chocolaty her aunt had brought home from Joyful Delights Café, a small bakery and bistro her aunt owned. Callie's recent weight loss from all the stress of the past few weeks gave her plenty of wiggle room to not worry about her carb intake.

Another mile marker zoomed by, making Callie's stomach twist with anxiety. Even after four days of driving, she still didn't have any answers about how she was going to provide for her family. She was a single mother of four-year-old twin boys, only had a high school education and a new songwriter's notebook without anything written in it. Ever since Boone's betrayal, Callie hadn't been able to write a single line. She also hadn't been able to sing . . . or hadn't wanted to sing. It was like the music in her heart and head had been stolen from her along with her work.

Her fingers gripped the steering wheel tightly as another mile-marker flew by. She needed to find a way to prove the song was hers. Why had she been so hesitant to share it with anyone? If she would have at least mentioned the title or lyrics in a text or an email then she'd have a leg to stand on, but her fear of failure had held her back.

Sighing, she glanced in the rearview mirror and looked at her beautiful children. Maybe it was time to grow up and stop dreaming about becoming a country music star. She needed to focus on her boys.

"Are we at Aunt Joy's house?" Gage asked, waking up from his nap. "This trip is lasting so long."

"I know, sweetie." Callie looked over her shoulder and merged into the right lane. "But we're almost there." The boys had done incredibly for such a long drive. Thank goodness for modern technology. Watching movies had helped pass the time, giving Callie plenty of hours to contemplate what she was going to do if she didn't have her music.

The exit for Sunset Falls loomed ahead. It had been over

three years since she'd come for a visit. Traveling with twin boys all by herself was miserable so Aunt Joy had always come to Nashville for holidays. She was beyond excited that Callie was coming home. Although she hadn't wanted her to move away, she had always believed in Callie's talent. She'd also made sure everyone in town knew that Callie was innocent and that the song was her original work. If only her aunt's word was enough to clear her name.

"This is it, boys," she said as she eased off the gas pedal. While she wasn't thrilled about the circumstances that had brought her back home to the lakeside Montana town, she had missed a lot of things about her childhood home. Callie had only been twelve when her parents had died in a car accident, and Aunt Joy had stepped in to finish raising her. She had very little memories about her mom and dad and wondered if they would've been proud of her or if they would've been disappointed with her marginal success in the country music world.

Driving past the grade school, Callie made a mental note to register the boys for kindergarten. They were turning five soon and would start school in the fall.

Gage and Max grew excited when they saw the school's playground. "Can we play there now?" Max asked. "They have a fire truck."

"Not today." She'd made a point to stop at several parks along their route. Since they'd made a stop at a park in Missoula a few hours earlier, she didn't feel too bad telling them no. Slowing down, she made a right turn. "I'll bring you tomorrow once we unpack the car," she said, before either child launched a verbal protest.

She passed the high school football stadium, bringing back many memories of cheering for the Sunset Warriors with her best friend Lauren. She and Lauren had lost contact with each other soon after Callie moved to Tennessee. Lauren had been hurt that Callie never told her about her intention to move to Nashville. She'd always thought they would room together at college. Even so, the lack of communication hadn't been intentional. At least not on Callie's part. She'd been too caught up in trying to be discovered while keeping herself fed and sheltered.

Since Lauren was never one for social media, it had been easy to lose touch, especially when she'd gone to college. Aunt Joy had kept Callie somewhat informed on Lauren's life until Lauren's parents had relocated to Florida. The last thing Callie knew was that her friend had finished her accounting degree and then married a military man. She had no idea where Lauren was now or if she was still married or had any children.

Callie's brief and tumultuous marriage had been a bad decision, yet had given her the greatest gift. She knew people counted the relationship as an epic failure on her part, but how could she ever regret marrying her two-timing ex-husband when she'd been gifted with her boys? Motherhood was something Callie excelled at. No, she wasn't perfect and often had no clue what she was doing, but she loved being a mother.

Skirting the outside of the lake, she spied the red tin roof of Aunt Joy's cabin. The home was huge in comparison to Callie's two-bedroom apartment in Nashville, but relatively small when compared to the home adjacent to it. Aunt Joy had sold off two acres a few years earlier, using the money to pay off her mortgage. She'd told Callie over and over that she didn't need to find a job right away and could focus on being a mother. Callie appreciated the offer but she didn't want to be a loafer. She knew Aunt Joy was ready to retire and sell the café. More than likely, she didn't really have a need for another employee, but Callie would work whatever hours she could until she found something else.

"Look at that big camper," Max shouted.

"Can we get a camper like that?" Gage asked.

"I don't think so." Callie caught sight of the trailer and frowned. She wasn't a big fan of camping. Not even in something as fancy as the shiny motorhome. "But I'll bet Aunt Joy has a tent we can set up in her backyard."

That appeased her boys, but seeing the large camper brought back a memory Callie hadn't thought about for a while. Lauren had an older brother that every girl in Sunset Falls had been in love with, including Callie. Ty Carter had been both smart and athletic, not to mention drop-dead gorgeous. Since he was three years older, he'd always treated Callie like a little sister. But the end of his senior year something had changed. Ty had acted differently around her, teasing her in a flirty way that made Callie think he might like her too. She hadn't dared say anything to Lauren. Knowing her friend, she would have flat out asked her brother if he was into her best friend.

The perfect opportunity to see if Ty really did like her had come the week after he'd graduated from high school and subsequently broken up with his longtime girlfriend. Lauren's family had invited Callie to come on their annual camping trip with them. Ty had also invited a friend, but his friend had to work and wouldn't make it to their campsite until the next day.

She would never forget how nervous and excited she was when Ty had asked her to take a walk with him down by the lake that first night. Lauren had eaten something that made her stomach upset so she'd gone to bed early. Mr. and Mrs. Carter had also gone inside the trailer to watch a movie, leaving Callie and Ty roasting marshmallows by the campfire.

Callie still remembered how it felt when Ty took her hand to help her jump over a stream. Once they were on the other side, he didn't let go and instead threaded their fingers together like they were a real couple. At fifteen, Callie had never held a boy's hand before. She'd never been kissed before either. She wasn't sure why she'd felt the need to give Ty that information. But what he did afterward made her glad that she had.

A shiver ran down her spine when she thought about what had happened next. With the full moon shimmering across the lake, Ty had pulled her to a stop and told her that he wanted to be the first one to kiss her. Time seemed to stop as he gently cupped her face with his hands and lowered his mouth to hers. Inexperienced, she hadn't known what to do and stood there without moving. Her mind had finally engaged, and she'd kissed him back. Passionately. She had no idea how long the make-out session had lasted, but when it ended Callie was head-over-heels in love with him, and she knew he was the man she would marry someday. Of course, she had to ruin everything by blurting that out as well.

The second the words left her mouth, she knew she'd made a big mistake. Eyes wide, he'd let go of her and stumbled back a few steps. "Whoa, kid, that was just a few kisses," he'd said with a laugh. "It doesn't mean anything."

Those words had knifed through her young heart, piercing her until she felt like she'd bleed out from the pain. Embarrassed, she'd run all the way back to camp. Tears had blurred her vision, and she'd fallen a few times, skinning her knee when she jumped over the stream and crashed into a jagged rock. Thankfully, Lauren was still sound asleep when she'd climbed into her sleeping bag and silently cried herself to sleep.

That wasn't the worst part. The next day, she'd overheard Ty telling his best friend all about the kiss and her confession of love afterward. Callie had been so humiliated, especially when Ty looked up and saw her standing there. She'd texted Aunt Joy to come and get her. Although her aunt tried to find out what had happened to make her so upset, the only thing she'd said was that Ty Carter and his friend were jerks, and she didn't want to talk about it. She had never told Lauren what had happened, but her friend knew Ty had done something to hurt Callie.

Even after ten years, Callie still felt embarrassed about the whole thing. Now that she was an adult, she could see how her declaration of love must have come off to a teenage guy. And, to be fair, he had tried apologizing several times to her over that summer, but she never allowed him the opportunity. She deleted any email messages and blocked his number so he couldn't text her. He'd even sent her a hand-written letter in the mail, which she'd thrown away. Callie had been relieved when he'd gone to college, and she hadn't seen him since. Then she'd moved to Nashville the day after graduation and fell for another man that broke her heart.

No wonder she'd promised herself to never fall in love again.

Her focus was on being a mother and now finding a new career. She just had no idea what she would do outside of her music. Was she too old to go back to college?

Some of her worries dissipated as she made the turn toward her aunt's house. The boys were going to love Aunt Joy's yard. Having only ever lived in an apartment complex, Max and Gage didn't have the luxury of playing in a fenced-in back yard. The daycare they'd attended the last few years had a playground, but the boys couldn't play whenever they wanted. At least here they would have the same kind of freedom she'd enjoyed as a child.

Before reaching her aunt's driveway, Callie slowed down to admire the beautiful log home next door. Her aunt hadn't talked too much about her new neighbor, only saying that she frequently took meals over since he was a bachelor. Callie had shut her aunt down before she got a chance to try and set her up with the new homeowner. The last thing she wanted to worry about was dating.

Her aunt's cabin looked the same, only with a fresh coat of stain to the large front porch. Wildflowers blossomed along the front of the house, making Callie wonder if her aunt had planted the flowers all by herself or hired a gardener. She'd always helped with the gardening. It was something she'd missed while living in her small apartment for the past few years.

Aunt Joy appeared on the porch steps as she pulled into the driveway. Gage and Max were out of their car seats and out the back door before Callie had unclicked her seatbelt. Her legs felt stiff as she climbed out of the vehicle. Pride swelled inside her as she watched her two boys hug her aunt.

"Let me see if I can guess who's who," Aunt Joy said, crouching down in front of the twins. They were identical in looks and had similar personalities. Callie could tell them apart, but that was only because she was their mother. Early on, she'd had to dress them in different colored clothing to help her differentiate them. She'd kept it up for their daycare providers.

Aunt Joy placed a hand on top of Max's head. "You must be Gage."

"Nope," Max said with a giggle. "That's Gage." He pointed to his brother. "Remember, he always wears blue shirts, and I wear red?"

"Hmm," Aunt Joy said, "I guess I remembered wrong."

Her aunt's memory wasn't faulty. Callie just needed to provide her with an updated color code chart. The boys didn't like wearing the same colors all the time. Callie rotated their clothing and kept track of it on her phone. This week was Gage's turn to wear blue, green and black.

"Can we go play in the backyard?" Gage asked. Callie had been talking up all the benefits of moving to Sunset Falls, and the boys were eager to see if what she'd said was true.

"You sure can." Aunt Joy stood up and pointed to the gate at the side yard. "Head on back through the gate, and your mom and I will be there shortly."

Max and Gage took off in a dead run. "Be careful," Callie said, hoping they didn't crash into each other to open the gate first.

"They look like they've both grown an inch since I saw them at Christmas," Aunt Joy said. Then she held out her arms to Callie. "And you, my dear, look exhausted."

Callie reached out and gave her aunt a warm hug. "Is that a nice way of telling me that I need to freshen up?"

"Yep." Aunt Joy squeezed her before pulling back. "You still look beautiful, just tired."

"It was a long road trip."

Joy tipped her head to the side and studied Callie's face with the eyes of a mother. "It's more than just the road trip, honey. The past couple of months have taken a toll on you, haven't they?"

Swallowing back the tight feeling in her throat, Callie bit her bottom lip and nodded her head. Her life had been in chaos ever since Boone Redford had come into it.

She'd known of his connection with Laney Loveland in the music industry and had been flattered when he'd shown up three nights in a row to hear her sing during open mic at the café.

Although Boone had tried coming onto her initially, he'd been smart enough to back off and shift into business-manger mode. Callie hadn't signed a contract with him. She wasn't sure he was the right person to represent her work. Besides, he seemed solely focused on Laney and finding her new music to record.

Callie had written a few originals that were okay but nothing show-stopping. She mostly sang covers, but Boone said she had raw talent. Boosted by his encouragement, she'd focused on her writing. "Catching Sunlight" was the result of her hard work. Callie knew the song was good but hesitated going public with it. She'd been rejected so many times and felt like this song would either make or break her music career.

Against her better judgment, she sang the song for Boone when he'd stopped by her apartment one evening. He'd been quiet and calculating during the number. As she strummed the last note on her guitar, he'd studied her for a long moment and then predicted the song would be a big hit. His compliment was quickly followed with criticism about her vocals, telling her she could make more money as a songwriter than a singer.

"Laney is hot right now, and her voice is perfect for this song." Boone had leaned in close and gave her a white-toothed smile that made her even more suspicious of his motives. "Think about it, Callie. You could make a name for yourself. I know a hit when I hear it. If you were to write a few more songs for Laney's next album, then you could be one of the first songwriter's to nab a Grammy."

Callie wasn't interested in selling her songs for someone else to record. At least not until she knew that having a solo career was out of the question. She'd decided to keep the song to herself until she had enough money saved to record a demo she could then submit to a few reputable agents.

Boone was not on her list, but that didn't stop him from trying. Over the next few weeks, he relentlessly pressured her to sell the rights to the song, often stopping by unannounced with food or gifts for the boys to soften her up. It was becoming a little on the weird side, and her boys were getting used to Boone bringing them gifts. She finally got the courage to tell him that she would never sell him the rights to her music and asked him to stop contacting her.

Imagine the shock she felt when a couple of weeks later she heard Laney Loveland singing her song, "Catching Sunlight." Boone was right. It was an instant hit, topping the country music charts in downloads. It even crossed genres, becoming the number one downloaded song in pop music for over two weeks.

Sick to her stomach, Callie had confronted Boone. He'd smugly denied the accusations and told her to leave his office before he called the police. That's when she'd learned that he'd already leaked a story about her accusing Laney Loveland of stealing her work. Determined to prove her innocence, she'd gone home to find her notebook to show the world who the liar was. Only she couldn't find her notebook. Without it, she had absolutely no proof the song was hers.

In a matter of hours, Callie's life was ripped apart. The café she'd worked for fired her shortly after everything hit the fan. She was sure Boone had somehow pressured the owner into it. Mr. Crosby had had tears in his eyes when he'd given her the news. He'd also asked her not to sing at his establishment anymore. In fact, every place Callie ever sang at had banned her because of the scandal.

The only proof of her innocence was the notebook. She still didn't know how Boone had stolen the book, but she knew he was behind it.

"Let's get you settled in while the boys play outside," Aunt Joy said.

Callie nodded her head but wanted to make sure the boys knew not to venture beyond the yard. They knew how to swim, but a lake was very different from the small community pool within the apartment complex. "I better check on the twins first and tell them they need to stay in the back."

"Sure, but just so you know I have a new security system with motion sensors, cameras, and an advanced locking system on the gate. I had it installed when I knew you and the boys were coming."

"Thank you, Aunt Joy," Callie said, leaning in to give her another hug. "I don't know what I'd do without you."

Before unloading her car, they went through the gate to check on the twins. They found the boys laughing and playing on a brand-new swing set with a two-story fort and slide connected to it. "Aunt Joy, you didn't need to buy this. The old tire swing and sandbox would've kept them happy for hours."

"I know, but there was only one tire swing and two boys." She wrinkled her nose. "Besides, the sandbox had become a stray cat's litterbox. If the kids want to play in the sand, then we'll take them to the lake."

"Can we go to the lake right now?" Gage asked.

Callie shook her head, fatigue hitting her like a bad cold. Every muscle was weary, and she felt light-headed. It was like her body had decided to check out now that Aunt Joy was here to take over for her. "Not tonight, sweetheart." She yawned. "Mommy is so tired."

They weren't happy with the answer, but Aunt Joy distracted them with the promise of helping her frost a batch of cupcakes after supper.

It took several trips to unload the car. Deciding to unpack only the essentials for tonight, Callie took a quick shower. She braided her dark hair in a single braid that hung over her shoulder and skipped reapplying any makeup. Then she went out back to call the boys to come inside. They were each in a swing, having a contest about who could go the highest.

"Hey guys," she said, leaning against the door. "It's time to come in for supper."

Gage dragged his feet along the grass to slow him down, but Max continued swinging higher and higher. Knowing her son could hold out for a few more minutes, she crossed the backyard, passing by Gage as he rushed inside the house to use the bathroom. "Max, please get off the swing."

"But I'm going so high."

"Yes, I see that." Her head was dizzy just watching him. She was hoping the boys would go to sleep early. Curling up in bed with a good book sounded so good to her. "But it's time to come in now."

"Just a sec," he said, keeping up the momentum.

Callie was too tired to reason with him. She resorted to bribery, telling him they wouldn't go to the lake the next day if he didn't immediately get out of the swing.

She'd expected Max to drag his feet the same way his brother had. What she hadn't expected was for him to jump out of the swing. In slow motion, she watched Max fly through the air and crash to the ground head first. At the last second, he put his hands out to brace the fall.

"Max!" she screamed as she rushed to her son's side. His face pale, he wailed loudly and gripped his left arm. Callie took one look at the arm and guessed it was broken. Panicked, she tried to calm Max down, but her voice sounded borderline hysterical. "It's okay, honey. Everything is going to be okay . . . Mommy's here."

Her words did nothing to calm her or Max down. She needed help. Since her cell phone was inside charging, she turned toward the house to yell for Aunt Joy and was startled to see a man wearing a brown cowboy hat vault the fence and jog across the yard.

"I saw the whole thing from my deck," he said, kneeling

next to her. "Hey there, Superman," he said to Max in a gentle voice. "Do you mind if I take a look at your arm?"

Max continued to scream and shook his head, guarding his arm from the stranger.

"Please don't touch him," Callie said, covering her mouth with her hand to prevent the sob choking her. She couldn't stand to see her little boy hurting and didn't know how to help him. "He needs a doctor."

The cowboy looked at her from beneath the brim of his hat, piercing her with sea-blue eyes. He looked vaguely familiar to her, but with the trimmed beard she couldn't place his face. "Well," he said with a smile, "I happen to be a doctor."

"You're really a doctor?" Callie asked, tempted to throw her arms around the man's neck. It was a relief to have someone who knew what they were doing take over in case she passed out. She turned to comfort Max. "This nice man is a doctor, sweetie. He's going to help you and make you feel better."

Max stopped crying as the cowboy moved in closer. Callie watched her son's face go a shade whiter. She recognized the signs and didn't have time to issue a warning before Max vomited all over the front of the doctor's shirt.

That's when Callie's brain clicked, and she knew why the guy looked so familiar. Her son had just thrown up on Ty Carter.

TWO

Ty tried not to react to the pungent smell emanating from the front of his clean shirt as he looked once more at the beautiful woman. Callie Jackson had grown up and was even prettier than he remembered. "Hey, Callie." Her hazel colored eyes narrowed, and she pressed her lips into a flat line. Apparently, she was still mad at him. Not that he blamed her. He'd been a total jerk. "I guess I probably deserved that, huh?"

She glanced at his shirt, and the tiniest smile flickered at the corners of her mouth. "Maybe a little."

That made him smile and released some of the guilt he'd carried around for how he'd treated her so long ago. It was one of his main regrets, and he hoped he'd finally get a chance to apologize.

"I threw up," her little boy said with a whimper.

Callie's eyes softened as she stroked her son's head. "It's okay, baby. Mr. Carter ... I mean, Dr. Carter isn't angry, and he knows how to help you."

Ty opened the emergency backpack he'd brought with him to look for a package of wet wipes. He should clarify what kind of doctor he was but decided it could wait until after he stabilized the kid's arm. "I'll do my best," he said, handing her the package of wipes. Their fingers inadvertently made contact during the transfer, sending a zap of electricity straight up his arm. *What the heck was that?* There was no way that was attraction. At least he hoped it wasn't. He looked up and saw a slight frown marring Callie's forehead.

"Thank you," she said, briefly meeting his gaze. "I'm sorry about your shirt. I'm sure as a pediatrician that happens a lot."

She didn't seem rattled by the physical contact. Of course, her focus was on her son. "I'm not a pediatrician."

"You're not?" Callie asked, looking mildly alarmed.

"But I do have experience with kids," he said, not wanting to upset her or the little boy further. He caught another whiff of his shirt and was glad he had a strong stomach. His job required it since he often encountered less than appealing smells.

While Callie wiped her son's mouth, Ty dug through his emergency kit to find a sling. As part of the county's search and rescue, he usually kept the bag in his truck. He'd brought the backpack inside to replace items he'd used on a rescue earlier in the day so it had been easy to grab.

"What's that for?" Callie asked when Ty unfolded the triangular cloth.

"I'm making a sling to help stabilize his arm."

The child's eyes went wide. "I don't want him to staple my arm."

"He's not going to staple your arm, sweetie," Callie said. "He'll put a cloth bandage on to make your arm feel better."

"That's right, buddy," Ty said. "This will help keep your arm steady until you get a cast."

Mentioning a cast was the right thing to say because the crying immediately stopped. "I get a cast?" the kid asked with obvious interest. "Can I pick out the color?"

"I'm sure you can," Ty said with a smile. "What's your name?" he asked as he carefully wrapped the cloth around the boy's arm and secured the ends around his neck.

"Max Michael Stewart," the little boy answered. "I'm almost five."

"Nice to meet you, Max." Hearing Callie's married name made him curious about her marriage and divorce. Something he knew about because Joy repeatedly told him that her niece was divorced, and Ty repeatedly told Joy that Callie's marital status didn't matter because he wasn't interested in dating. Not after his ugly divorce a few years earlier.

Once the sling was secure, Ty pulled his cell phone from his pocket. "I'll call the urgent care and let them know we're on our way."

"I can call." Callie patted her back pocket and sighed heavily. "I forgot my phone's inside. If you don't mind calling that would be great. Thank you."

With a nod, Ty turned away from her and tapped on the screen to bring up his contacts. "Hey, this is Ty Carter," he said when Linda Barnes answered the phone. Before she started in on him about taking out her granddaughter again, he told her the reason for the call and gave her an ETA of twenty minutes.

Joy opened the back door just as he ended the call. "Oh my, what happened?" she asked, hurrying across the yard. While Callie gave her a brief synopsis, Ty noticed a child trailing behind her. He was an exact replica of Max.

Wow, Callie had two kids. Aside from the public scandal involving Callie and Laney Loveland, he wondered what else had happened to her in the last decade. Joy made sure everyone within the county knew her niece was telling the truth and that it had been Laney's manager who had stolen Callie's song.

"Guess what, Gage?" Max said. "I get a cast."

"Cool! Can I get a cast too?" Gage asked his mother.

"Not today," Callie said. "Hopefully not anytime soon," she mumbled under her breath.

Gage took the news well, asking if he could ride in the ambulance.

"There isn't going to be an ambulance," Callie said. "Mommy is going to drive him."

"Let me take you," Ty said without thinking it through. He almost recanted his offer but stopped when he saw the relief in Callie's eyes.

Still, she was hesitant to accept his offer. "You really don't have to drive us."

"Let him help you," Joy said. "That way you can sit in the back with Max."

"Okay." She fingered the end of the long braid hanging down her shoulder and met his eyes. "Thank you."

"Can I come too?" Gage asked.

"Not this time," Callie said.

Ty waited for the kid's protest, but Joy provided the perfect distraction. "If you go then who will help me ice the cupcakes?" Joy asked. Without giving it a second thought, the little boy took off for the house. "Ty," Joy said, "thank you for helping Callie and Max. It sounds like you've had a busy day."

"No problem." He zipped the bag closed. "Glad I was home."

"Callie, let me know what the doctor says," Joy said before heading back inside her house.

"I will." Callie rubbed her lips together and looked at Ty. "I'm fine driving him to the clinic if you don't have time."

"I've got time." His partner was taking calls for emergencies, so Ty knew his evening was free. "Think you can walk?" he asked the little boy. He would offer to carry him but didn't want to jostle his injured arm. Plus, his soiled shirt was starting to smell.

"Yeah," Max answered.

Ty got to his feet. "I just need to change my clothes, and then I'll drive the truck over to pick you all up."

"Sorry about the shirt," Callie said again. "I'll be happy to wash it for you."

"Not necessary." He slipped the strap of his backpack over his shoulder. "I'm used to laundering far worse than this."

Jogging back to the fence, he vaulted it easily. Once he was on the other side, he unbuttoned his shirt and slipped it off as he mounted the porch steps to his back door. Pinching the shirt with his fingers, he dropped it in the washing machine. He peeled off the white tee and added it with his other shirt. At least the kid was little, so there wasn't too much volume. He wasn't lying when he'd said that he had encountered worse. As a rural vet, he got hit with all kinds of things that usually came out of the backside of an animal.

He turned the washer to soak and then hurried into the bathroom for a quick spit bath with soap and water. After fishing out a clean shirt from the dryer, he made sure he had his wallet before he grabbed the keys from the hook by the door to the garage.

Callie and her little boy came outside as he pulled into the circular driveway. Putting the truck in gear, Ty set the emergency brake and hopped out of the vehicle. "Ready?"

"Yes, but I need to get his booster seat out of my car." She unlocked a silver Subaru with Tennessee plates on it.

Ty stood behind her, trying not to notice the way her jeans hugged her curves. "I've got it," he said when Callie turned around.

"Oh, thanks." She hesitated a moment before transferring the seat to him in a handoff so quick he almost dropped it.

Ty installed the seat, wondering if the quick exchange meant she didn't want to touch him again. He stepped back, and she helped her son into the vehicle. Her eyes flickered to

Ty's and held before she thanked him and slid in the truck next to her son.

"Clinic isn't far," he said once he was behind the wheel. The drive didn't take long, and he didn't try making polite conversation. Instead, he listened to Callie softly soothing her son. The tender words let him know she was a good mom. She continued to comfort her son as she helped him down and led him to the front entrance.

Closing the door, Ty hurried to catch up to them. He should have set the record straight about his vocation. Aside from his position on the county search and rescue, the only kids he'd ever treated had been during his training at a goat farm.

The clinic wasn't busy. Only one other person sat in the waiting area. Linda glanced up and grinned when she saw Ty. "You've had a busy day, haven't you?" She removed her reading glasses and let them hang down around her neck. "I heard Jess say you delivered two foals early this morning before going out with the sheriff's department."

"Yes, ma'am." Ty leaned against the counter and nodded toward Callie. "This is Joy Franklin's niece, Callie Jackson . . . uh, Stewart?" He glanced at Callie, and she nodded her head. "And this is her son, Max," Ty said, looking back to the receptionist.

"Max Michael Stewart," the little boy said. "I'm almost five."

"Well, hello there, Max Michael Stewart." Linda peered down at the child with a soft smile. "I can tell you're almost five," she said with a wink. "That must be why you're so brave."

"I get a cast," Max said. Then he scrunched up his little nose and looked at his mother. "Will it hurt, Mama?" he asked in a trembling voice.

Before she could answer, Jess Tanner opened the door. The doctor was a good friend of Ty's and a little on the silly side, which kids loved about him. Today Jess wore a yellow Minion shirt underneath his white doctor's lab coat. "Hi there," he said, crouching down in front of Max. "You must be the young man who tried flying."

"No," Max said as his eyes filled with tears. "I jumped out of the swing and breaked my arm."

"Hmm," Jess said, rubbing his clean-shaven jaw. "I think we need to take a picture of your arm with my special X-ray machine."

"Does it hurt?" Max asked, pressing against his mother's leg.

"I'll do my very best not to hurt you," Jess answered. Then he leaned in close. "How about we have your mom come with us?"

Max nodded his head. "Can Dr. Carter come too? He told Mama he's an expert with kids."

"Sure." Jess got to his feet and gave Ty a curious look. "I can always use an expert with kids."

"He means I have experience with kids," Ty said, feeling his neck flush. Most of his close friends knew he wasn't an expert with kids. Otherwise, his ex-wife would have allowed Ty to stay involved in his stepdaughter's life. Kayla made it perfectly clear that Ty wasn't father material when she cut him off and allowed her new husband to adopt Evie.

"Good to know." Jess grinned and looked between Ty and Callie. "So how do you two know each other?"

There were several beats of silence before Callie answered the question. "We knew each other in high school."

Ty saw the speculative look in Jess's eyes so he quickly added on, "Callie and my little sister Lauren were best friends."

"That's great," Jess said with a broad grin. Before he could say anything else, the radiology tech stepped out into the hall and called out Max's name.

Ty trailed behind the group, wishing he could duck out and wait for Callie and her son in the lobby. If Max hadn't specifically requested he be in there with him, he would do just that. He wasn't sure why he'd insisted on driving Callie here. He liked helping people, but he didn't want to give her or anyone else the wrong impression.

After his marriage had ended two years earlier, he'd decided to dedicate his life to his vet practice and being an uncle to his sister's children whenever they visited from Italy. Lauren was married to an Air Force fighter pilot and had three boys. They were currently stationed in Italy but whenever they were stateside, Ty made sure to spend plenty of time with the boys, teaching them to ride horses and taking them fishing.

He would email Lauren about Callie moving back to Sunset Falls as soon as he got home. He knew his sister had lost touch with Callie when she'd moved to Nashville right after high school graduation. A few years back, he'd finally confessed what he'd done to hurt Callie. His sister hadn't been happy with him. She'd said that Callie had changed after that camping trip. Ty already felt bad enough about what he'd done. He'd even considered trying to apologize to Callie again but didn't want to bother her. Now she was here, giving him the chance to make things right. He just hadn't counted on feeling attracted to her after all this time.

Shoving his hands in his pockets, he watched her from under the brim of his hat as memories of her flooded his mind. He couldn't pinpoint the exact time or event of when he'd first been aware of her. She was always at their house, and he'd viewed her like his kid sister. It had taken him by surprise when the first spark of attraction had hit him. All of a sudden, she didn't look like a little girl. Curves he hadn't noticed before made her appear much older than fifteen. Her music added depth and confidence to her personality that his sister and other girls in high school lacked.

He hadn't planned on kissing her that night by the lake. He certainly hadn't planned on his reaction either. The truth was, Callie had shaken him that night. He'd kissed plenty of girls but nothing compared to what he'd felt when he'd kissed Callie Jackson. It had scared him, especially when she professed her love and that she wanted to marry him. She was only fifteen. Technically, he was an adult since he had turned eighteen a week earlier, so that made her even more off-limits.

As if she knew he was thinking about her, Callie turned and caught him staring at her. Ty swallowed hard when her lips curved up into a smile. The impact felt like a stallion had just kicked him in the chest. He needed to put a stop to these feelings before they got him in trouble again.

His phone buzzed in his pocket and, he gratefully took it out and stepped out to take a call from his partner. Olivia McBride rarely called on Ty when it was his day off. He hoped nothing serious had happened.

"Hey," he said. "Is everything okay?"

"Yes and no." Olivia let out an exasperated sigh. "Madge Smith brought her dog in for a tummy ache—her words, not mine," Olivia said with a snicker. "She's insisting it's more serious and wants you to stop by and check Chester for an appendicitis."

"I'm assuming you explained to her that is anatomically impossible?" Ty asked.

"What do you think?" Olivia said dryly. Then she whispered into the phone. "There is nothing wrong with Chester. I wish I could say the same for his owner."

Olivia's comment pulled a laugh out of him. She always

made him laugh, which was one of the things he liked about having her as a business partner. He'd heard a few of the gossips question his judgment by bringing her on as a partner. With her blonde hair and blue eyes, Olivia was beautiful and looked like a young Reese Witherspoon, but Ty viewed her only as a friend and colleague. Besides, she was happily married and just announced she and her husband were expecting their first baby.

"Tell Madge that I'll stop by her place later this evening."

"Ty, you shouldn't cater to her," Olivia said. "It will only encourage her to keep doing this."

"I know, but she's a friend of my grandma's. Besides, if I make a home visit she won't be back in tomorrow."

"Good point." Olivia thanked him and quickly ended the call.

Ty smiled and slipped his phone back into his pocket as he turned and saw Callie and Max walking down the hall. Jess was right behind them.

"Come back in a couple of days for a follow-up X-ray," Jess said. "If the swelling is down then we can switch the splint for a cast." He crouched down in front of Max. "No more jumping out of any swings, okay?"

"Yes, sir," Max said with a sniffle. He was a tough little kid.

Callie thanked Jess as she shook his hand. Ty picked up on a slight southern drawl, making the husky tone of her voice even more appealing.

"Ty," Jess said with a nod of his chin. "Beth just texted and said she's worried about Holly. Says the mare's limping, but she couldn't find the cause. If you get a chance, maybe you could swing by the house sometime this weekend?"

"Sure, I can come over later this evening. I've got to stop by Madge's and check on Chester anyway."

"Thanks, buddy," Jess said before stepping into another exam room.

"You're a veterinarian, aren't you?" Callie asked Ty as they walked to his truck.

"Yeah," Ty said with a grin.

"What's a vegetarian?" Max asked.

"A veterinarian," Callie corrected her son. "It means that Dr. Carter takes care of animals, not people."

"I take care of people too," Ty said, opening the back door of his truck. "I'm also an advanced EMT and volunteer for the county search and rescue." He helped Max climb into the backseat.

"Like Paw Patrol?" Max asked.

Ty looked to Callie for clarification. He had no idea what the kid was talking about. His stepdaughter had been into all things princess. "Paw Patrol is a show about rescue pups." She gave him a small smile. "It's Max and Gage's favorite show."

"Cool," Ty said, stepping back so Callie could sit beside her son. "Hey," he said before she took a seat, "I didn't mean to deceive you. I just wanted to help keep everyone calm."

She met his eyes and considered him for a long moment. "Thank you," she said, her husky voice almost a whisper. "And thank you for driving us."

"You're welcome." He stood close enough to see the flecks of green and gold in her brown eyes. Awareness zipped through him when his gaze dropped to her full lips. It happened so fast that he sucked in a quick breath and stepped back. "That's what neighbors are for."

Confusion etched a line between her eyebrows before she turned and slid onto the seat next to her son.

Ty closed the door and quickly went around to the driver's side. He should've stayed away from his little sister's friend when she was a teenager, and he needed to stay away now. Callie was a grown woman with two children. As much as Ty loved kids and wanted to have a family someday, he couldn't let himself get involved with her.

He'd already done that and it hadn't ended well. Kayla's daughter might not have been his, but he'd loved the little girl like his own. It had killed him when Kayla remarried shortly after their divorce and then refused to let him see Evie any more. He went from seeing the child every other weekend to absolutely no contact when Kayla's new husband, Jeff, said he wanted to adopt Evie.

Frustrated and angry, Ty fought it, even going as far as hiring an attorney to sue for joint custody. He knew he didn't have a case and, in the end, the judge sided with Kayla since Ty wasn't Evie's biological father.

Jerking open the door, he got in behind the wheel and headed for home. He ignored the occasional whiff of Callie's perfume floating on the air and tried not to look in his rearview mirror. Because every time his eyes connected with hers something deep inside him stirred, simmering like a lone ember from a fire waiting for the right accelerator to coax it back to life.

For two years he hadn't met a single woman that sparked any kind of attraction. There were plenty of sparks where Callie was concerned. He needed to make sure those sparks didn't ignite a fire.

Joy met them outside when he took Callie and Max home, thanking him again and reminding him about dinner after church services on Sunday. Ever since he'd moved in, Joy had issued a standing invitation for Sunday dinner at her house. Although Ty usually ate dinner with her, he had already decided to find an excuse not to show up.

THREE

CALLIE STOOD IN front of the mirror and added a touch of mascara to her naturally dark lashes. Tugging on the end of the pale pink tee, she wondered if she should find something else to wear that didn't fit quite so snug. Losing weight hadn't lessened her bra size, and the shirt hugged her curves perfectly. With her hair pulled back into a ponytail, she almost looked like she had back in high school. Almost. She now sported a few worry lines that had appeared over the past few weeks.

Turning off the bathroom light, she slipped on her walking shoes and grabbed her purse. She didn't want to be late for her first day on the job. Aunt Joy had arranged for Callie to help cover the lunch hour. She knew it was more for charity since her aunt and the current staff handled the afternoon shift just fine. But she couldn't turn the offer down. The hours were short and would give her time to find another job. Plus, there was a daycare across the street, so she didn't need to worry about finding someone to watch the twins.

"Boys," she called out. "Are y'all dressed?" Before starting her lunch shift, she needed to take Max back to see Dr. Tanner for a follow-up and to get a cast. The broken arm hadn't slowed her son down very much. She couldn't wait until he had a permanent cast on, so she didn't worry about him causing further damage.

"They're down here, hon," Joy hollered from the kitchen. "And both of them are dressed and have their shoes on."

"Thank you," Callie said when she came into the kitchen. "By the way, have you seen my cell phone?"

Joy pointed to the twins who huddled close together in a little alcove taking selfies with her phone. A few months earlier, Gage and Max had discovered the camera on her cell and the silly filters available. Since they didn't need the passcode to access the camera, they often confiscated her phone when she was getting ready. She didn't mind because it kept them out of trouble.

The only downside was when they grew bored with the activity and set her phone down without remembering where they put it. Callie had finally purchased a watch that had an app to locate her phone, but now that was lost too. It was probably buried inside her oversized backpack that doubled as a purse.

"You look very pretty," Aunt Joy said, untying the apron from around her waist. "I'll bet business surges once the single men learn you'll be working in the café again."

"Thanks," Callie said. "But I think it's the food that brings in the customers." She turned toward the boys, wondering if Ty was one of those single men who frequented the café. Part of her hoped to see him again while her other half wanted to avoid him. Much like she suspected he was avoiding her. She hadn't seen him since he'd dropped her and Max off a couple of days earlier. The man hadn't even come over for Sunday dinner, messaging Aunt Joy that he'd been called out for an emergency at a horse ranch on the outskirts of town.

It shouldn't matter to her that he'd canceled dinner. It shouldn't matter to her that he hadn't followed up on Max. It shouldn't matter . . . but it did. Much to her dismay, it had only taken a few minutes of being around Ty Carter to resurrect her teenage crush on him. She wasn't even angry with him anymore.

The one good thing to come from their brief encounter was her renewed friendship with Lauren. Ty had at least been thinking about her long enough to tell his little sister that she'd moved back to Sunset Falls. Lauren had emailed Aunt Joy to get Callie's contact info, and they'd chatted through text messages and set a time when they could make a video call. Lauren planned on calling her the following weekend once she had her children in bed. With the time difference between Montana and Italy, it was difficult to find a time when they were both available. Sunday was the perfect day.

She heard her phone chime an incoming text. Gage looked at her and held up the phone. "Someone wants you, Mama," he said.

"Thank you, baby." She crossed the floor, hoping the someone wasn't another reporter. Her attorney had advised her not to talk to anyone about the accusations. Until she could prove Boone stole her work, he suggested she lay low. Besides, defending herself made Boone dig in his heels deeper.

Glancing at the screen, she let out a big breath of relief. The text was a reminder of Max's appointment with Dr. Tanner. The family practice doctor was in his regular office today. He and a few other physicians took turns at the urgent care on the weekends. Luckily, he was accepting new patients and accepted her insurance. While her ex-husband wanted nothing to do with the boys, he at least paid a minimum amount of child support and kept them on his insurance policy. She'd opened a savings account for both boys and tried not to use the child support money unless it was an emergency. The loss of income and the move had left her with no choice but to dip into it.

Replying to the text with a yes, she herded the twins out

to her car, telling her aunt she'd see her at the café after Max's doctor appointment.

"Look, Mama," Max said, darting in front of Callie. "There's the vegetarian."

Before she could process what he meant, Max ditched getting in the car and made a beeline for the neighbor's driveway. Turning to call him back, Callie watched Gage sprint across the yard to join his brother.

"It's veterinarian," Callie muttered under her breath. Squinting against the afternoon sun, she watched Ty greet her boys with a wide grin as he crouched down to talk to them. He wore a light-colored straw cowboy hat, jeans, and a fitted tee that emphasized well-developed biceps and a firm chest. A man shouldn't look that good in such simple clothing. She tugged on the pink shirt again, wishing she'd donned one of Aunt Joy's aprons.

She heard her aunt come out the front door. "That is one handsome cowboy," Joy said, coming to stand beside Callie. "Why aren't you over there too?"

"I don't want to bother him."

"He doesn't look bothered at all." Her aunt nudged her in the arm. "You're the one who looks bothered."

Maybe that's because she was. How could her long ago crush still be so powerful, even after all these years? Ty laughed at something one of the boys said and tousled Gage's hair as he straightened up. Then he looked directly at Callie and unleashed his grin on her.

"Hey there," he said, pushing the brim of his hat back a little.

"Hey," she said, lifting her hand to wave at him. She leaned toward her aunt. "I don't suppose you'll go get the boys, will you?" she asked from the corner of her mouth.

"Nope," Joy said with a small laugh. "I need to get to the café."

"Sure you do," Callie said, knowing perfectly well her aunt ran the business part of the café these days. Rolling her shoulders back, she drew in a fortifying breath and made her way across the yard. Ty tracked her progress, never once taking his eyes off of her. Just as she made it to the driveway, her boys took off after a butterfly. "I'm sorry if they were bothering you." She glanced at Max and Gage running around in circles. "Obviously, a broken arm hasn't slowed Max or his stunt double down at all."

"Stunt double is pretty accurate," Ty said. "How can you tell them apart?"

"I'm their mother." Her lips lifted into a sheepish smile. "But I admit that the first year of their life I painted one of Gage's toenails blue and Max's red to keep them straight."

Ty laughed. "I guess you couldn't keep that up for too long."

"No, but now I have a schedule for what color they wear to help their preschool teacher tell them apart." Her gaze flickered to the twins. "I've thought about styling their hair a little different, but they love looking like each other. I guess someday they may want to look different, but for now the clothing color schedule works."

"Hey, Mister," Max called out. "Do vegetarians take care of bugs too?" he asked, holding out his hand. Callie saw the butterfly wasn't moving, and she hoped they hadn't accidentally killed it. Before either she or Ty answered, the butterfly took off and flew away.

"That was a close call," Callie said. "You almost had to perform first aid on an insect."

"Not sure how that would've played out." A grin crossed his handsome face. "By the way, I'm not a vegetarian."

Callie giggled. "Sorry about that. I'll work on helping them understand the difference."

"Don't worry about it. It's kind of cute." His eyes slowly traveled over her, making her wonder if he thought she was cute too. When his blue gaze connected with hers, her pulse bounded wildly as if she'd chased the butterfly alongside her boys. "Maybe you . . . " Ty paused, the muscle in his jaw tightening as if he hadn't meant to speak out loud. Swallowing, he rubbed a hand across his bearded jaw. "Maybe you could bring the boys to my office some time so I can explain a little better about what I do?"

Warmth pooled in her stomach as she considered him for a few heartbeats. While Callie loved her boys and made time to play with them, they were starved for male attention. She knew they'd latch onto someone like Ty and not want to let go. Boone wasn't warm and fuzzy, but he'd showered the boys with little gifts and treats. It had been hard on Max and Gage when he'd stopped coming by the apartment. It was risky letting them get too close to Ty. Even riskier for her to get close to him. She didn't have a whole lot of faith in men. Still, something made her smile and nod her head yes.

"I think they'd like that. Thank you."

A smile crinkled the corners of his eyes. "Okay. My clinic is across from the hardware store." His cell phone trilled from his pocket. "Excuse me, but I need to take this call," he said when he looked at the screen.

Callie didn't mean to invade his privacy, but she had a clear view of his screen and the beautiful woman calling him. "Sure." She took a step backward. "I need to get Max to Dr. Tanner's office anyway."

"That's right. He's getting his cast on today," Ty said as he swiped his thumb across his phone to connect the call. "I hope it goes well."

"Thank you." Callie waved goodbye and quickly walked toward the twins. Jealousy pricked her heart when she heard

Ty warmly greet someone named Olivia and then apologize for leaving her alone for so long. She should've known a man as handsome and nice as Ty wouldn't be single.

Even though she tried not to think about him, Callie obsessed over who Olivia was and whether she was Ty's girlfriend. She'd almost asked Dr. Tanner about it when he'd put the blue cast on Max's arm. A few times she'd almost questioned her aunt. She even went as far as introducing herself to any woman who came into the café who resembled the blonde, blue-eyed beauty she'd caught a glimpse of on Ty's phone. None of them had been named Olivia.

"It's nice to see you so friendly," Joy said after a pretty woman named Christina left the café. "You've made a few new friends today and gotten reacquainted with a few old ones."

Despite her motivation behind her friendliness, Callie was glad she'd put herself out there. Annie, a girl she and Lauren had hung out with in high school, had come in with her two children. The youngest was a boy and was the same age as the twins. She and Annie were going to meet the next day after her shift for a playdate for the boys at the park. Maybe she knew who this Olivia was.

"I enjoyed it," Callie said, wiping down the countertop with a disposable cleaning wipe. It really hadn't been bad. Much better than her job as a waitress in Nashville. The only time she'd been uncomfortable was if someone asked her about Laney Loveland and what she was going to do. No one acted like they thought she was guilty, but they were very interested in her association with the new country music singer.

Gina, a long-time employee and friend of Aunt Joy's, came out of the kitchen carrying a platter of orange rolls. "Callie, I'm sure glad you were here today," she said, placing the plate on the countertop. "It was extra busy today, and with Natalie calling in sick it could've been a disastrous day."

"I'm glad I was here too." Callie glanced at the clock. "I'm going to get my boys unless you need me to do something else?"

"I don't think there's anything else." Gina glanced at Joy and raised one of her brows. "Did you talk to her about our idea?"

"Not yet." Aunt Joy cut Callie a glance and then looked back at her friend. "I've been waiting for the right time."

Callie narrowed her eyes. "Talk to me about what?"

"Well, Gina and I have been discussing a few ideas to bring in more customers." Her aunt fiddled with the jar of pens situated in front of the cash register. "We thought about adding live music like an open mic night or afternoon since lunch is the busiest time."

Callie's stomach twisted with anxiety at the thought of performing live again. She wasn't sure she had it in her. What if her music career was over for good? She hadn't even picked up her guitar for over two weeks. "That's a great idea."

"It is?" Both women said at the same time.

"Yes, of course it is." Callie tucked a loose strand of hair behind her ear. "But I'm not going to do it if that's what you're really asking. I'm giving up music."

A slight frown wrinkled her aunt's brow. "You don't mean that."

"I do." Callie lifted her chin. "I have two kids who rely on me to take care of them. It's time I grew up and got a real job."

She swallowed back the fear pressing against her throat. She truly had no skills that could provide a decent income. It was only a matter of time before Aunt Joy sold the café to Gina and her daughter, Chloe. The mother-daughter duo had taken over all of the baking in the morning. Ron, Chloe's husband, worked the grill. And their two teenage daughters helped out as well.

"Music is part of who you are," Joy said. "You have a God-given talent for writing and singing. Even if you decide to stop performing, don't give up on writing. 'Catching Sunlight' is proof of that."

Callie glanced down at her hands, feeling the calluses from her guitar as she rubbed her thumb and finger together. She hadn't told anyone, including her aunt, that the music had died inside of her. The melodies and lyrics that had floated in her head were as silent as her parents' graves. "I can't write anymore."

"Can't or won't?" Aunt Joy asked in a soft voice.

Lifting her face, she met her aunt's gaze straight on. "Can't." She bit down on her quivering lower lip. "I don't know if it will ever come back."

Gina and her aunt both looked at her with tenderness and concern. Callie felt like a black rain cloud, blotting out the light and sunshine. It was the complete opposite of her song, "Catching Sunlight." She didn't want to be a downer or take away from their idea. She would've loved to have had a venue to play her music in when she'd been in high school.

"That doesn't mean I can't help you get things set up though." Her voice wavered. She cleared her throat and forced her lips into a smile. "I'll come up with some design concepts, but right now I need to get my boys."

Needing a minute to compose herself, she grabbed her purse from behind the counter, waved goodbye, and hurried out the door. A second later, she slammed into a hard wall of masculine muscles. She caught a glimpse of sea-blue eyes before she landed on top of Ty Carter.

FOUR

Ty opened the door to the café and didn't have time to move out of the way as Callie crashed into him. Knocked off balance, he barely had time to wrap his arms around her before he hit the pavement with a thud. The breath rushed out of him when Callie landed on top of him.

"Hi there," he said when her eyes met his. "You're just the person I came to see."

"You came to see me?" she asked, pressing her palm against his upper torso to push up. "Wow, that is one solid chest you have," she said, patting his chest lightly. She groaned and squeezed her eyes closed like if she couldn't see him, then he couldn't see her. "I did not just say that out loud."

"Thanks," he said with a laugh that made his chest bounce.

Callie's eyes flew open. "Oh, sorry," she said, scrambling to try and get off of him. He grunted when her knee came awfully close to the part that made him a man. "Oh my gosh!" she said, scooting away from him. "Sorry again."

Chuckling, Ty pushed up on his elbows and righted his cowboy hat. "No problem." He felt a twinge in his back as he got to his feet. He'd tweaked it earlier in the day when trying to catch a kitten chased by a yappy, little dog. "You okay?" he asked, holding out a hand to help Callie stand.

"Uh-huh." Cheeks a pretty shade of pink, she studied his

outstretched hand as if debating if it was safe to touch. Slowly, she pressed her hand to his and then sucked in a quick breath. Ty was having a hard time breathing himself. The zing of heated electricity shooting through him was like getting hit with a cattle prod.

He pulled her up to stand and was disappointed when she quickly withdrew her hand from his. "Thanks." She slipped her purse strap over her shoulder and looked up at him through her dark lashes. "So you were looking for me?"

"Yeah." Ty noticed the two women watching them through the café's front window. He waved at Callie's aunt when the woman grinned widely and gave him the thumbs up. "Were you headed somewhere?" he asked, looking at Callie once more. It would be nice to talk without an audience.

"I was on my way to pick the boys up from preschool."

"Little Boots Daycare?" Ty asked, nodding his chin in the direction of the preschool. He and Olivia had given tours of their clinic to some of the older children over the past couple of years.

"That's the one." Curiosity burned in her hazel eyes. "Do you have a child who goes there?"

Ty's chest felt tight when he thought of Evie. Many times he'd been the one to pick her up from daycare when Kayla hadn't answered her phone or was late picking the little girl up. "No, I don't have any children." He scuffed the toe of his boot against the sidewalk. "The preschool has come on a field trip to the clinic a few times."

"Oh, my boys will love seeing where you work." Callie caught his eye, and they both smiled. "Who knows, maybe one or both of them will end up being a vegetarian."

Ty grinned at the running joke and shoved his hands into the front pockets of his jeans. "That's what I wanted to talk to you about."

"My boys becoming vegetarians?" she teased.

"I hope not. This is cattle country."

Lips tilted up, she considered him for a long moment. "We can talk on the way," Callie said, turning to walk toward the daycare.

Ty fell in step with her as they headed down the sidewalk. "I need to check on newborn twin lambs that are only a week old. Their mother was killed by a cougar shortly after they were born."

Callie gasped and glanced up at him. "That's so sad."

"Yeah, the family is pretty upset. They've been bottle feeding both of them, but I promised to look in on them this week to make sure they're thriving." They stopped at the crosswalk and waited for the light to change. Ty hesitated for a second, knowing that what he was about to ask her wasn't really a big deal. It was the why behind the question that was a big deal. Callie intrigued him, and he wanted to get to know the grown-up version of her. "So, I was wondering if you and the boys wanted to come with me? They could help feed the lambs and then see how similar a checkup for a baby lamb is to a child visiting the doctor's office."

Callie didn't answer right away. Even though he'd told himself he shouldn't spend any time with her, Ty hoped she would say yes. He liked her and wanted to get to know her better. Besides, it would give him the opportunity to finally apologize for how poorly he'd treated her ten years ago.

"I think that would be fun," she said, giving him a soft smile. "Thank you for thinking about them."

Yeah, he had been thinking of her boys, but she was the one that he couldn't get out of his head. "Great." Ty returned the smile and their eyes held for several heartbeats. A chirp indicated the light had changed. Without thinking about it, he placed his palm against her lower back, nudging her forward. Touching her did crazy things to his insides. Good crazy things that made him want to hold her hand. He remembered the last time he'd held her hand and what had happened by the lake. He wouldn't mind repeating the whole thing, minus his idiotic reaction when the kiss had ended. "I don't think we'll be too long," he said when they were almost to the other side. "Maybe we can stop by the Burger Barn on the way home to grab some dinner?"

"The Burger Barn?" she asked once they made it across the road. He heard a hint of alarm in her voice and braced himself for the rejection.

"Unless you're actually a vegetarian," he teased.

She giggled. "I'm not a vegetarian." Her steps slowed, and he matched her pace as he waited for her final answer. "I guess that would be all right," she said with a trace of uncertainty. "But this isn't a date, right?"

He looked at her sidelong, wondering if she wanted him to say yes or no. "Do you want it to be a date?"

"No." She followed up the quick answer by a nudge to his arm. "No offense, but I don't date."

"None taken," Ty said. "I don't date either."

They stopped in front of the daycare's front entrance and turned to face each other. Callie's lips twitched as if she fought off a full-blown smile. "Okay, good," she said. "I'm glad we're on the same page."

"Definitely."

Amusement danced in her eyes. "Should I follow you or do you want us to ride with you?"

"Ride with me," he blurted out. He inwardly cringed at how eager he sounded. "I mean if you're okay with that?"

"Yes," she said. "I'm okay with that."

Ty wanted to pump his fist in the air and shout out a loud yes. Instead, he took a step backward. "I'll go get my truck and then meet you by your car to get the booster seats."

"Sounds good. I parked behind the daycare." The facility's door opened, and a mom with three rambunctious children came outside. "See you in a few," Callie said before disappearing inside the building.

After getting his truck, Ty parked next to Callie's Subaru. She and the twins came around the corner, and he got out of his truck to help her with the booster seats.

"I got my cast!" Max shouted when he saw Ty.

"Slow down," Callie called out, but it was too late. Both Max and Gage raced toward Ty.

"You sure did," Ty said. "It looks awesome."

"I don't have a cast," Gage said. He held up his finger, wrapped in a colorful bandage. "I just have a Band-Aid."

"Me too," Ty said, showing the kid a plain colored bandage he'd wrapped around his pinkie finger. Working with animals was an occupational hazard. The kitten he'd saved from the dog paid him back by nipping his finger.

He noticed Callie struggling to get one of the seats free from her car and hurried over to assist her. The boys each wanted a window seat, which meant Callie would ride in front with Ty. Although she'd already been in his truck, this time seemed more intimate. While she circled the back of the truck, he opened the passenger door and waited for her.

"Thank you," she said, slipping past him to step up on the running board. The strap of her purse got hung up on the edge of the door, jerking her backward and straight into his arms.

"Careful," Ty said, maintaining his balance as he righted her. She turned toward him, and he unhooked the strap and handed it to her.

"Oh, thanks." Her fingers brushed over his, leaving a trail of heat across his skin. The air thickened and awareness crackled between them as she peered up at him. "I'm not normally this clumsy."

"Then it's a good thing I was around."

She bit her bottom lip and nodded her head. Turning, she climbed onto her seat without further incidence.

Once they were on the road, the twins immediately plied him with questions about where they were going. Ty had hoped he and Callie would have a few moments to talk. Lauren had emailed him this afternoon, asking him if he'd finally apologized. He needed to get that out of the way.

He had no idea two little boys could talk so much. Evie had always been so quiet and timid. Ty fielded their questions the entire ride to the small farm. The moment he rolled to a stop, he heard rustling from the backseat.

"Hey you two," Callie said, twisting around to look at her boys. "I need you to stay beside me and listen to everything Dr. Carter says, or you will have to sit in the truck."

"Yes, ma'am," the boys answered in unison.

Ty wanted to open Callie's door, but she exited the truck at the same time he did. Like they'd done this a hundred times, they opened the rear doors to help the two boys out of their booster seats. Gage expertly unbuckled the straps and jumped down. Then the little boy wrapped his small hand around Ty's fingers. The feel of the child's soft skin reminded him of his stepdaughter and all the times she'd held his hand, hugged him, or asked him to hold her. It wasn't fair that he had no contact with Evie, but there was nothing he could do about it.

"Olivia said they would be in the barn," Ty said when Callie and Max met them at the front of the truck.

A shadow crossed Callie's features. "Olivia?" she asked. "Is that who lives here?"

"No," Ty said, trying to get a read on Callie's cool tone. "Jed and Natasha Merrill own the farm. They just moved here from Missoula a couple of months ago."

Callie lifted her chin and narrowed her gaze. "Who is

Olivia then?" She moistened her lips. "Your girlfriend?" She shook her head. "Never mind. You don't have to answer that."

Ty tried not to smile but it was hard not to. Callie sounded jealous and was doing her best not to show it. "I don't have a girlfriend. Olivia is my partner."

"Your partner?" The grooves around her mouth deepened. "Well, that's good to know," she said, looking away from him.

"Let's go, Mama," Max said, tugging on his mother's hand. "I want to feed the lamb."

"Me too," Gage said, pulling Ty along with him to keep up with his sibling.

With the kids on the outside, Ty and Callie walked side by side. She looked straight ahead, her lips pressed firmly together. "Just to clarify, Olivia is my business partner," Ty said.

Callie looked at him sharply. "She's a veterinarian too?"

"Yes. Olivia and her husband moved to Sunset Falls at the same time I came back home. We were both interested in buying out the former vet when her husband suggested we go into an equal partnership."

Callie's steps faltered a little. "Oh, that's great."

"Isn't it?" he teased.

She shot him another look that wasn't nearly as hostile. "I look forward to meeting her."

Holding back a laugh, Ty gave her a satisfied smile. "You can stop by any time."

She looked away but not before he caught the small smile on her lips. Rounding the corner of the barn, they found Jed Merrill helping his daughter feed one of the lambs. The man glanced up and grinned. "Hey, Dr. Carter." He let the little girl take over the feeding and wiped his hand across his jeans. "Thanks for stopping by."

"No problem." Ty shook the man's hand. "And please call me Ty."

"All right." Jed glanced at the little boy holding Ty's hand and then to his look-alike brother. "Looks like you've got a set of twins too. How old are your boys?"

The muscles in Ty's shoulders went taut. "Oh, I'm not . . . they're not my boys." He wasn't sure why the denial bothered him. "Let me introduce you to my friend, Callie Stewart, and her sons, Max and Gage."

"Hello," Callie said, shaking the man's hand. "It's nice to meet you."

"Jed Merrill." He pointed to his daughter. "This is my youngest daughter, Penny."

"It's nice to meet you both," Callie said.

"How old are your boys?"

"Almost five," Max answered for her. He held up the bright blue cast. "I breaked my arm."

Gage let go of Ty's hand and held up his bandaged finger. "I got a sliver," he said, moving to stand next to his mother's side.

"Sounds like you all like to have fun adventures," Jed said with a wink.

"Never a dull moment at our house," Callie said. "By the way, this is Max." She pointed him out since he'd moved closer to the pen. "And this is Gage," she said, smoothing her hand over the child's brown hair.

"Glad you boys could come for a visit." Jed turned when his wife and other daughter came into the paddock.

"Hi there," Natasha said, handing her husband the feeding bottle she was carrying. "I didn't know you had twin boys, Dr. Carter."

Jed made the correction this time and then introduced his wife to Callie. After the two women exchanged a greeting,

Jed tugged on the end of his daughter's braid. "Lilly is our oldest," he said. "She had a birthday yesterday and turned nine."

A pang of sorrow squeezed Ty's heart. Evie would be nine next month, and he couldn't even send her a birthday card, let alone a gift.

"Do you boys want to help feed the lambs?" Jed asked.

Max and Gage didn't hesitate and dashed toward the gate. They bounced up and down with pent-up energy while they waited for Jed to open it. "Boys, don't run," Callie said. "And listen to everything Mr. Merrill says."

"Yes, ma'am," they answered in unison.

"They're adorable and so well-mannered," Natasha said. "Do I detect a southern accent?"

"We just moved from Nashville," Callie said, looking at her boys with pride.

That got the two women talking about their children, sounding like they'd been friends forever. Deciding Callie was in good hands, Ty focused on what he'd come here to do. While he examined the lambs, he explained everything to Max and Gage. They asked a lot of questions and wanted to try doing everything Ty did. The lambs were patient and doing well with the bottle feedings. After discussing the feeding schedule with Jed, his daughters volunteered to let the boys take a turn with the rest of the feeding.

Max had a hard time holding the bottle with one arm, so Lilly helped him out. Gage held onto the bottle with both hands, laughing as the lamb suckled the contents dry. Since Callie had gone inside the Merrill's house to use the restroom, Ty took out his phone and took a few pictures. He would text them to Callie later on. It was the perfect reason to ask for her number.

"Daddy, can we show Max and Gage the new kittens?" Lilly asked when they finished.

"If it's okay with their mom." Jed took his cowboy hat off and wiped his brow. "Guess they're still up at the house."

"Just ask their daddy," Penny said, pointing to Ty.

"We don't have a daddy," Gage said.

"Yeah," Max said. "He doesn't live with us."

Jed put his hat back on and looked to Ty. He had no say over the kids. He and Callie weren't even dating. "I think it'll be okay if they go take a look," Ty said. He jerked his thumb over his shoulder. "You could go with them, and I'll go find Callie and let her know where they're at."

He spun around on his boot heel and headed toward the direction Callie and Natasha had gone earlier. As he walked, he thought about Callie's ex-husband and wondered why he wasn't part of his kids' lives. Was it by choice or was Callie keeping him from them?

A pit formed in his stomach as he came around the corner and spied the women talking. The lowering sun cast a golden hue over Callie, bringing out reddish highlights in her dark brown hair. He watched her for a minute, feeling that same pull he'd felt when they were just kids. It would be so easy to fall for her . . . as well as her little boys. But how smart was that? He had no idea how long she planned to stay in Sunset Falls. If she proved that she'd written the popular song, then she'd most likely move back to Nashville to continue with her music career.

Resolve settled over him like armor. He needed to stop flirting. He had no business getting attached to Callie or her children. It would hurt too much if he lost them just like he'd lost Evie.

Callie glanced up and caught him watching her. A radiant smile blossomed on her face, making her look even more beautiful. It would hurt to lose her too.

FIVE

CALLIE DECIDED FIVE days was long enough to wait and see if Ty was ignoring her or if he was just busy with work. She wasn't sure what had happened, but somewhere between the Merrill's farm and the Burger Barn, his whole demeanor had cooled. She was stressing way too much about it and needed to get an answer so she could move on.

Tiptoeing out of the house, she closed the door behind her, hoping the boys wouldn't wake up. The scent from the plateful of freshly baked cookies wafted on the slight breeze as she walked toward Ty's house.

A moth fluttered around her head, and she swatted it away, crinkling the tinfoil covering the still warm snickerdoodles she'd baked after the twins were in bed. She wanted to thank Ty for taking the boys to the Merrill's farm and for buying them hamburgers and fries. She also wanted to find out why he had all but disappeared from her life. The only communication from him was through her aunt. Ty had texted Joy a few pictures he'd taken of the boys feeding the lambs. It hurt that he hadn't asked for Callie's cell number if only to text her the pictures. Glancing at his house, she saw the lights were on. Good, that meant he was home . . . hopefully alone. Just because he wasn't dating Olivia, didn't mean he wasn't dating someone else. She pulled her sweater tight and sidestepped a divot in the grass. True, Ty had said he didn't date, but maybe he'd said that because of her no dating stipulation.

The wooden step creaked under her as she approached the front door. Taking a deep breath, she raised her hand and knocked a couple of times. Her stomach felt like a hive of bees had been let loose. She wasn't sure what she was going to say to him. If Natasha hadn't turned out to be such a good friend, she might not be here at all.

The two women had become close over the past week. Natasha worked part-time at the hair salon, and her girls went to the same daycare as Max and Gage. Since Callie's shift started at noon, the two new friends met at the café over Natasha's lunch break a half hour before Callie's shift started. It turned out they had a lot in common, including their love of country music and playing the guitar. Natasha had agreed to dust off her guitar and play at the café once the open mic stage was ready if Callie would do it too. Callie hadn't decided anything yet, but she wasn't sure how much longer she could repress the yearning to sing and play.

Not only had Natasha managed to get Callie to open up about her music and what had happened with Boone, but she'd also dragged out the whole story about Callie and Ty's kiss by the lake and what had happened after. Natasha firmly believed Ty was still attracted to Callie but was just running scared. Callie knew Ty was married before, and the marriage had ended a couple of years earlier, but she didn't know any details.

Shifting her weight, Callie was about to press the doorbell when she saw a shadow approach the door. Perspiration dotted her hairline when she heard the click of the lock and Ty swung the door open. One look at Ty made her mouth go dry and her mind go blank as she took in the incredibly sexy man standing in front of her. He wore a snug black tee, worn jeans, and his dark hair was damp from a recent shower.

"Hi," she said, suddenly feeling as nervous as she had on her first open mic gig. She thrust out the plate of cookies. "Sorry to bother you so late, but I made you cookies to thank you for dinner and everything the other night."

His bearded jaw was tight, but the lines in his face softened as a slow smile spread across his handsome face. "You didn't need to do that." He took the plate and lifted it to his nose. "But I'm glad you did."

"Aunt Joy said snickerdoodles are your favorite."

"They are. Thank you." He held her in his blue gaze, the pull between them pulsating like her bounding heart.

"You're welcome," she said, wishing she knew if he felt it too or if it was just her latent crush making a comeback. Several beats of silence followed and her hopes of talking to him dwindled when he didn't invite her to come inside.

At least she could report to Natasha that she'd tried. Moistening her lips, she pulled her sweater together. "Well, I won't keep you." She turned to leave. "Good night, Ty."

"Don't go," he said gruffly. She froze and then slowly turned to face him. "Do you want to come inside?" he asked, his voice a deep rumble. A muscle ticked in his jaw, making her wary of accepting the invitation. It was the husky *please* he added that changed her mind.

"I'd like that." She crossed the threshold as he stepped back and opened the door wider. Callie's breath caught as she took in the beautiful foyer. It looked like something you'd see at a home show with hand-hewn wood floors and polished wood beams overhead. "This is beautiful," she said, turning in a slow circle to take it all in.

When she stopped spinning, Ty was uncomfortably close. Her senses came alive as she caught his masculine, spicy scent. "You smell really good."

He laughed as she widened her eyes and slapped a hand

over her mouth. "I can't believe I did it again," she said through her fingers. What was it about him that made her blurt out her thoughts? She wasn't a teenager anymore.

"Did what again?" he asked with a deep, throaty laugh that sent a tremor all the way down to her toes.

"Say the first thing that comes into my mind." Dropping her hand to her side, she let out a big breath. "I feel like I'm that twittering, idiotic, fifteen-year-old girl again."

Instead of laughing, his face sobered. "You weren't the idiot, Callie. I was."

"Oh." She didn't know what else to say.

A buzzer sounded from the kitchen. "Let me get my dinner out of the oven before it burns and then we can talk."

"I don't want to interrupt your dinner."

"It's a frozen pizza, so I think it'll be okay." He motioned for her to go in front of him. "Kitchen's down this way."

She padded down the hallway, acutely aware of the man following closely behind her. While she wanted to talk about that night, she also wanted to forget it had ever happened. She wished things could've gone differently and that she hadn't put him on the spot like that. When she'd expressed her undying love for him, what had she really expected him to say? That he was madly in love with her too and that he would wait for her to graduate so they could get married?

Her thoughts slammed to a halt when she stepped foot into the most gorgeous kitchen she'd ever seen. Off-white cabinets with dark granite countertops, new appliances that looked like they'd just come off the showroom floor.

"Wow, this kitchen is amazing." She ran her hand over the smooth granite that was free from little boy messes and fingerprints. "It's stunning."

"Thanks," he said, turning off the buzzer and grabbing a hot pad to pull the pizza from the oven. "I admit I'm not much of a cook though." He smirked as he set the hot pan on the granite. "This isn't exactly gourmet food."

"Is it even considered food?" she said, eyeing the unappetizing glob of melted cheese and red sauce. "You should probably apologize to your oven for insulting it like this."

The corner of his mouth tilted into a crooked smile. "I'll just add it to my list of apologies I need to make."

Shoot, she hadn't meant to bring that up. Feeling her face go hot, she walked over to the French doors that opened up to a large deck. The view of the lake was breathtaking. The smooth water shimmered under the light of the full moon. "You have a beautiful view of the lake."

"It's even prettier in the morning." He came to stand beside her, his arm brushing hers. "I love when I have a chance to get there right as the sun comes up. The fishing is good too."

"Max and Gage have never fished before," she said, vaguely remembering a time when her dad had taken her fishing. "I may have to brush up on my fishing skills and take them one morning."

"I have a boat," Ty said. "We could all go if you want."

She angled her face up, and their gazes clashed, sending a rush of tingling heat directly to her heart. "I didn't mean to try and get an invite from you."

"I know." His eyes roamed her face, his expression serious. "Callie, I need to apologize for what I did to you that night by the lake." His jaw tightened. "And for what I said to Justin the next morning. I was immature and an idiot, and I'm sorry about it all."

Did that mean he was sorry that he'd kissed her too?

"Ty, please don't worry about it." She smiled and lifted one shoulder in a shrug. "It happened a long time ago. Besides, you tried many times to apologize, but I wouldn't let you."

He stared steadily at her, then his eyes briefly dipped down to her mouth. "I wish I could have a do-over."

Her breath caught in her chest. "You want to go for a walk by the lake and kiss me again?" His lips twisted into a wry grin, and she knew that wasn't what he'd been thinking. "Forget I said that," she said with a light laugh. "I know that isn't what you meant."

"It's not a bad idea." He inched closer, narrowing the distance between them so that the tips of his boots touched her shoes. "Would you like to go for a walk by the lake?" he asked in a low voice. He didn't mention anything about a kiss, but his smoldering blue eyes implied that was part of the invitation.

She should tell him no. He probably wasn't serious anyway, just teasing her because she had blurted out yet another embarrassing thought. So why on earth did she lean toward him and ask, "Isn't it too far?"

"There's an ATV trail that goes right to the lake's edge." His fingers lightly brushed her hand. "I own an ATV."

His touch burned through her, flaming her teenage crush into a roaring fire. "Okay." She licked her lips. "What about your pizza?"

"It can wait." His hand wrapped around hers. "Come on, and I'll get you a sweatshirt. It may be a little chilly by the water."

The next thing she knew she had on one of Ty's hoodies and sat behind him on the back of his ATV with her arms wrapped firmly around his chest. This was totally crazy. She was a twenty-five-year-old mother of two, heading to the lake to kiss Ty Carter. A smile slipped across her face as they zipped past the edge of her aunt's property. It might be crazy but it also felt free.

The 4-wheeler bumped along the trail, forcing her to tighten her hold so she didn't fly off the back end. "Sorry," Ty said when he hit a rut that made her squeal. "We're almost there."

Yikes, why did that make her want to jump off the machine and run back to her aunt's house? It had been over five years since she'd kissed a man. What if she didn't remember how to do it or said something stupid?

But what if it was amazing? There was nothing wrong with kissing. Even friends kissed or so she'd heard. Besides, kissing didn't equate commitment. It didn't mean they were dating. It would just be two adults recreating a moment that had ended badly. And this time she would keep her thoughts to herself—no more declarations of love or spouting off visions of marriage.

As they approached the lakeshore, Ty slowed down and veered to the right. They went a few more yards before he brought the ATV to a stop near a picnic table and a path that led to a long dock. She shivered when he climbed off, exposing her to a light breeze that seeped through the fabric of the borrowed sweatshirt.

With shaky legs, she climbed off the recreational vehicle and looked across the lake.

Ty moved next to her, sending a rush of electricity through her when his shoulder brushed against her. Her hand bumped into his, and she didn't pull away. Warmth spread through her, chasing away the chill when Ty intertwined their fingers together.

They were holding hands. Now what? Were they supposed to make small talk, pretending they hadn't come to the lake to make out? No, not make out. She was too old to make out. Kiss. Just one kiss between friends. It would mean nothing other than they were mature adults and had moved on.

While Callie contemplated about who would make the first move, Ty tugged on her hand, and they started walking down the path that led to the dock. "Tell me about living in Nashville."

Apparently, kissing wasn't on his mind. It was just as well and much safer for her heart.

"What do you want to know?" she asked. "I lived there for eight years."

"You could start at the beginning and tell me about Max and Gage's dad." The muscles in her shoulders stiffened. Life in Nashville wasn't her favorite subject right now. "But only if you want to," Ty said, leading her onto the wobbly dock.

Feeling unsteady, she gripped his hand tighter and paused until she regained her equilibrium. Once they started walking again, she told him all about meeting Paul Stewart on open mic night at the diner where she worked as a waitress. She'd fallen for him fast and hard. He was a big shot attorney for a well-known record label and made her all sorts of promises, including to love her forever. "I didn't know that he had a mistress or that he and Heidi already had a baby together." She sighed as they approached the end of the dock. This part of the story was humiliating.

"Heidi was married to someone else but wouldn't divorce her husband. Apparently, she'd made him believe he was the baby's father and wasn't sure she wanted the scandal her affair would cause. I can't begin to understand her thought process, but she was stringing Paul along until he'd finally had enough. Paul married me not because he loved me but because he wanted to show Heidi how it felt. It was the catalyst to make her leave her husband. Paul served me with divorce papers the day Heidi's divorce was final."

Ty used a mild expletive when he expressed his disgust for her ex. "I'm sorry that happened to you," he said, giving her fingers a gentle squeeze.

"I was young and so naïve." The unpleasant memories were hard to think about, and she needed a little space. Letting go of his hand, she leaned on the railing. "He was my biggest mistake, but I'd do it all over again to get my boys."

Ty joined her at the railing but kept enough distance away from her that she didn't feel crowded. The silence stretched between them as they gazed out over the water. With the moonlight illuminating the surface of the lake it was easy to see the fish rising to the top to snatch a late-night snack.

"What about the boys?" Ty asked. "Does your ex-husband have any contact with them?"

"No, he granted me full custody." Callie sighed and turned to find Ty watching her instead of the jumping fish. "His new wife didn't want the twins interfering in their life."

Another curse word slipped through his tightly pressed lips. "What about his financial obligations as a father?" he asked.

At least that was one thing she'd done right. During mediation, Callie agreed to go away quietly and forfeit any of his assets or receive alimony if he agreed to pay child support and provide insurance for Max and Gage. "He's kept his end of the bargain, and I've kept mine. I try to save what I can so the boys will have a college fund, but there are times when I have to use the money like for daycare, food, and clothing for them."

Ty studied her contemplatively, the hard lines in his face softening. She sure hoped he wasn't going to try and kiss her now. Then she would forever associate the kiss with her pathetic choice of a husband.

"What if he wanted to see them?" Ty asked. Pain flashed in his eyes, and he glanced away. "Would you let him?"

"I would have to consider his motivation, but if he truly wanted a relationship with them, then I would never deny my boys that chance."

Ty swallowed hard and wordlessly stared across the water. Callie would bet money he wasn't looking at anything in particular. He rubbed his bearded jaw and then told her all about his ex-wife and the stepdaughter he loved and thought of as his own, but was denied any contact with because he wasn't the biological father.

"Kayla's husband was a widower and had two daughters from his previous marriage." Ty leaned on the railing, his hands clasped in front of him. "He wanted to adopt Evie. I tried fighting it, but there was nothing I could do about it. Besides, Evie was so happy to have sisters."

"I'm sorry," Callie said softly. She wanted to comfort him with a hug, but she sensed he was the one who needed the space now. It appeared that the do-over kiss was no longer on the table, having been replaced by airing their dirty laundry.

"Life can be hard," he said after a moment, "and not always because of our choices."

"That's sad but true." Since she'd already shared her ugly marriage, she told him all about Boone Redford, the missing notebook, and how it was the only proof she had that the hit song was hers.

"So you really don't have it written down anywhere?" he asked with concern. "No notes on your computer or phone?"

She shook her head and shrugged. "Stupid, I know."

"You're not stupid, Callie." The tone of his voice held a note of protectiveness in it. It made her feel vulnerable but not in a negative way. Like she was a girl, and he was a superhero ready to defend her against the evil villains in the world.

She stared into his eyes, wondering what her life would have been like if she'd married someone like him. Afraid she might actually voice her musings aloud, she cracked a smile. "Wow, I didn't mean to tell you my life story." She tapped him playfully on the chest. "Guess I killed the mood for our walk around the lake." Her eyes widened, and she snatched back her hand. "Not that there was a mood to kill." Biting her lower lip, she looked down at her feet, wishing she could slip through the cracks of the wooden dock and disappear. Why couldn't she ever keep her thoughts to herself?

Ty hooked a finger under her jaw and gently lifted her chin until their eyes met. An electric current of awareness zipped between them as if a live wire connected them. Her insides lit up with nervous energy as his eyes moved slowly over her face before settling on her mouth.

The kiss was back on the table.

SIX

Ty's pulse pounded in his ears as his gaze dropped to Callie's mouth. He knew he wasn't smooth and that his man-radar might be totally out of whack, but if he read her correctly, then she wanted to kiss him as much as he wanted to kiss her.

Vulnerability flickered in her eyes along with desire as her full lips parted slightly, and she slanted forward. Pushing out thoughts about if this was a smart move or not, Ty lowered his mouth to hers and touched her lips softly.

He meant to keep the kiss short and sweet but just like the last time he'd kissed her, his brain short-circuited, and the world around him began to blur. With a soft moan, Callie melted against him, her lips demanding more. Sliding his hands along her neck, Ty held her face and adjusted the angle of her head to deepen the kiss. He took his time, exploring her mouth, tasting and breathing her in. When he was tempted to let his hands make an expedition, he knew it was time to stop. He slowed the kisses before he drew back and pressed his forehead to hers. "Thank you," he said in a raspy voice.

"You're welcome." Her breathless tone came out in a sexy whisper that made him want to devour her all over again. "Wait," she said, edging back just enough to look up at him, "why are you thanking me?"

He chuckled, liking how she didn't hold anything back or play stupid games. "For one, thank you for giving me a second chance and graciously accepting my apology." He rubbed his thumb over her smooth cheek. "And for trusting me enough to tell me about your life."

Ty hadn't planned on delving so deeply into Callie's personal life or spilling his guts about Kayla. It had been hard to hear what Callie's ex-husband had done to her, but at least he knew she didn't deny her boys a chance to be with their father out of spite. In fact, now that he knew the story, he wasn't so sure the guy deserved one ounce of consideration if he ever decided he wanted a relationship with his children. What he'd done to her was the kind of thing you heard about and didn't believe it was true.

"And finally," he said, moving his thumb down to run along the bottom of her lip, "thank you for letting me kiss you."

"Oh." Moonlight illuminated her face, her eyes sparkling with a mischievous glint. Her grin widened, and she broke out into a song from the *Moana* movie. "Well then, what can I say except you're welcome." He'd watched the animated show with Evie a few times. The memory of his stepdaughter still caused him pain, but it paled in comparison to what Callie had experienced. After hearing her story, he was now grateful Kayla's husband had wanted to adopt Evie.

"Cute." He dropped his hands to cup her shoulder. "But I'm not going to sing back to you."

"Sorry," she said with a giggle. "I'm such a dork."

"A pretty cute dork."

"Oh my goodness!" she said with a huge smile. "I just sang. Like actually sang."

"Yes, you did," he said, feeling a little confused. "Isn't that kind of what you do?"

"It was, but I haven't wanted to play my guitar or sing since Boone stole my song." She patted him on the chest again, resting her palm flat against his chest. "Who knew that kissing you was the key to getting my voice back?"

Ty did something he never thought he'd ever do in his life. He sang the same song back to Callie. It was only the one line, and he knew he sounded nothing like Dwayne Johnson's character from the movie, but the look on Callie's face was worth the embarrassment.

"That was probably the sexiest thing a man has ever done for me." Then she rose up on her toes and kissed him slow and sweet. He had no idea how much time passed, but when they finally drew apart, Ty was the one who wanted to profess his undying love for her and then drop to one knee and beg her to marry him.

"We didn't just make out, did we?" Callie asked.

Ty wasn't sure how to answer her. He couldn't get a read on whether she was serious or just messing with him. "Uh . . . we can call it something else if you want." That made her smile, but there was enough moonlight to let him see she was genuinely distressed. "You want to tell me what's going on in that pretty head of yours?"

She watched him, worry lines marring the smooth skin on her forehead. "I guess I'm scared."

He almost said that it was just a kiss but then remembered that's what he'd told her the last time he'd kissed her. Back then, he'd said it to protect himself. Now, he wanted to say it to comfort her, letting her know they didn't have to rush into anything.

Still, he got what she was saying. Hadn't his fears kept him away from her the past few days? "I understand." He ran his hands down her arms, linking their fingers together. "We can take things slow."

Her expression remained solemn, and it suddenly occurred to him that he had no idea if she even wanted to keep seeing him. She'd told him she didn't date. He'd responded in kind because at the time that was exactly how he felt. But now . . . now he'd changed his mind. Callie, however, might not feel the same way.

Even though he felt exposed, he went ahead and asked the question. "That is if you want to go out with me?"

"I do want to." Her chest rose and fell as she drew in a big breath. "But I have my boys to consider. They already like you so much. I don't want them to get hurt either."

"Callie, I would never do anything to hurt them intentionally."

The guarded expression slowly melted away, and she nodded her head. "I believe that."

"Good." He squeezed her hands. "Now I better get you back home."

"Okay." A tiny smile appeared on her lips. "Just to clarify . . . going slow doesn't mean we can't kiss anymore, right?"

Grinning, Ty slipped his hands to the lower curve of her back and pulled her into his chest. Their eyes locked as he slowly lowered his head. Just before their mouths touched, her eyes fluttered closed. A fire burned through him as he closed his eyes and lost himself in her kiss. "Does that answer your question?" he asked a few minutes later.

"Perfectly," she said on a sigh.

Ty walked her home as soon as they returned to his house. As much as he wanted to invite her inside, he remembered his promise to take things slow. Being with her had unlocked a door he'd closed after his marriage had ended. He wasn't the type of guy to push for a physical relationship just to satisfy his needs, but he didn't want the temptation. And she was very tempting.

"If things aren't too crazy tomorrow, I'll stop by for lunch," he said, walking her across the moonlit yard to her aunt's house. "If not, will you have dinner with me?"

"Yes," she said after a brief hesitation. "But I'll need to check with Aunt Joy to see if she can watch the boys."

"The invitation includes them too," he said, glancing down at her. He wasn't sure if her reluctance was because she didn't want him to get to know her boys better or if she didn't want to leave them out. "But I'm cool with whatever you want."

"I'd like them to come along," she said as relief washed over her features. "But they don't sit still very long, so maybe we can have dinner at your house instead of going out?"

"Sure. Do they like pizza?" he asked.

"Yes, but not the stuff you have in your freezer," she teased. "I'll bring everything over to make homemade pizza."

The idea of her cooking in his kitchen made him smile. "My oven and I thank you very much."

Laughing, she rose up on her toes and gave him a quick peck on the lips. "I'll see you tomorrow."

The next day proved to be a busy day. It started with an emergency call to a stud ranch in the next county over. One of the stallions had gotten tangled up in barbed wire and needed stitches. The horse was ticked off and tried kicking Ty in the chest. When he'd dodged the hoofs, Ty fell into a fresh pile of manure. His cell phone fell too, and the stallion stepped on it before the owner of the horse or Ty could pick it up.

The rest of the day was just as crazy. Ty wasn't sure he was going to make it home in time for dinner with Callie and her boys.

Olivia pushed him out the clinic's door just before six. "I've got this. Besides, Charlie's working late so it'll just be my dogs and me tonight."

"Thanks," Ty said, grabbing his keys. "I promise I'll return the favor."

"That's what partners are for." She leaned against the door and smiled. "By the way, I really like Callie."

"When did you meet her?" Ty asked.

"You mean our summer intern didn't tell you where your lunch came from?"

"No." Ty rubbed his beard, trying not to be irritated. Their summer intern wasn't as helpful as she'd promised during her interviews. The girl focused on two things. Planning her wedding and planning her wedding. This wasn't the first time she'd failed to tell Ty something important. "She just said my lunch was in the fridge."

"I'm so sorry. Today was nuts, or I would've followed up with you sooner," Olivia said with a sigh. "Your girlfriend brought lunch for you and was nice enough to include food for the rest of the staff."

Girlfriend? How had word spread that quickly? They'd only just decided to start dating the night before. He was fine with it. It was Callie he was worried about. She wanted to take things slow. Being labeled as his girlfriend in less than twenty-four hours wasn't complying with her stipulation. "Shoot, and I didn't even thank her." He reached for his phone only to remember he didn't have it.

"Don't worry, I told her what happened to your phone." Olivia pushed away from the door. "She is so beautiful, Ty. Do not screw this up."

"How am I going to screw this up?"

"You're a guy. It's kind of in your DNA."

"I'm going to ignore that sexist remark."

"Yeah, forget I said that." She rubbed her stomach. "My pregnancy hormones are making me crazy."

"Are you still having morning sickness?" Ty asked.

"Morning sickness? How about morning, noon, and night sickness?" She snorted a laugh. "I'll bet you a hundred bucks a man came up with that term."

"I'll go ahead and ignore that sexist comment too."

Olivia laughed and pointed to the door. "Go before I change my mind."

Ty made it home fifteen minutes later. Callie was coming over at six-thirty, which meant he had exactly seven minutes to shower and get dressed. He pulled a clean shirt over his head just as the doorbell sounded.

"Hey guys," he said when he opened the door and found Max and Gage standing on the porch. He spied Callie coming up the walk, carrying two grocery sacks.

"We're making pizza at your house," Max said, racing through the door.

"And ice cream," Gage said as he tripped over the door jam, trying to follow his brother.

"You okay, bud?" Ty asked, helping Gage stand up.

"Yep." He gave him a thumbs up and then raced toward the kitchen. Ty hoped he hadn't left anything dangerous out on the countertop.

"Sorry about the boys just barging in," Callie said. "They've been asking me every two minutes when it was time to come over."

He walked across the porch to help her. "They're fine." He reached out to take the grocery sacks but froze when their hands connected.

Throughout the day, he'd questioned whether the chemistry between the two of them was really as powerful as he remembered. He still couldn't believe he'd taken her down to the lake for the express purpose of kissing her. Ty wasn't that spontaneous eighteen-year-old kid anymore. Life had thrown a few curves at him, making him much more cautious. Right now, he wanted to drop the grocery sacks to the ground, wrap his arm around Callie, and kiss her senseless.

"Thanks," she said, breaking contact with him as she let go of the sack. "Did you just get home?"

"Yeah." He was having a hard time formulating words. Her long hair hung in loose curls, falling over her shoulders, and reaching nearly down to her waist. He wanted to slide his hands through her hair while he kissed her senseless. "I'm sorry I missed seeing you this afternoon. The tech forgot to tell me you were the one who brought lunch. I found out from Olivia just before coming home."

"I heard about your morning and your phone." She tucked her fingertips into the front pockets of her denim shorts that showcased well-toned legs. "Olivia was very nice. She's also very beautiful."

"That's exactly what Olivia said about you." He really wanted to drop the groceries and steal that kiss when they heard a loud crash come from the kitchen.

"Oh no," Callie said, rushing past him.

Ty was right behind her. So far, he hadn't heard a child's cry. He hoped that meant it wasn't serious.

"Gage Evan Stewart," Callie said. "What are you doing?"

The little boy stood on top of the countertop, the cupboard open, and a barstool knocked over on the floor. He held up a glass filled with water and grinned. "I got a drink all by myself."

"I see that." She lifted the little boy from the counter and set him down on the floor. "Where is your brother?" Callie asked as she righted the barstool.

Setting the sacks of food on the bar, Ty noticed the sliding glass door was slightly ajar just as Gage pointed to the back deck. What he saw made him laugh out loud. Callie just dropped her chin to her chest and mumbled something about failing as a mother.

"I'm sorry," Callie said. "He usually uses a toilet."

"It's no big deal," Ty said with a chuckle. "At least he's aiming toward the grass."

"Ha ha." Callie nudged him in the arm with her shoulder. "Do not encourage him by telling him that."

Max finished his task, pulling his shorts back up with his free hand. The pants were a little askew when he triumphantly marched toward the sliding door.

"Max, you know better than to go potty outside," Callie said when the little boy came back inside.

"It's okay, Mom. It was a mergency," he said simply.

Ty snickered, earning a censuring look from Callie. "What?" he asked with a wink. "He's probably right since he's never been in my house before."

"It was not an emergency because I made both of them use the bathroom before we came over," Callie said in a low voice. "I let them go from the side of the road a few times on the road trip from Tennessee, and now they think it's the best thing ever." She glanced at her boys before leaning toward Ty. "We were at the park the other day, and they decided it was more convenient to go behind a tree."

Ty didn't tell her that every little boy thought the same thing at one time or another. "I wouldn't worry too much," he said, leaning down to whisper close to her ear. "Eventually, they'll grow out of it." The clean scent of her hair tempted him to linger and get a better whiff. Before he did something crazy like pushing a lock of hair to the side and kissing her neck, he felt a tug on his hand.

"Hey, Mr. Doctor, do you have any toys?" Gage asked.

"You can call me Ty," he said, ruffling the kid's wavy hair. "And I do have some toys for when my nephews come to visit."

"Can we see?" Max asked.

"Please?" added Callie.

"Please," Max repeated.

"Sure." He looked at Callie. "I'll be right back."

Ty escorted the kids to his family room. He opened the storage closet and pulled out the box of toys he'd purchased the last time Lauren and her family came to see him. At the time, his nephews were into Star Wars and Marvel superheroes. Gage and Max were excited with both options.

He left them happily playing and made his way back to the kitchen. Callie had her back to him, humming as she loaded the makings for homemade ice cream into his fridge. He hung back and watched her for a few moments. He liked having her here and knew he wouldn't mind coming home to find her in his kitchen every day.

She continued to hum softly as she rearranged the space on the second shelf to accommodate the new items. Even though she was only humming, Ty could tell she had a beautiful voice and hoped he'd get to hear her sing sometime. Maybe she would sing something to him if he kissed her again. It had worked last night.

Closing the fridge, she turned around and caught him staring at her. A small smile flirted at her lips. "I hope you don't mind me makin' myself at home," she said, the southern drawl more pronounced than usual.

"I don't mind." Ty pushed away from the doorjamb and crossed the wood floor. "I was just thinking how much I like having you here."

"Oh yeah?" she said as she tracked his progress. "Is that because you don't like cooking or because you like me?"

"Definitely because I like you." He took the final steps, narrowing the space between them and pulled her into his arms. "In fact, I like you so much that I'm going to kiss you."

"I'm okay with that," she said, sliding her arms around his neck and lifting her face to his.

Lowering his head, he felt her warm breath against his lips before he caught her mouth with his. Callie melted into his embrace as he inhaled her scent, every one of his senses acutely aware of her. Threading his fingers through her hair, he curved his hand around the back of her neck and kissed her deeply.

This wasn't the first time he'd kissed this woman, and he didn't want it to be the last. Still, he didn't want to move too fast. Reluctantly, he ended the passionate exchange and just held her until his breathing regulated.

"Ty," she said with a soft sigh. "I definitely like you too."

"Good." He wanted to swoop down and capture her mouth again but settled for a kiss to the top of her head when the twins came racing down the hall. "We'll finish this . . . conversation after the boys are asleep," Ty whispered as Callie stepped out of his embrace.

"Conversation?" Laughter glittered in her eyes. "Is that code for meet me down by the lake?"

"Sounds good to me," he said, snagging her hand before she got too far out of his reach.

Max and Gage burst into the kitchen, eager to help make the pizza. The evening was crazy busy. Through it all, Ty and Callie cast longing looks at each other and touched as often as possible. As the boys dug into the homemade ice cream, Callie came up behind Ty and whispered in his ear, "The lake is too far away. I think the porch swing is the perfect place to have our conversation."

SEVEN

CALLIE SLIPPED OUT of bed, unable to wait another moment. Glancing at the clock, she knew she was going to regret getting up at four-thirty in the morning, but she was too excited to sleep anymore.

Crossing the room, she opened the bedroom closet and pushed back the clothes until she located her guitar. Pulling it free, she returned to her bed and laid the case down. Her hands shook as she opened the lid. Her Gibson guitar didn't look all shiny and new, but she loved it and it still sounded amazing.

Wishing she had a sound-proof room she could go to, she lifted the instrument and hugged it to her. Boone Redford might have stolen her song, but he hadn't stolen her music. It was hiding under a mountain of grief and stress. Perhaps, she would have eventually discovered it, but after spending every spare second with Ty the past three weeks, she felt alive. And she could hear the music again. It had come back to her gradually like spotty cell service. But something had happened last night that boosted the signal, and she could hardly wait to play the melody she heard in her head.

Her fingers itched to strum the opening chords, but she didn't want to wake up the boys too early. They'd had a late night with Natasha and her girls so Ty and Callie could have an evening alone. Ty was taking all of them fishing later on, and her boys would be total grumps if they didn't get at least ten hours of sleep.

Putting the guitar back inside the case, she opened the drawer of the nightstand and picked up the empty notebook. Cracking open the cover, she smoothed her fingers over the bare pages. She could easily see the notes and chords and wanted to get started before the quiet ended with the rising of the sun and her boys. The music always came first for her. Lyrics were harder for her, but they usually came once she had the melody written down.

With the notebook in hand, she dug through the inside pocket of her purse and searched for her pen she only used to write music. A feeling of panic twisted her stomach when she couldn't find it. It might be silly, but she always used the same pen until the ink ran dry. Then she'd buy another one exactly like it. She had a new package of the pens packed away somewhere, but she didn't want to go find them. Finally, after realizing she may need to clean out her purse, she grasped the pen laying in a side pocket, tucked obscurely at the very bottom of her bag.

Clicking the guitar case closed, she picked it up along with the notebook and pen and quietly made her way downstairs. She wouldn't be bothering her aunt since she'd already left for the bakery an hour earlier. Joy was covering for Gina and her daughter this week while they were at a baking convention in Idaho. Callie knew it was only a matter of time before her aunt sold the café to the pair. She didn't feel quite as panicked about that prospect because she had a plan to make money with her music without the hassle of agents and the grind of Nashville.

In preparation for the café's first open mic night, Callie had helped Natasha brush up on her guitar and vocal skills as well as tips for performing in front of a live audience. Word had spread through Sunset Falls, probably because Natasha told everyone who came in for a haircut about Callie helping her, and now Callie had men and women of varying ages wanting to sign up for private guitar and voice lessons. After calculating tuition prices, she knew it was enough money to provide for her little family.

Settling on the edge of the loveseat next to the fireplace, Callie lifted her Gibson from the case and began tuning it. The strings were stiff, and the calluses on her fingertips had softened a little but not enough to cause any problems.

Over the next hour or so, the melody flowed out of her. It was thrilling how easily it came back to her. Finally, she penned the last measure of music and turned to a new page. The lyrics came next, talking about letting go of fears and finding her heart again.

By the time the sun peeked over the eastern mountains, Callie had most of the song finished. She was stuck on the ending. Knowing that it didn't help to force her creativity, she went upstairs to get ready before the boys got up.

After taking a long, hot shower, Callie wove her hair into a single braid that hung over her shoulder. Glancing at the clock, she quickly dressed in jeans and a graphic tee. Max and Gage woke up immediately when she reminded them about the fishing trip. They were dressed in record time and eating breakfast when Ty knocked on the door.

Her lungs seized when she opened the door to let him inside. Wearing a ball cap instead of his usual cowboy hat, he looked sexy in jeans and a simple tee that barely contained his well-developed biceps and broad shoulders.

"Good morning," she said, stepping into his open arms for a hug. "Oh, you smell so good," she whispered against his neck.

He made a low growling noise and pulled back just

enough to look at her. "Where are the boys?" he asked in a husky voice.

"Eating breakfast."

Something hot flared in his eyes, making her stomach flutter with anticipation. "Good, that gives me time to do this." His palms framed her face as he crushed his mouth to hers, kissing her with a hunger that made her body feel weightless. "I've missed you," he whispered against her mouth.

"I've missed you too." She pressed her lips to his and lost herself in another toe-curling kiss.

"Mama?" a little voice said from behind her. "Is Ty going to be our new daddy?"

Startled, Callie broke the connection and turned around to find both of her boys staring at her. "Hey guys," she said in a shaky voice. "Are y'all done with your breakfast?"

Gage and Max didn't fall for the detour. "Are you getting married?" Max asked. "Penny said that if you kiss someone you have to marry them."

Ty laughed, and she gently elbowed him to quiet him. "Well, that's not always true," Callie said, wondering what else the boys had discussed with the Merrill girls last night.

"It is in this case," Ty whispered in her ear.

Callie froze at his words. What was he saying? "Well, I think it's time to go fishing," Callie said, trying to distract her sons as well as the man whispering things he shouldn't be saying. He hadn't even told her he loved her, and yet he had just insinuated that he wanted to marry her. "Run upstairs and get your shoes on and then we can go."

The tactic worked, and the two kids raced up the stairs. Feeling like she'd overloaded on sugar, Callie's insides shook as she slowly turned around to face Ty. He wore a teasing grin, but his eyes held a serious note that made her knees go weak. Was she ready for this conversation?

"Hey," he said. "Did I tell you how beautiful you look?"

"No." She moved closer, never taking her eyes from his. "Are you trying to distract me?"

He lifted a brow, his grin widening. "Sweetheart, if I wanted to distract you I wouldn't do it by telling you how beautiful you look." He snagged her around the waist again and leaned down to kiss her.

Callie put her finger over his lips and shook her head. "I think we need to talk."

He held her gaze, his blue eyes sobering. "I think we do too."

"Ty, did you mean what you said?" she asked in a soft voice.

"I did." Uncertainty flickered across his face as he visibly swallowed. "I'm falling in love with you, Callie. I know I promised to take things slow and it's probably too soon to say that, but I can't keep it inside anymore."

Her throat thickened with emotion. While she wanted to confess her growing feelings, she wasn't sure she was ready to take that step. Max and Gage had just asked her if Ty was going to be their new daddy. Hearing them ask the question reminded her there was more at stake than her heart.

The lyrics to the song she'd started writing flitted through her mind. Yes, she was afraid. Giving her heart to someone was risky, but some risks were worth taking.

"I think I'm falling for you, Ty." She licked her lips. "I'm still scared, but I don't want to be."

"That's a good start." He reached for her hand, pressing a kiss to her palm, then drew her closer and murmured against her hair. "I'm a patient man, Callie Stewart."

Ty proved just how much patience he had. Fishing with two four-year-old's wasn't easy. First, Gage dropped his fishing pole into the lake. Ty made a valiant attempt to snag it with another rod but almost ended up in the lake himself. Then Max knocked over the can of worms. Callie couldn't bring herself to help clean the wriggling creatures up. She shuddered when her sons dug through the dark soil and pinched the fat worms between their fingers.

"Where are his eyes?" Gage asked, holding one of the worms up close to his face for inspection.

"That is a good observation," Ty said, winking at Callie. "They actually don't have eyes."

While Ty cleaned up the mess, he explained all about earthworms. Max and Gage were fascinated, asking Ty question after question. Callie loved watching him interact with her boys. He was kind and tolerated their endless questions. Since they'd spent so much time at his house over the past three weeks, it had given her plenty of time to get a sense of his true nature. No matter what chaos or mess her boys made, Ty never got too riled up.

Gage handed Ty his worm and then put his arm around Ty's neck and leaned in close as he watched his worm squirm around on top of the dirt. Callie quickly pulled her phone from her pocket and captured the sweet moment. It was obvious her little boys had fallen in love with Ty Carter.

And that's when she knew she loved him. She just didn't know if she was brave enough to tell him. While she knew Ty wouldn't react the same way he had ten years earlier by telling her it was just a kiss and it didn't mean anything, she was almost more afraid of what he would say this time. He'd basically said he wanted to marry her. Was she really ready to take that next step?

The rest of the afternoon was fairly uneventful. By the time they motored toward the dock, Gage and Max were as hooked on fishing as the trout they'd caught.

"Sit tight," Ty said as he killed the boat engine and

jumped out on the dock to wrap a rope around one of the cleats. "I'll be right back with the trailer."

She admired his athletic body as he jogged toward the parking lot. She could almost see him in his high school football uniform as he ran out onto the field. It was hard to believe that the Warrior's tight end she'd fantasized about as a teenager was now her boyfriend. Callie couldn't wait to tell Lauren the next time they talked. Her friend was all for Ty and Callie getting together, especially since her boys would get new cousins.

She snapped to attention when she saw the boys trying to climb over the boat from the corner of her eyes. "Hold it right there," she said, pulling them back inside. "Y'all need to stay in the boat with me while Ty gets the truck."

"I want to look through the cracks for fish," Gage said. "I won't fall in the water."

"Me too," Max said.

When they'd launched the boat this morning, Callie had told them to lay on the dock and look for fish so she could keep an eye on them. She pulled her phone from her pocket and opened the camera app to distract them. "Here, y'all can take silly pictures of yourself to show Aunt Joy."

That kept them occupied long enough for Ty to back the trailer down the boat ramp. But when Ty unwound the rope from the cleat and guided the vessel onto the trailer, both boys immediately went to the edge to watch him.

Callie stayed nearby in case one of them tried to go overboard. She completely forgot about her cell phone until Max informed her that it just fell in the water.

"I got it," Ty said, wading through the shallow water to scoop up the phone.

"Sorry, Mama," Max said, his lower lip quivering.

Callie couldn't scold him. It was an accident, and she

should've taken the phone back after they finished taking pictures. Thankfully, she'd backed up her phone online. "It was an accident, sweetie," she said, hugging her son. "I'm not mad at you, okay?"

Sniffing, he nodded his head and sat down next to Gage.

"Thank you," she said as Ty handed her the phone. "I guess we'll see if this new model is really as water resistant as they claim."

"I'm impressed," Ty said, gazing up at her from the water.

She quirked an eyebrow. "That my phone is water resistant?"

"No," he said with a chuckle. "That you didn't yell or get angry." The blue in his eyes deepened in color. "You're an amazing woman, Callie. And an incredible mother."

Callie was so tempted to jump overboard so she could give Ty a hug and a kiss. His words meant more to her than any accolades the country music industry could ever bestow upon her. "That is one of the nicest things anyone has ever said to me."

Her body heated under his stare as if the mild temperature had jumped to a scorching summer day in the desert. "Then I better voice my thoughts more often," he said, his voice an octave lower than normal.

"I need to go potty," Gage said, shattering the moment.

Ty laughed and offered to take him to the nearby outhouse. Callie hated the smell of those buildings and looked longingly at the copse of trees flanking the parking lot. Ty seemed to read her mind, which was one more point for him.

"Come here, sport," Ty said, climbing onto the trailer, so he was fairly level with the edge of the boat. "The grass by the trees needs watering."

"You may live to regret that when the grass by your deck turns brown," Callie said dryly. "But thank you so much."

"I need to go too," Max said.

Before she thought of a plan to take her other son, Ty volunteered to take him too. "Be right back," he said, holding a child in each arm.

Callie sighed as she watched him put those impressive muscles of his to good use, carrying the boys as if they weighed nothing. Once he was on even ground, he galloped with them toward the trees, eliciting adorable laughter from each of her sons. Tears of amazement, gratitude, and happiness pressed at her eyes, and she blinked to hold them back.

She really had no idea how wonderful it was to have a partner to help her with the kids until now. It almost scared her how much she'd grown to rely on Ty to help with dinner and bedtime.

Her heart expanded with love until she thought it would burst through her chest as she watched Ty and the boys emerge from the cover of the trees. Instead of carrying them, he held their hands with Gage on one side, and Max on the other.

It was time to be brave. She decided that the first moment she got Ty alone, they were going to have a conversation . . . a real conversation and not just a make-out session. A smile curved her mouth as the song she'd started this morning played in her head, and she knew how it would end.

EIGHT

Ty leaned against the doorway, watching as Callie kissed her children goodnight. He'd helped her with their bedtime routine for a couple of weeks now, and tonight he knew those kids weren't getting out of bed for a drink or a snack. They were exhausted after their day of fishing and then helping him prepare the fish he'd fried for dinner.

A band of emotion tightened around his chest as he watched Callie smooth a lock of Gage's hair away from his forehead. He loved Callie. Heck, he'd been in love with her since she'd flattened him on the sidewalk and landed on top of him. It was getting harder and harder to comply with her edict to take things slow. Not when all he wanted to do was tell her how much he loved her and then whisk her off to the nearest church and marry her.

Callie leaned across Gage and pulled the blanket to cover Max's arm. The kid was getting his cast off next week, and he wanted Ty to be there with him. Swallowing back the lump rising in his throat, Ty acknowledged another kind of love taking root in his heart. He also loved her boys. They were incredible little human beings. Funny, full of life and so smart they frequently astounded him with their questions and observations.

Pressure built behind his eyes as another wave of emotion crashed over him. He wanted this family to be his.

Wanted it more than success or the material possessions he owned or ever hoped to own.

Callie backed away from the beds, pausing to look down at the boys one last time before she turned and walked toward him. "I think we wore them out," she whispered. "They have never fallen asleep so quickly."

"Good," he said, taking her hand and leading her down the hallway. "Now I get you all to myself."

"It was a wonderful day, Ty." She leaned her head against his shoulder. "Thank you so much."

Joy looked up from her knitting as he and Callie came into the family room. "Are they asleep already?" she asked.

"They were asleep the second their heads hit the pillow." Callie glanced up at Ty and then back to her aunt. "Are you okay listening to them for a little while?"

"Of course." Joy peered at them over her close-up glasses that had slipped down her nose. "You two go have some fun together." Her eyes twinkled with mischief. "I'm sure it'll be nice to cuddle up without those two rug rats getting in on the action."

"Sounds good to me," Ty said with a grin. Both Gage and Max were affectionate children and rarely let Ty and Callie hug without one or both of them wiggling into the middle for a group hug. A quick peck on the lips was the only kissing that happened when they were with the twins.

While he and Callie needed to talk, there was going to be a lot of kissing involved.

"I've got my phone if you need me to come home," Callie said.

"I'll be fine," Joy said. "I've got season two of *The Paradise* to watch, so I'm not going to bed any time soon."

Eager to get home, Ty led Callie to the front door and opened it for her. The temperature had dropped a few degrees. A shroud of clouds dimmed the light from the lowering sun, the smell of pending rain thick in the air. Ty loved summer rainstorms and the clean scent that came with it that smelled like fresh cut wheat fields.

"Rain is coming," he said, leading Callie down the porch steps. "If it's still raining tomorrow, maybe we could take the boys into Missoula after church services to see that new movie they've been talking about."

"They would love that." She squeezed his hand. "You're too good to us," she said softly. "I don't know what I'd do without you."

Ty heard the catch in her voice. He looked at her sidelong, hoping her emotions were a good thing. "I'm not going anywhere," he said gruffly.

She didn't say anything, just gave his hand another gentle squeeze. He sure hoped she wasn't about to break things off with him. Otherwise, the engagement ring he'd purchased a couple of days ago would be pointless.

Callie met his eyes briefly as he held his front door open for her. He tried to gauge the array of emotions reflected in her hazel eyes, but she looked away and quickly crossed the threshold.

Pulling the door closed, Ty followed her down the hall toward the family room. It was their favorite place to talk or kiss if the twins weren't around. Instead of taking her usual spot on the loveseat, Callie stood in front of the fireplace with her hands clasped together.

"Do want anything to drink?" Ty asked as he slowly approached her.

"No thanks." She didn't take her eyes off of him, and the weight of her stare physically pressed down on his shoulders. She obviously had something to say. The question was whether he was going to like it or not.

"Hey," he said, not sure if he should take hold of her

hands. She clasped them so tightly he figured he'd have to pry them apart. "What's got you wound up so tight?"

She dropped her hands to her sides and drew in a deep breath. "I'm just going to come out and say it."

Unease constricted Ty's airway as if somebody had slipped a rope around his neck and tightened it. "I'm listening," he said, feeling like ice had replaced the warm blood in his veins.

Her eyes widened. "It's not bad." She rubbed her lips together. "At least I hope you don't think it's bad."

He mentally told himself to cowboy up and take whatever she had to say like a man. "Callie, please just tell me what you're thinking."

Lacing her fingers together, she covered her stomach with her hands. "I'm in love with you."

She said it so quickly, he almost didn't catch it. A huge smile split his face as her words finally registered. "Well, it's about time," he said, swooping her into his arms. She laughed as he spun her around and sat down on the loveseat, settling her on his lap. "Don't ever scare me like that again," he said just before he covered her mouth with his. Holding her close, he kissed her thoroughly, breathing in her scent and tasting the cinnamon on her tongue.

Callie kissed him like a woman in love, holding nothing back. Her arms wound around his neck, and she pressed closer like she couldn't get enough. Deepening the kiss, Ty's hands moved to her back as want and desire coursed through his veins like liquid lava. It was hard to keep his hands from exploring the curves of her body, and he knew he needed to stop before they crossed a line that would make it impossible to go back. They both were married before, and they knew what they were missing.

Easing the pressure on her mouth, he gave her a series of slow kisses before drawing back to catch his breath. "We need to do something else like maybe take a walk in the rain," he said when her eyes fluttered open to look at him.

"Probably a good idea." She untangled her fingers from his hair and slid her hands down to rest on his chest. "But first, could you do me a favor?"

"Anything," he said.

"I'm pretty sure after the way you kissed me that you love me too . . . but I want to hear you say it."

He'd said it so many times in his head that he couldn't believe he'd failed to voice his feelings aloud. "I love you, Callie," he said, kissing her on the forehead. "And I love your boys."

"They love you too." She gave him a watery smile. "Thank you for loving us." Then she brushed her lips over his, giving him a sweet kiss that conveyed even more than the hot kiss a few minutes earlier ever could.

They spent the rest of the evening talking about their future, including getting married. Ty was ready to get the ring out of his top dresser drawer and propose to her tonight. In his mind, there was no reason to wait. He could easily provide for Callie and her boys. She wouldn't have to worry about work and could focus on her music if that's what she wanted to do. She'd told him that she was writing again, but her end goal wasn't to be a country superstar anymore. She was excited about helping local artists achieve their dreams by managing the café's open mic endeavor. On top of that, she had a list of guitar and vocal students wanting her to teach them.

Still, he wanted the proposal to be special. His little sister would kill him if he didn't do anything romantic. Maybe he would buy a camping trailer and take Callie and the boys camping to the same spot his family used to go. They could invite Jed and Natasha to come with them. The boys loved playing with the Merrill girls. They could keep watch over the twins while he took Callie back to the lake so he could really have a do-over. It would be the perfect setting for a proposal.

Distant thunder rattled the window followed by a flash of lightning. Callie cast a worried look outside. "Gage and Max are afraid of thunderstorms. I better get home in case they wake up."

Grabbing one of his coats for Callie to use, Ty quickly walked her next door. "I love you," he said, brushing his lips across hers. The rain was coming down hard, so he kept the kiss goodnight short. "I'll see you tomorrow."

"I love you too." She let go of his hand slowly, the tips of her fingers sliding across his skin to prolong the connection. A clap of thunder made her jump. "You better go."

He ran back home, hating how cold and lonely the house felt without Callie there. Waiting to ask her to marry him didn't seem like such a good idea right now. Stripping out of his damp clothes, he took a hot shower and considered different options that didn't involve planning a camping trip. Pulling on flannel pajama bottoms, he grabbed a T-shirt and went downstairs to get his phone. It wouldn't hurt to search for creative ways to propose.

Ty couldn't remember where he'd left his phone and finally found it wedged in between the cushions of the loveseat. Alarm swept through him when he saw the screen had several missed calls from Callie. Hoping nothing bad had happened to the twins or her aunt, he quickly called her back. "Sorry, I was in the shower and left my phone downstairs. Is everything okay?"

"Yes," Callie said with a hiccup that was either a laugh or a sob. "But I need you to come over here as soon as you can."

"Are the boys okay?" he asked, grabbing a clean pair of socks.

"They're fine . . . I . . . " She hiccupped again. "Oh, Ty, I found proof that 'Catching Sunlight' is my song."

NINE

CALLIE'S HEAD WAS spinning, not only from a lack of sleep but also from the whirlwind of events that had occurred over the past few days. She clutched Ty's hand tightly, grateful he'd been by her side every step of the way.

"I think I'm going to throw up," she whispered. "What am I supposed to say to her?"

"Exactly what you told your attorney and me." Ty brought her hand to his mouth and kissed her knuckles. "It's going to be okay, honey. Just try to relax."

Nodding her head, she kept her eyes trained on the conference door. Laney Loveland would be walking through that door any moment now. The country music star had arranged for this meeting. Laney wanted to apologize for Boone Redford's deception personally.

Callie wasn't sure why Laney felt responsible. Boone had deceived her too.

Feeling like she'd stuffed her mouth full of toilet paper, Callie reached out with her free hand and picked up the glass of ice water from the coffee table. Her hand shook, rattling the ice against the side of the glass. Taking a sip, she set the glass down and closed her eyes. This whole thing was so crazy. She still couldn't believe her little boys had been the ones to exonerate her name and nail Boone Redford with irrefutable evidence that he'd stolen Callie's song and lied about it.

The video had been on her phone all along, accidentally recorded when Max and Gage had taken her phone to take their silly selfies. She remembered giving them her phone to keep them occupied when Boone had stopped by her apartment, pleading with her to let him hear her song.

The boys had accidentally selected the video mode and then hit record. Although the video only lasted under a minute, the timing had been perfect. Not only had they caught the last few lines of "Catching Sunlight," but they'd also captured Boone's face clearly as he campaigned to buy the rights for the song so Laney Loveland could make it a hit. The whole spiel about Callie possibly winning a Grammy as a songwriter was there too. The new category had only recently been added, and Boone was clearly using that as a ploy to sweeten the deal.

Callie gripped Ty's hand tighter as the conference door opened. Mack Layton, the entertainment attorney from Missoula that Callie had hired to represent her, gave her a warm smile. "Callie, Ms. Loveland and her attorney just arrived and want to come in," Mack said. "Are you ready to meet them or do you want a few more minutes?"

A few more minutes sounded nice, but she didn't want to put off the entourage. Not when they'd gone to such great lengths to meet with her in Montana. They'd offered to fly Callie and her attorney to Nashville, but Callie wasn't sure she wanted to return to the city. Besides, she wanted Ty to be with her.

"I'm okay." She and Ty both stood up from the leather couch. Ms. Loveland had requested an informal setting so they could talk without feeling like they were here on business. "Just stop me if I say something stupid."

"You'll be fine," Mack said.

Callie appreciated his kind words and was so glad she'd asked him to represent her. She'd fired her attorney in

Nashville when all he could talk about was filing a lawsuit against Laney Loveland and her record label. Callie didn't want to sue anyone other than Boone Redford. And even then she only wanted what was fair, not the millions of dollars her attorney said he could easily get for her.

"You won't say anything stupid," Ty said. "Remember, you did nothing wrong."

Before she could argue that Ms. Loveland hadn't done anything wrong either, a handsome man wearing an expensive suit walked in and shook Mack's hand. "Mack, I'm Perry Daniels. It's a pleasure to meet you in person."

"Likewise," Mack said. He swept his hand in front of him and introduced Callie and Ty.

Mr. Daniels looked more like a GQ model than a high-powered attorney, but Callie supposed that's why he was representing the rising music star. "Ms. Stewart," Perry said, coming around the table to take Callie's hand in both of his. "Thank you for taking the time to meet with us."

"You're welcome." Callie's eyes darted to the open door and then back to Mr. Daniels. "Please, call me Callie."

"Thank you, Callie." Still keeping her hand sandwiched between his, he applied gentle pressure before releasing her hand to address Ty. "Perry Daniels," he said, holding out his hand.

"Ty Carter." The two men shook hands and then turned to the doorway.

As if on cue, Laney Loveland walked in. The stunning red-head was much taller in person. Pinning Callie with her dark green eyes, the music star parted her red-painted lips into a brilliant smile. "Oh my goodness," she said in a southern accent that made her instantly likable. "You are as pretty as your picture." She didn't bother taking Callie's hand and went straight in for a hug. "I'm so happy to finally meet you."

Surprised by the warm greeting, Callie hugged her back, catching the subtle scent of her expensive perfume. The woman had soft curves but was clearly toned. Callie liked her all the more because she felt real. "Thank you," Callie said. "I'm happy to meet you too."

Laney stepped back but kept her hands on Callie's shoulders. "I just want you to know how sorry I am for what happened. That Boone Redford is as crooked as a barrel of snakes. I swear I didn't know that he'd stolen your song."

"Laney," Perry said, clearing his throat. "Remember what we talked about?" Her attorney's warning was clear, but Laney didn't pay him any mind.

"Oh, you hush up, Perry Daniels," Laney said sweetly as she shot her attorney a censuring look. "This girl has been through enough. I came here to apologize, and that's what I plan on doin'." She met Callie's gaze and winked at her. "We girls need to stick together, right?"

"Right," Callie said with a laugh. She'd heard that Laney was a genuinely nice person and very down to earth. After meeting her, she believed it was true.

"Now who is this handsome man?" Laney said as she turned all the down-to-earth charm on Ty. "Montana sure has a lot of good-lookin' cowboys. I think I'll look here for a few to be in my next music video."

The tips of Ty's ears turned red as he introduced himself. "Ty Carter, ma'am," he said, sounding a little bit starstruck. "I'm here with Callie."

Callie wished they were engaged and he could introduce himself as her fiancé, but with everything that had happened all their talks of marriage were on hold. Still, he could have said he was her boyfriend.

"Are you here professionally or personally?" Laney asked, her southern voice now sounding sexy and sultry instead of sassy.

"Personally," Ty blurted out. "We're dating. Seriously."

One of Laney's perfectly shaped eyebrows lifted as a slow smile curved her mouth. "I seriously believe you," she said, amusement making her eyes sparkle like emeralds.

Ty rubbed a hand across his bearded jaw and exchanged a look with Mack. "Let's all have a seat," Mack said, obviously able to read the distress on Ty's face.

"Callie and I are going to sit right here," Laney said as she took Callie by the hand and led her to the matching loveseat. "Y'all can sit wherever you'd like."

Callie wanted Ty to sit with her too, but what if Laney insisted he sit next to her instead? She wanted to hug and kiss him when he pulled up a chair and took a seat on her side. "Serious boyfriends are invited, right?" he said, sounding a little more like the confident man she'd fallen in love with.

"Absolutely," Laney said. "You don't have a twin brother by chance, do you?" she asked.

"No ma'am, but did you know Callie has twin boys?"

That got the conversation off to a good start. Callie told Laney about Max and Gage, proudly showing her pictures on the temporary cell phone her attorney wanted her to use. Although the video was backed up online and there were copies made of it, Mack wanted to have her phone to hand over to the authorities once formal charges were filed against Boone.

Once that was out of the way, Laney was very direct about how she wanted to make things right with Callie. "Look, sugar, I've been in this business long enough to know how tough it is to catch a break." She took a sip of her Diet Coke and then set the glass down on the coaster. "I was lucky enough to be noticed by Phillip Jacobs when I was in the top ten on *The New Voice of Country Music*. While I didn't win a contract with his record label, he invited me to perform as one of his opening acts for his last concert tour."

"I watched the season you were on and voted for you," Callie said. "I thought you should've won."

"Ah, thank you," she said. "That is so sweet of you to say." She tucked a luxurious strand of her red hair behind one ear, revealing a dangling diamond earring. "I want to give you a break, Callie. What Boone did to you was wrong, and I want to make things right."

The air in Callie's lungs felt trapped in her throat. What exactly was Laney offering her? "What do you mean?" The entire room went silent as she waited for Laney's answer. Callie reached for Ty's hand, feeling like she needed to be anchored to him.

"I'd like to have you as the first opening act for the rest of my tour, which ends in Nashville the first week of December."

Callie's heart thrummed so loudly in her ears that she had to strain to hear the rest of Laney's offer. She could hardly think straight but felt Ty's muscles go rigid before he withdrew his hand.

Thousands of questions pinged through Callie's mind. She wanted to turn and look at Ty to include him in the discussion, but her first priority was Max and Gage. "What about my boys?" Callie asked. "I don't want to leave them."

"We can discuss definite plans once we draw up a contract, but we only do two shows a week. My voice can't handle more than that." Laney gave her a soft smile. "Since the last six months of my tour are in the southern states, you could have your home base in Tennessee and go home in between concerts."

Tennessee? Callie didn't want to move back to Tennessee. At least not permanently. But six months wasn't forever. Once the tour was over, she could move back to Montana. She tried pushing out more intrusive thoughts like what if she was a big success and she headlined for Laney again or maybe someone like Phillip Jacobs? But where did that leave Ty? Would he be willing to relocate to Tennessee? She had no idea if he would even consider the idea. A buzzing in her head was making it hard to process. She was overloaded with questions and felt like she was going to explode.

"You could have your sons go on the road with you a few times, but it's hard on children," Laney said, unaware of the inner turmoil Callie was battling. "With what you'll make on royalties from 'Catching Sunlight' and your salary, I'm sure you could afford to hire the help you need as well as travel accommodations for your family."

Her mind snagged on her song title. "Royalties on 'Catching Sunlight'?" she asked. "I don't understand?"

"Laney," Perry said in a firm voice. "We are not discussing that in this meeting."

"I'm not naming numbers, Perry," she said with an eye-roll. "Y'all can work that out legally. I just want her to know she is getting royalties on her song. It's only fair."

While Laney sparred with her attorney, Callie turned to see what Ty thought about all of this. He sat ramrod straight, his attention focused on the wall. "Hey," she said, touching his arm.

A muscle ticked in his jaw as he turned toward her. She withered inside when he looked at her with eyes as cold as marble. "Hey," he said, his chiseled face carved with tension that wrapped around her heart and squeezed.

"Talk to me," she whispered.

"Not much to say until you get all the details." He glanced away from her. "You need to listen to everything Ms. Loveland has to say before you make a decision."

Before she made a decision? What happened to *them* making decisions together?

Hurt by his cool reply, she turned her attention back to

Laney. "This is a lot to take in," she said, unsure of what else Laney and her attorney had said.

"I know, sweetheart, and I'm sorry if I've caused any problems." Her eyes flickered to look at Ty. "I just want to make things right."

"I appreciate it," Callie said. "When do you need a decision?"

Laney looked to Perry and lifted a questioning brow. The man cleared his throat. "We're in no rush. You and your boyfriend take your time thinking about everything." He nodded toward Mack. "Mr. Layton and I will be working together on behalf of our clients."

"One more thing," Laney said as she lightly touched Callie's hand to get her attention. "I'd love for y'all to come for a visit to my ranch this weekend. My treat, of course. My publicist has rescheduled my concert tour this week, so I only have one show on Wednesday and the weekend off. Y'all could bring your boys, and we could get to know one another better."

"That's very kind of you," Callie said, licking her lips. "My boys will love it."

"Good." Laney got to her feet. "I'll have my assistant get you the travel information. I just need to know how many will be traveling."

"I'm covering the clinic this weekend," Ty said without looking at Callie. "So unless Callie brings her aunt along it will be three traveling."

"All right." Laney held out her hand. "It was a pleasure meeting you, Mr. Carter."

"Thank you, ma'am," he said, giving the woman a quick handshake. "What you're doing for Callie . . . " His voice caught, and he gently cleared his throat. "It's very admirable and shows great integrity."

Surprise lit Laney's eyes, and Callie caught a spark of attraction flicker there too. "Integrity is a quality my granddaddy instilled in me. It means a lot to me for you to say that."

Callie wanted to point out that integrity usually also meant that someone didn't hit on another woman's man.

"I'll leave my contact information with your attorney," Laney said before leaning into to wrap Callie in another warm hug. "I hope everything works out with you and your boyfriend."

Did she really? Now Callie wasn't so sure about how genuine and down to earth Laney was. After all, this visit could all be for good PR. She would want to capitalize on all the media attention while looking like a hero.

Callie hated this ugly jealous side of her. It's not like Ty was going to go after Laney. But what if Laney went after Ty? She pulled away from the music star, catching another whiff of her expensive perfume. "I'll stay in touch," she said. "Thank you again for everything."

"Of course." Laney looked at Ty and gave him a smile that signaled her interest. "If you change your mind about this weekend, Ty, the offer for you to come still stands."

Feeling like she needed to stake a claim on her man, Callie stepped in front of him. "Ty and I will talk about it. Maybe he can switch his schedule and come with us."

With one last long look at Ty, Laney gave Callie a sweet smile and left the room.

"Wow," Mack said, once Perry followed Laney out of the room. "This is an incredible opportunity, Callie," he said with a bark of laughter. "You and Ty have a lot to discuss."

"It's not up to me," Ty said. He crossed the room and shook Mack's hand. "Thanks for everything you're doing for Callie." Then he strode out of the room.

"I hope he remembers I rode with him," Callie said, trying to lighten the heavy mood.

"Go talk," Mack said. "He's probably as overwhelmed as you are."

"I am completely overwhelmed and don't know what to do."

"Perry and I have a conference call set up for tomorrow to discuss real numbers," Mack said, walking Callie to the door. "We can set up a meeting once I have more information to give you."

"Thank you." She hugged the man. "I don't know what I'd do without you."

"I'm happy to be of service," Mack said.

Callie had almost forgotten she'd hired the man and that he was going to make a substantial percentage. Still, it was nice to have someone in her court.

Pushing the door open, Callie was relieved to see Ty's truck parked in the same place. He sat in the driver's seat, his posture rigid. She needed to remember how he must be feeling and not just think about herself. She worried her bottom lip with her teeth as she made her way toward the parked vehicle. She couldn't help thinking that maybe their relationship was over before it started. The thought physically hurt, but she needed to take whatever was coming without falling apart. She had weathered a lot of storms, and she had her boys to think about.

The wounded part of her hoped Ty would get out of the truck to open her door for her. The tough-girl part of her remembered that she'd been on her own for a very long time. She could open her own door.

Once she was inside, he said absolutely nothing to her. Just shifted the gear and headed for home. The tension in the truck was tighter than a new pack of guitar strings. She battled with wanting to yell at him to stop being an idiot or telling him it was over. Either way, she wanted to cry.

Turning her face to look out the passenger window, she fought the tears stinging her eyes. She and Ty had been so happy, and now everything was a mess.

"I'm sorry," he said in a gruff voice. "I know I'm acting like a jerk, but I don't know what to tell you."

How about you love me? She thought to herself.

"I love you, Callie," he said, the words crumbling the wall she was rapidly building to keep from getting hurt.

She turned and saw his hand stretched across the middle console with his palm up. "I love you too," she said, reaching out and placing her hand in his. A tear slipped down her cheek when he curled his fingers around her hand and held on tight.

"I don't want to hold you back," he said. "But I don't want to let you go either."

She angled her body toward him, wishing his truck had a bench seat so she could scoot over and sit next to him. "Why does it have to be one or the other?"

"I can't relocate my vet practice. Not this close after doing it two years earlier."

"Six months isn't forever," she said. "You could come out for visits until the tour is over and then I'll move back home to you."

Home. She hadn't really thought of Sunset Falls as home. Ty was the one who made it home.

"You have a gift," he said, his voice a low rumble that vibrated through her. "If the country music folks are smart they'll offer you more opportunities." He swallowed hard. "You could be bigger than Laney Loveland."

"Speaking of Laney Loveland," Callie said, unable to mask her jealousy, "I don't like the way she was looking at you."

That made him laugh. "You have nothing to worry about, sweetheart." He squeezed her fingers and cut her a quick sideways glance. "I only have eyes for you."

"That sounds like the title of my next song," Callie said. She could already hear the melody forming in her mind. "So we're good?" she asked.

He took a long moment before he nodded his head. "Yeah, let's take this one day at a time."

That sounded like another title of a good country song. She just didn't know if it was a tear-jerker ballad or a sweet love song.

TEN

Ty pulled the brim of his cowboy hat down as he watched Callie, from the wings of the stage, sing the last line of her latest hit, "I Only Have Eyes for You." It was December, and this was her last performance. He hoped her next gig would be just as successful and fulfilling. The pay wasn't nearly as good, but hopefully the benefits would offset the lower income.

He'd been right. Callie was a smashing hit. Nashville loved her. Once Laney had gotten over her brief infatuation with Ty, she had become a good mentor for Callie. She was a good friend too and happy for Callie's success.

"You ready to do this, cowboy?" Laney said from beside him.

"Past ready," he said, even though it felt like a herd of stampeding cattle had been let loose in his chest. "Thanks for your help."

"You are very welcome." She touched him on the elbow as the crowd clapped loudly for Callie. "Your sister's in the audience with the boys, right?"

"Yes, ma'am."

"Well, all righty then," she said, squeezing his arm. "Let's do this."

The lights went low, and a hush fell over the crowd. "Ladies and gentlemen," the announcer said. "We have a special performance for you." A drum rolled dramatically for several seconds. "Put your hands together for Nashville's sweetheart, Laney Loveland!"

One of Laney's songs blasted the air as a spotlight pinpointed her walking onto the stage. The crowd went crazy with applause and whistles. Sure, this was Laney's concert, but she wasn't due to perform for at least another forty-five minutes. Laney waved and blew kisses, raising the noise level a few more decibels. Ty was glad Max and Gage had pediatric hearing protection given to them by the stage manager.

The spotlight followed Laney as she made her way to center stage and then broadened to encompass Callie when Laney stopped beside her. Ty saw Callie's lips move, her eyes wide with confusion. The sound guy made her mic go live, catching the end of her sentence. "I don't understand what's going on." She snapped her mouth closed and looked around like she wasn't sure if that was her voice or not.

"Good evening, Nashville!" Laney said. "I've been working on this song with a friend who is new to country music." She took the guitar one of the stagehands offered her and put the strap over her shoulder. "I hope y'all like it."

Callie started to back away, but Laney reached out to stop her with her hand. "I need a chair for Callie," Laney called out. Magically, a stool was produced from another stagehand.

"Um, okay," Callie said, taking a seat. "Thank you."

Laney strummed the opening chords, and the audience quieted, eager to hear a brand new song for the first time. "Not everyone gets a second chance to fix something from the past. One shot is sometimes all you get, reaping consequences that last a lifetime."

Ty watched Callie's face as Laney wove a spell with her vocals that had made her a country music sensation. Technically, he hadn't helped write the lyrics. He'd commissioned Laney to do that. He'd just provided the idea and the last line of the song.

She continued singing the ballad that talked about how sometimes things needed to go wrong in order for them to go right. About forgiveness and having courage to love again.

Ty's gut twisted with apprehension as the song neared the end. It was his cue to walk on stage. "This way, Mr. Carter," the girl assigned to take him on stage said as she gripped his elbow and led him toward Callie without the aid of a light.

No one noticed him—not even Callie. Laney had positioned herself to block her view. Ty got down on one knee and a few beats later another spotlight landed on him, revealing his presence. The audience gave a collective sound of astonishment as Callie gasped and covered her mouth with her hand, her pretty eyes brightening with tears.

Laney's voice sounded crystal clear as she sang the final line. "Take a leap of faith; don't grip the reins tight. Give this cowboy his second go to make the wrongs right."

The song ended, and the audience roared to life. "Hey," Ty mouthed to Callie. Only his mic was live, so it echoed around the stage.

Laughter filled the theatre but quickly quieted when Laney put a finger to her lips and signaled the audience to settle down. Every eye was on Ty. Sweat beaded along the brim of his hat and his mouth felt dry. Why had he thought this was a good idea? He looked into Callie's shining face and had his answer. Because he loved her and wanted her to be his wife.

"Callie Stewart," he said, his voice not nearly as shaky as he felt. "You gave me a second chance to tell you how much I love you. Now I'm asking you to take another chance and agree to be my wife." The audience made a loud *ahh* as if they were at a firework show. "Will you marry me?"

There was a beat of silence before the spectators began chanting *yes, yes, yes, yes.*

"Yes!" Callie said, loud enough to make the sound system screech. "Yes," she said a little softer.

Ty got to his feet and took her hand, slipping the sparkling diamond on her left ring finger. "It's beautiful," she breathed as she held up her hand.

Amidst the clapping, the crowd started chanting *kiss, kiss, kiss, kiss, kiss.* Ty heeded their prompting and pulled Callie to him. Lowering his head, he took possession of her lips, softly at first, then more urgently when she wrapped her arms around him and pressed closer.

He heard a commotion on the stage as comments from the crowd filtered through the chaotic noise like *those are her twins* and *look how cute they are.* He'd almost forgotten about Lauren bringing Max and Gage on stage until the two little boys wiggled their way in between them for a family group hug.

Ending the kiss, Ty picked up Max and handed him to Callie. "Hey, baby," she said, kissing the little boy's cheek. The sound guys had cut the mics, so her words didn't make it past their little circle.

"Come here, little man," Ty said as he lifted Gage into his arms. Then he leaned over to give Callie one more sweet kiss. "By the way," he murmured against her mouth, "this is going to be a very short engagement."

"How short?" she whispered back.

"Less than twenty-four hours," he said. "You'll be mine just as soon as the sun rises."

"Sounds perfect," she said, brushing her lips over his. "And you just gave me an idea for my next song, but I'm not writing it until after our honeymoon."

Ty grinned and slowly lowered his mouth to whisper in her ear. "Sweetheart," he said in a low voice, "our honeymoon is going to be the inspiration for your entire next album."

Cindy Roland Anderson writes clean, contemporary romance with a combination of humor, romantic tension and some pretty great kissing scenes. She and her husband, John, live in northern Utah, and have five amazing children. Their family has expanded by adding a son-in-law, a daughter-in-law, and seven adorable grandchildren. She is a registered nurse and has worked in the NICU as well as the newborn nursery. She loves to read, almost as much as she loves writing. And she loves chocolate, probably a little too much.

To contact her or to see other projects she is working on go to www.cindyrolandanderson.com

www.ingramcontent.com/pod-product-compliance
Lightning Source LLC
LaVergne TN
LVHW021234080526
838199LV00088B/4345